Your name is Hannibal Fortune and you are (1) resourceful (2) highly trained (3) the most competent choice for the job (4) the hope of the world (5) in all probability the best secret agent in the history of secret agenting.

EMPIRE is the reason you're here, and putting a ruptured time-line back together is the only problem you've really got time for since you discovered you and Webley were cut off from help. . . .

Just you and me, Web, we're on our own
the two of us against the world
and what has the world ever done for us?

But are you sure you feel all right?

T.E.R.R.A.

This is the fourth exciting AGENT OF T.E.R.R.A. adventure. See page 256 for information on the first three books in this fast-action series.

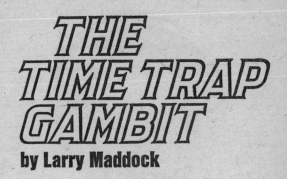

THE TIME TRAP GAMBIT

by Larry Maddock

AN ACE BOOK

Ace Publishing Corporation
1120 Avenue of the Americas
New York, N.Y. 10036

THE TIME TRAP GAMBIT

Copyright ©, 1969, by Ace Publishing Corp.

All Rights Reserved.

CONTENTS

ONE: THE LITTLE FIX-IT-SHOP
IN THE MIDDLE OF THE GALAXY

THE JET BLACK EYES of Pohl Tausig, rotund
Operations Chief of the Temporal Entropy Restructure
nd Repair Agency, peered out from above an equally
lack forest of beard at his handsome, debonair visitor.
This one seems cut out for you, Fortune," Tausig rum-
led in a voice like a temple gong.

"Earth again?" inquired the Special Agent, easing his
anky frame into a chair opposite Tausig.

"Northern coast of Africa," Tausig confirmed. "The
esident Team there reports that a war of conquest is
oing the wrong way. The rightful victors are rapidly
ecoming the vanquished."

"That doesn't sound like something Empire'd take a
and in," Hannibal Fortune protested. "Who's involved?"

"Rome and Carthage."

The agent whistled softly. "I see why you said it
eems cut out for me. I've always wanted an excuse to
eet my namesake."

"General Hannibal hasn't come into it yet," Tausig
id. "The report comes from Mark 2775."

7

Mentally, Fortune translated the year into Earth-terms, then nodded. More than sixty years had passed since he'd done his thesis on the Punic Wars, and some of the details were hazy. "Let's see, it's still Scipio and Syphax against Hasdrubal, right?"

The bulky, fierce-bearded administrator shook his head. "Wrong. Hasdrubal and Syphax against Scipio."

The agent frowned. "I can't have forgotten that much about it, Pohl."

Tausig smiled dryly. "Your memory is all right. Wi'in will be available for empathy in eight days. You should be ready for departure then." He closed the folder in front of him and moved it aside. "How does it feel to be back in harness?"

"Great." Fortune grinned. "I guess that means I passed all the tests they've been throwing at me in the ten days since we got back."

Tausig patted the folder. "It's all in here. Your recovery seems to be complete. In fact, PsychSec tells me you've matured a bit."

"That's what a good woman'll do for you, Pohl. And speaking of Luise, I'd like to recommend considering her for Special Assignment, instead of sending her back to finish out her Residency."

"I'll think about it." He gazed blandly at the agent for a moment, his eyes twinkling with rare amusement. "She must be extraordinary for you to stay interested for a full year. I wonder, however, if your view of her is entirely objective. Still, if you wish, I'll talk to her."

"You won't regret it, Pohl."

"Meanwhile, get started on this Rome-Carthage thing. I've already notified the supporting sections. Your schedule." Tausig passed him a sheet of paper outlining eigh days of pre-assignment preparation. "It should keep you fairly busy."

Quiet understatement, Fortune mused, was characteristic of T.E.R.R.A.'s Operations Chief.

The huge artificial planet in the exact center of the galaxy represented the most ambitious attempt to preserve the status quo in galactic history. Each of its ten thousand occupants realized that not only their future but their present existence depended upon maintaining the past as it had already happened. And each of the ten thousand others—T.E.R.R.A.'s Resident Agents, scattered along the time-lines of forty-seven Galactic Federation planets—were equally aware that their world could suddenly cease to exist if they failed to spot a single significant deviation from history-as-they-knew-it.

Thus, Vango and his symbiotic partner Arrik, stationed in the ancient city of Carthage on G.F. Planet 38 in the Earth-year 203 B.C., were duty-bound to report Scipio's failure to conquer the nearby and still more ancient city of Utica in the time history said he'd conquered it.

As the only one of T.E.R.R.A.'s Special Agents whose field of academic concentration was Earth-history, Fortune was familiar with the ruthless, efficient way Publius Cornelius Scipio had forced Utica and Carthage to surrender. He'd forgotten the exact number of troops involved on each side, but he recalled that Scipio's legionaries and Syphax' barbarian warriors had hopelessly outnumbered every defense Utica had been able to muster, including the Carthaginian army under General Hasdrubal. It had taken but a few weeks to bring Utica to her knees, annihilating Hasdrubal's forces in the process, after which Scipio and Syphax had marched on Carthage itself to begin the year-long siege which destroyed Carthaginian domination of the ancient world and assured Rome's ascendency. Hannibal, busy harassing Rome's home front, had been unable to return to Carthage in time to save the city.

But now, according to Vango, King Syphax had switched sides, Utica had *not* fallen, and further delay might see Scipio—and Rome itself—wiped out instead of Carthage. The probable consequences of such a discrepancy could not be ignored. There were relatively few events along any given time-line, Fortune realized, which were crucial enough to shake the foundations of base-time reality—but the obliteration of a civilization was one of them. History demanded that Rome utterly liquidate Carthage. Anything which threatened to change the outcome of that conflict endangered the security of the Galactic Federation.

Vango and Arrik had been planted in Carthage for the same reason the honeycombed headquarters of T.E.R.R.A. Control had been built in the middle of the galaxy: to thwart the ambitions of a criminal genius named Gregor Malik, who had already become Tyrant of the planet Borius when Rimaud Rudnl and Linz Lipnig had built the galaxy's first workable time machine in what corresponded to Earth-year 2552. The then-68-year-old Galactic Federation had immediately outlawed it as a threat to the thousands of time-lines which supported base-time reality. Rudnl, piqued at having a lid summarily slapped on his life's work, took the invention to Gregor Malik. Recognizing the device as a way to extend his tyranny over the known universe, Malik was delighted to become Rudnl's patron. By G.F. year 72 Malik had recruited enough of the galaxy's top criminal minds to form the plundering organization known as Empire.

In G.F. 74, the Galactic Federation was forced to create T.E.R.R.A. and equip it with the very device it had so abruptly outlawed six years earlier. In the ensuing fifteen years, T.E.R.R.A. had waged a relentless battle to detect and correct Empire's meddling with the time-lines of the Federation's forty-seven member planets. And although Malik himself had been removed from the action, apparently his henchmen had kept Empire rolling right along, looting the past and disrupting the history of the G.F. planets.

The twin tasks of (a) finding out how Empire hoped to profit from the Second Punic War, and (b) setting everything straight again, rested squarely on the shoulders of one man, Hannibal Fortune, and his symbiotic partner, Webley.

TWO: HANNIBAL, VEGETABLE

OR MINERAL?

DAY 76: For a while it seemed as if rest and mild exercise might be all you needed—until a moment ago when you woke up screaming.

All of your sensory inputs are scrambled. . . . You hear a sharp prickly odor; your eyes cringe from a grinding, thumping noise; you taste too-bright colors; a sweet-sour pressure pricks your skin and a pungent scratchiness flays your nostrils.

Endure. Even though your senses can't identify the familiar environs of *Time Out* you know that's where you are. You know who you are and you're fleetingly aware that the alien pressure inside your head is Webley's attempt to shunt the more violent shocks away from your screaming pain centers. You envy him his ability to effect extensive self-repairs at the moment of injury, and you're agonizingly aware that Hannibal Fortune isn't built that way.

Or rebuilt that way.

You try to laugh but what comes out is a candy-striped obscenity fringed with slime-slippery giggles. You feel Webley's answer as a muted wetness of staccato violins. With a purple shrug you retreat into warm nothing studded with random shards of disaster.

You close your eyes and fall through boiling red mists. Mud-brick roughness chills your naked back and you know you're chained to a wall alongside a girl you'd like to get to know better but her screams tell you Poplvf and Malik are torturing her again and the Solupsine is in your blood, leisurely nibbling at your nerve cells. . . .

The wiry, white-bearded authority on military technique welcomed Fortune with a grin. "I'm told you're slated to play around with one of my favorite campaigns," he remarked.

"I should have realized you'd be a Punic War buff, d'Kaamp," Fortune replied.

"Do you know which army you'll be in?"

"That decision'll have to wait until I have a chance to survey the existing situation. Better prepare me for both."

"Both?" countered the instructor. "There are five different armies involved. Scipio's, which is quite conventionally Roman; Hasdrubal's, which is just as conventionally Carthaginian; Hannibal's, which started out mainly with Carthaginians, Gauls and Numidians, but has picked up a considerable number of Italians in several years of campaigning around Rome; the barbarians under Syphax, drawn from all the tribes in North Africa, including a healthy force of Numidian horse; and to some extent at least, Masinissa's Numidian horse. You, I recall, are already a competent horseman."

"I do all right," Fortune replied modestly.

"Let me warn you: the Numidians ride without any furniture at all—no saddle, bridle, reins or anything."

"If I have to play that role, d'Kaamp, my partner will be able to control the horse. He did so well on one assignment he earned a reputation as the God of Horses.* I don't think I'll have any trouble in that respect."

*See Agent of T.E.R.R.A. #2, The Golden Goddess Gambit.

"Good. Shall we begin by breaking you in as a Roman legionary? You'll notice two swords on the bench. The first is a standard Roman short sword for use in battle. Next to it is a practice sword, with a blade just twice as heavy as the first. Legionaries spend at least an hour a day working out with the practice weapon to develop an arm that won't tire easily. Put on your battle garb and I'll show you how a well-trained legionary handles himself in combat."

In another part of the synthetic planet, Luise Little eased the gleaming induction hood from her head and sat immobile in the fatigue-proof chair for several minutes, thinking in Chinese. The high-speed teaching apparatus had just transferred to her brain the contents of a cerebrotape which held the entire vocabulary and grammar of the dialect spoken in the central provinces during the early part of the Shang Dynasty on G.F. Planet 38. And that, she thought wonderingly, was four thousand fifty-four years ago. It was a difficult thought to entertain in the Shang dialect, because the Chinese numbering system couldn't conveniently handle the figure 4054. The cumbersomeness annoyed her, as mathematics was her forte. The simplest technical jobs in the whole T.E.R.R.A. organization required mathematical competence—even the basic concept of time travel itself, on which the agency was built, was mathematical.

The arbitrary nature of time, she reflected, was never so apparent as when you try to revise your body rhythms to fit a completely alien time scheme. In sixteen Earth-years her body had adjusted to Earth's curious cycles and even more curious clocks and calendars. She had difficulty remembering her childhood with its roomy hundred and forty-four ork days. Earth-days were only eighty orks from sunup to sunup. And on *Time Out,* where she'd just spent a year's sabbatical with Hannibal Fortune, the days were shorter still—a scant sixty-three and a half orks.

Even the G.F. Standard Year they'd spent together, recuperating from the deadly Solupsine injections they'd received during the Special Assignment on which Fortune and Luise had met, was sixteen hours shorter than an Earth-year. But since the days were shorter, too, there were more of them: 454.54 to be precise, or 104.54 more days than she would have counted in the same length of time at T.E.R.R.A. Control.

DAY 152: With more days, more sunsets . . . and more chances to lie here in the sand watching them alongside Hannibal.

You tell him that and he smiles.

"Measured in my time," he adds, "these days are almost exactly fourteen Rus and forty-eight Arus."

The expression is meaningless. "How many Arus to the Ru?" you ask.

"Sixty-four. Where I grew up we had thirty-two Rus in each day."

"And where was that?"

Fortune looks scoldingly at you. "Special Agents never tell anyone their planets of origin."

"I know," you reply, adding, "or their real names."

In shared silence you watch the sunset. After a while you snap off a brittle cheno shoot and use it to scribe figures in the sand.

"What's that?" he asks.

15

"I call it my Tracking Down Hannibal Fortune Formula. Observe. We knew that a day on this planet equals seven point seven standard G.F. Time Units, right? In terms of my time, that's the same as sixty-three orks six, or sixty-three and a half orks. But Hannibal Fortune calls it fourteen Rus forty-six Arus, or fourteen point seven two Rus, right?"

"Right," he agrees, somewhat admiringly.

"We also know," you continue, warming to your topic, "that your planet's day is exactly thirty-two Rus long. I was born into a twelve-talo day—that's one hundred forty-four orks. By cross-multiplying here, canceling these two quantities out—aha, just as I thought. Thirty-two Rus is exactly six orks less than my regular hundred forty-four ork day. Therefore, Hannibal Fortune is a native of G.F. Planet Seventeen."

Fortune looks from your computations to your face. "Luise, my love, you are fantastic."

"Just good at math." You laugh. "I started out as a communications technologist, remember? Transposing from base twelve to base eight isn't so difficult."

"No, but matching the inferences is tricky business. Given enough clues, you'd eventually come up with the fact that the gens Wokajeni once called me Drajne."

"Drajne," you repeat softly. "May I?"

He grins. "I think we're safe from Empire ears."

"And eyes," you add, moving closer to him under the darkening sky. "My darling Drajne. . . ."

She smiled. Yes, it had been a good year together. She'd learned a lot since that day in Mohenjo-daro when she'd called for help and T.E.R.R.A. Control had sent

Hannibal Fortune and Webley to her rescue.* She'd considered most Special Agents, and Hannibal Fortune in particular, "Professional Heroes." But after they'd faced death together and fought their way through a kill-crazed mob of invading barbarians she'd begun to find out what makes men like Hannibal Fortune tick.

It takes a peculiar sort of person, she learned, to be a successful secret agent. The vast majority of them are male. They're not the easiest men in the world to like, because there are too many human traits they simply can't afford.

Each agent, she discovered, finds his own way to compensate for his exclusion from the good things ordinary people often take for granted—things which he must deny himself to stay alive in order to protect the ordinary people. Often what he substitutes isn't pretty; sometimes he must manufacture contempt for values other men cherish, and he's frequently forced to cling fiercely to his loathing, or risk losing everything.

When the Ordinary Man takes that risk and loses, he's the only loser.

But men such as Hannibal Fortune are not Ordinary Men. When they lose, the toll in lives can easily exceed the average person's comprehension.

She learned that on all the planets, in all the cultures and in every century where such men have been called to action, secret agents considered themselves a breed apart, viewing the laws of Ordinary Men with contempt, condescension, and sneering disdain. If an agent were sufficiently colorful, flamboyantly clever and talented at

*See *Agent of T.E.R.R.A. #3, The Emerald Elephant Gambit.*

17

tweaking the collective probosci of the Ruling Minority, the best he could hope for in any age would be the grudging admiration and the distant applause of a few Ordinary Men, but it would be most unusual for any of them to invite him to dinner or introduce him to their sisters, for Ordinary Men are uniformly uneasy in the presence of the Extraordinary Man. Furthermore, most of them could sense the wall of arrogance a secret agent must erect to protect himself from the sort of friendships he knows he can't afford. Thus, meaningful involvements outside his own envelope of skin become increasingly impossible.

Hannibal Fortune had logged over sixty years as a secret agent, avoiding the traps built into being human, overcoming the biological tendencies characteristic of his species, honing his survival reflexes, and knowingly, rationally and continuously propagandizing himself with the attitudes and beliefs which would keep him in the select group of Special Agents of T.E.R.R.A., those who'd been granted the coveted License to Tamper.

At first all she'd seen was his protective wall of arrogance, which was why she'd labeled him a "Professional Hero." But in their year together at *Time Out*, that wall had gradually eroded away, until they'd both genuinely regretted their return to duty status.

The white-bearded instructor smiled tightly in approval and stepped back from his heavily armored student. "Once more," he directed. "Keep working on my face—thrust! Thrust!"

Grinning, Fortune surged forward and feinted an underthrust designed to decoy the opposing shield away from his enemy's face. The rhythm of this Roman-style swordplay was like a dance: *one*, two, *three*, four and you're back in position to feint and thrust again. He'd already pulled the heavy blade back and thrown his weight into the three-count when he realized d'Kaamp's shield was still up and moving higher, while the instructor dodged lightly to Fortune's right, then stepped in under Fortune's upraised weapon to force it even higher with his shield. Fortune's entire right side was exposed, and d'Kaamp's blade darted at him from below—

Ooops.

He tried to twist away but the momentum of his thrust worked against him. The instructor's point ticked his ribs.

"You're dead," d'Kaamp said curtly.

"I know," the agent acknowledged ruefully.

"The fighting precision of the Roman army is its greatest strength, but leaves little rooom for flexibility except at the top. A Roman infantryman can survive almost everything but an unconventional opponent."

"I'll remember that."

"You'll overcome it," d'Kaamp corrected, "if you intend to stay alive. The wisest approach is to keep entirely out of battle situations. If you *must* indulge in swordplay, remember that the Romans are the only ones you can count on to be consistent. The others are a motley lot at best, but among them are some surprisingly talented warriors. Tomorrow we'll go into the military philosophy of the man you'll probably have to manipulate."

"Publius Cornelius Scipio."

"*Skeepeeoh*," the older man replied, nodding. "If you're

going to speak Latin, the least you can do is pronounce
it correctly."

Of all the diverse species working shoulder to thorax
in the fourteen separate environments maintained at
T.E.R.R.A. Control, none was more whimsically constructed than the one to which Webley and Ronel belonged. Exactly when on the evolutionary calender their
ancestors had learned to think was a mystery not even
T.E.R.R.A.'s remarkable temporal transporters could
help solve, but that time-shrouded event had led to
the most adaptable creature yet uncovered in the galaxy. It was the only life-form which could successfully
base its daily activities on wishful thinking. Not content
with merely being able to change its shape at will, this
curious species (which called itself *Torg*, meaning, quite
naturally, "people") was completely telepathic. One of
the Torg's close relatives, evolutionarily speaking, possessed neither its extreme plasticity nor its thought-
reading abilities, both limitations presumably resulting
from its having developed a rather rigid network of
nerves while the Torg themselves continued with totally
unspecialized cellular evolvement. Their lack of a formal
nervous system allowed a degree of self-awareness un-
paralleled in any other species, and was thought by
many G.F. biologists to be essential to the Torg's shapechanging and telepathic potential. The Torg had long
ago developed phenomenal control of and defenses
against their own mind-probing talents and had agreed
on rules of telepathic conduct to regulate the degree of
mental intimacy permitted between individual Torgs.
In most cases, a Torg felt more comfortable in a symbiotic relationship with a member of another species,

such as Webley enjoyed with Hannibal Fortune and Ronel had with Luise Little, than he would in a friendship with a fellow Torg.

Surprisingly, the two symbiotes had taken a thoroughly uncharacteristic shine to each other during the last desperate hours of Mohenjo-daro, paralleling their human partners' involvement with each other. What went on between Fortune and Luise at *Time Out* hadn't been of particular concern to Webley, for the crusty, sharp-tongued symbiote had learned from experience that questioning Fortune's intricate mental processes was foolish—the safest way to view Hannibal's enthusiasm for human females was to find it amusing and to try not to laugh too loudly. Fortune and the girl had earned their year's sabbatical; since she'd brought *her* symbiotic partner, Webley'd had enough fun and games of his own to distract him from whatever the two humans were doing.

Now however, with the training schedule underway, Webley began to worry about Fortune's reactions to his imminent separation from Luise. Yoked in his customary position across the agent's shoulders, he could feel the turmoil in his partner's mind as Fortune met Luise for lunch. The symbiote recognized a note of anguish completely foreign to the man he'd shared assignments with for the past sixty years. He decided it warranted watching; if it became much more severe he'd have no choice but to point it out to Pohl Tausig.

". . . finally had a chance to recommend promoting you to Special Agent," Fortune was saying.

"I'm still not sure I can handle it," Luise replied.

"*I'm* sure. And Pohl will agree with me. He wants to talk with you."

"When?" Nervously, she fingered a lock of gold-blonde hair.

"Soon, I think. He'll let you know."

"You still haven't told me where you're going," she reminded him.

"Carthage, 203 B.C. The Second Punic War."

"Back when the Roman Empire was young," she said.

"The Roman Empire didn't begin to exist until a century later. In 203 Rome was still a Republic," he told her. "What fascinates me is that I may have a chance to meet the man whose name I borrowed—Hannibal of Carthage."

Luise smiled. "The one who took the elephants over the Alps. I've never met that one, but I still think I prefer the Hannibal who rode an elephant into Mohenjodaro. When do you leave?"

Fortune's face became grave. "Eight days," he said softly. "We don't have much time left together, do we?"

"All we've really got is now," she responded. "That ought to be enough for anybody."

"*Humans!*" Webley snorted.

DAY 95: Of all the hypno-drugs, Solupsine is the deadliest and the trickiest. The rigorous physical conditioning demanded by your job helps insulate you from its full effects. That, and the ingenuity of several other T.E.R.R.A. Agents in getting the antidote to you in time. Another five minutes. . . .

You'd been recovering nicely, until now. The pain is more brutal than Gregor Malik's most sadistic tortures; nerves laid bare by the chemical onslaught, instead of healing properly, have become brittle; overloaded, the delicate ganglia are shorting out, causing you to hear odors and taste colors and experience varieties of pain for which you have no buffering thresholds. T.E.R.R.A.'s physicians have warned you that drugs would be useless so you resolve to live with the agony, fighting to apply the pain-blocking techniques you learned when you first became a secret agent, but even with Webley's help they no longer work.

You open your eyes and see what smells like

PING-ga-PING-ga-PING

aaaaaaaaaaaaaaaaaaaah

ga-PING-ga-PING

ssssssssssssh . . .

except it's the wrong color.

THREE: "PRETEND THESE LAST

FEW MINUTES DIDN'T EXIST."

"ONCE YOU understand what he believes in," d'Kaamp stressed, for perhaps the fiftieth time since Fortune had met him, "you can find a way to control him. Scipio, for instance, is not a 'typical' Roman. Intellectually he's in the avant garde—he scorns the old gods and the old traditions, although his social prominence forces him to participate in many of the popular superstitions."

"I'd better not come to him as a messenger of the gods, then," Fortune drawled.

"Exactly. Publicly, he claims Jupiter as his divine patron—Jupiter Optimus Maximus."

"The best and the greatest."

The white-bearded one nodded sharply. "Everything we know about him reflects a tremendous striving to *be* the best and the greatest. Because his family, the gens Cornelii, is the aristocracy's Most Powerful family, he measures himself against a very exacting yardstick. His own beliefs about what he is and what he's striving for determine his conduct as a man and as a general."

"You mentioned public superstitions," Fortune prompted.

"Yes. You're familiar with the Magna Mater cult?"

"Cybele, the grain goddess?"

"Part of Scipio's campaign for the Consulship concerns the Magna Mater," d'Kaamp related. "Hannibal was at the gates of the city, the people were panicky, so the Senate decided to stage a religious pageant to allay their fears. They had the King of Pergamum ship the

24

black stone believed to be the Great Mother of Rome. When it arrived, Scipio and (we are told) a band of virtuous matrons received it with impressive ceremony. I imagine Scipio had a good laugh later, especially when the Senate discovered this new deity had to be served by self-emasculated priests. There's no doubt he's a non-believer in *any* sort of superstitious nonsense, but in public he apparently considers it good politics to respect the gods."

"That makes him no different from most of Earth's politicians," Fortune observed with a grin.

"Of course he's stuck with the Megalesia because of it."

"Megalesia?"

"Feast of the great goddess," the other explained. "Because Hannibal didn't attack Rome after they'd moved the black stone there, the rank and file were convinced the Magna Mater had saved them. To show their gratitude they celebrated the Megalesia every April thereafter. Since Scipio had such a direct hand in it, he has no choice but to observe the holiday."

Fortune's eyes twinkled. "It could be awkward if he has to plan a campaign around it. I'll remember that."

"I wonder if you'd do me a small favor if the opportunity arises?" d'Kaamp asked unexpectedly. "Scipio is one of the key figures in my private collection of military geniuses—strictly a hobby, although from time to time it proves useful. I'd like a tape of his activities during part of this campaign. I'll give you a miniaturized recorder if you think you might have a chance. . . ."

"I'll do what I can," Fortune promised.

DAY 190: You've been here five months now, getting

25

stronger every day. Drajne's recovery has lagged a bit behind yours, but that was to be expected since the Solupsine had longer to work on him than it did on you. You've felt perfectly fine for almost two months, and you've had a lot of time to think. The discovery that you're in love with this fantastic man who calls himself Hannibal Fortune has come as a mild shock to you. You've examined it from every angle and you're satisfied that that's just what's happened. *You've* fallen in love. Once you accepted that fact, Drajne's behavior toward you began to make a lot more sense.

Yes, girl, you tell yourself wonderingly, two people from cultures which don't have the "in love with" concept have managed to fall in love with each other! So you spend hours daydreaming about sharing the rest of your life with this magnificent man, and the whole idea is impossible. You're both agents of T.E.R.R.A.; you don't have time for such silly customs as love. In fact, you doubt that anyone who hadn't specifically studied the customs of G.F. Planet 38 would have heard of Being In Love. It's so much more than merely a physical urge to mate, although you admit that in his presence you experience a distinct biological tingle. You enjoy the man, his strength, his intelligence, the tenderness that tells you he recognizes the uniqueness of you. Here you'd started out resenting him, categorically detesting him because he was a Professional Hero, and you wind up loving him. It doesn't make sense, but the feeling is so—what is the word you want?—delicious?

Today, for instance, he's teaching you some of the finer points of temporal navigation, and he's just sealed himself inside the time-craft to demonstrate the reality of skipping over a section of day. He'll press the button and the transporter will vanish; exactly fifteen minutes later it will reappear, but Drajne Wokajeni will not exist in the time he was gone as far as the time-line you're on is concerned.

The time-craft winks out and there's a sound like a small, sharp explosion; implosion, actually, as the air rushes in to fill the sudden vacuum. With it you feel a twinge of panic that he'll never be back. You know he's coming back, he's already fifteen minutes in the future, climbing out of the capsule, but for this instant he does not exist, anywhere, and you *feel* his absence. Ridiculous. How will you feel, you wonder, every time he leaves on Special Assignment, where his chances of being killed will be excellent?

Stubbornly, you don't want to be in love with this man. Or with anyone. You'd much rather just enjoy his company.

Another *pop!* and you stare at the gleaming time-craft; instead of fifteen minutes barely thirty seconds have elapsed since he left. Now the hatch sighs open and there he is, except that—

There's a fresh cut under his right eye. He looks as if he's been rolling in dust. There are black smudges all over his naked body, and ugly bruises.

"Drajne!"

He looks at you with a strange expression, his eyes lancing into you, his mouth grim for the instant it takes him to remember to smile. By the time he's swung himself down to the ground he's grinning foolishly.

"Where've you been?" you exclaim, seeing the extent of his injuries.

He puts a finger to his lips and whispers, "Classified." Then he grins more broadly. "I meant to bring you a present, but the natives weren't as friendly as I thought they'd be. Incidentally, darling, this visit is highly irregular. It might be dangerous for me to know about it later."

"All right," you say, puzzled but willing to cooperate, for you know that when Hannibal Fortune says something might be dangerous it's probably fatal. "I'll try not to mention it to you."

Suddenly he puts his arms around you. "I love you," he says with unexpected ferocity. "I love you as much right now as I did tomorrow."

You look blankly at him, trying to read behind his eyes, as he continues: "Time is arbitrary. You realize, we really can't afford each other. We . . ." You can see him groping for words, auditioning ideas, discarding them.

"We what, darling?" you say softly, promptingly.

"I love you no matter what you look like," he whispers, and then he's kissing you, holding you fiercely, and you see he's crying. You start to say something but he shakes his hand. "Don't ask me," he warns, his voice so low you have to strain to hear him. "We only have a few minutes."

You snuggle your face into the hard muscles of his neck and make an acquiescent sound. A moment later you realize he's saying something else.

"You have to pretend that these last few minutes didn't exist."

"I promise," you assure him. Suddenly the things you'd been thinking about a few minutes ago fall into place. "There's only now, isn't there?" you say. "For as long as we live, all we've really got is now. That ought to be enough for anybody."

You kiss him and he steps back and somehow you

know you can't follow him. Too quickly he clambers into the time-craft and the hatch swings shut after him. Seconds later it warps into otherwhen, leaving behind the tiny thunderclap. How long has it taken? Ten minutes? Twelve? Precious little time is left for you to wipe the traces of his visit out of your eyes. Your mind churns with the strangeness of it and you force intense concentration to burn each word into your memory. You must never mention it to him, and when he comes back in a minute or two he won't know about it. You'll examine it later, but right now you have to keep him from even suspecting that he was here. You imagine it's something like Earth-humans often did back in the days before they found how to eliminate cancer.

You're glad Webley and Ronel are busy somewhere else, because this is a burden you prefer to bear alone.

Hannibal Fortune stood in the scan chamber at the entrance to the library. Webley obligingly lumped himself on his partner's left shoulder, extruded an assortment of feet and jumped down to the floor, where he puddled himself compactly while the scanner satisfied itself that this truly was Hannibal Fortune and not an impostor with Fortune's ID. The machine flashed its readiness for a voice comparison; the agent recited the required words, "Hannibal Fortune, Special Agent, Temporal Entropy Restructure and Repair Agency." A green light glowed approvingly and the heavy door snicked open. Webley leaped back up and again became a yoke of living protoplasm.

Thinking like interstellar criminals came easily to the amphibious natives of Bortan III; T.E.R.R.A. had chosen the three most paranoid of them to design and refine the security system guarding the library's History Section. Gregor Malik's passion for plunder had inadvertently distorted past events often enough as it was; if Empire were to obtain truly accurate histories of any of the member planets, it might deliberately start a chain reaction which could lead to the wholesale destruction of key Federation segments.

The crafty Bortaneans' security precautions, although at times annoying, were a reassuring reminder that T.E.R.R.A. valued its agents. The origins of Hannibal Fortune and his fellows had been deliberately clouded lest the enemy invade an agent's past and get to him before he joined T.E.R.R.A. Ruefully, Fortune recalled the security violation he'd committed at *Time Out*: letting Luise know his pre-service name. In response to this thought, Webley snaked a speech tendril into the agent's ear and intoned melodramtically:

"Only the lovely Luise Little knows the Worldsaver's true identity. . . ."

Grimacing, Fortune retorted in loud-think: *Can't you find anything better to do than memorizing old radio serials?*

"Research," the Torg replied. "You're usually so busy loading up on historical facts that you neglect the niceties of accepted heroic deportment. *One* of us has to keep current on matters of style."

Historical facts. Fortune chuckled. He'd learned long ago that there is virtually no such thing as a historical fact. The best guidelines were guesses, weighted with probability factors. Until the development of the temporal transporter, enabling direct observation of events, history was the one field of study in which there were no primary sources. The closest thing to "raw material"

30

were eyewitness accounts written immediately after the event—but these had already been processed by the witnesses, colored by what each reporter chose to see, slanted by his philosophy, pre-censored by his culture's taboos, distorted by consideration for the impression he wanted to make on his audience, crippled by omission of material the witness deemed insignificant.

Compounding the frustration of later scholars were those cultures (over two hundred of them in the galaxy) which kept no formal records at all. These were largely societies whose languages had no words for time or the continuity of events. Several quite literally couldn't count beyond three. *Nerd, thort, ostu,* in the Upper Ptahrian dialect on G.F. Planet 26, translated: *one, two, more than two.* The most exact story of past events an Upper Ptahrian was capable of relating invariably began with the words, "Ostu roveen," the literal equivalent of an Earth-child's "Once upon a time." Outlanders were astonished at the high degree of civilization Upper Ptahr had attained without ever feeling the need to count beyond three. Visiting teams of social anthropologists soon leaned to ignore the natives' honest answer, "It has always been this way," to inquiries about various customs, because the same statement could apply with equal truthfulness to a centuries-old tradition or a ceremony invented night before last.

Even civilizations which recorded every significant event in meticulous detail sometimes stumbled over their own calendars, and frequently nullified their passion for exactitude by carefully noting the most useless information and ignoring everything of consequence.

The majority of "historians" in all cultures, Fortune had learned, were either deliberate liars, naively wishful thinkers, or fanatically distortive adherents of woefully inadequate philosphical "explanations" of how and why things happened.

"Thirty-eight," Fortune said. "Mark 2800 to 2750."

The Librarian gazed at him for a moment with a smile of contemplation on her lips.

"And a full-range cubicle," the agent added.

"Oh! Yes. Certainly, I was—ah—did you say thirty-eight, sir?"

"Thirty eight," Fortune repeated kindly.

"The catalogue will be on the left wall. The reference material will be waiting in"—she consulted a chart—"Cubicle B." Blushing, she handed him a vococall command unit.

Fifteen pounds of pliant protoplasm chuckled silently under Hannibal Fortune's shirt.

Tausig was startled by Luise Little's short golden hair and pale skin. When he'd last seen her she'd been a heavily-pigmented, raven-haired "native" of Mohenjo-daro. He didn't wonder that Hannibal Fortune had taken an interest in her. What surprised Tausig was that the swashbuckling agent had remained interested in her for more than his customary few weeks. Somehow it didn't seem in character.

He waited until she'd taken a seat, then rumbled, "Fortune tells me you might be a candidate for Special Assignment."

"He taught me a lot during our year together," the girl replied. "About the job."

The Operations Chief indulged in a rare chuckle. "That was the one thing I didn't expect to happen when you went off together. Frankly, I'm a bit surprised the

THE TIME TRAP GAMBIT

two of you seemed to get along so well for so long."

Luise shrugged. "We had to do something to fill the time. I found him quite charming, and I'm flattered that he recommended me for promotion."

"He seems very impressed with you. My question, however, is how do you feel about him?"

Tausig watched her closely as she groped for the right words. At last she said simply, "The vacation's over."

He nodded approvingly. "It's good you can see it that way. Now we come to my problem. I assigned you to a twenty-year Residency, four of which remain to be completed, by someone. It's not an insoluble problem at all. I doubt if I'd consider changing your duty status if you hadn't been the one to ask for that Residency in the first place. You do recall talking me into giving it to you? Good. And you proved to me you had the background for it. If you're equally sure you can handle the much more demanding duties . . ."

"I think so," the girl replied. "I'm willing to give it a try, at any rate."

Tausig frowned, mentally comparing her with his other Special Agents. Each of them fairly bristled with self-confidence, an almost egomaniacal lack of self-doubt, verging on grandiosity. Looking at Luise, he wondered.

"Let me put it this way," he said. "Do you want to try for Special Agent status?"

"My preference is unimportant," she answered. "I expect you to put me where I'll be the most useful to T.E.R.R.A."

DAY 389: "Drajne my darling . . . don't try to make it into something it isn't."

He smiles. "Am I really being that obvious?"

You nod and move closer to him, then rest your head on his arm and look up at the stars. You want him to be obvious—after all, by now neither of you has anything to hide. And tonight you're painfully aware that all too soon your joint sabbatical will be over. By temporal transporter, T.E.R.R.A. Control is less than forty-eight minutes away. In a little over two months, Earth-time, you'll be making that trip, returning to duty. If this man in whose arms you fit so wonderfully well can sell Pohl Tausig on the idea, you'll have a chance to try for Special Assignment. The challenge appeals to you; you and Drajne are so alike in so many ways, and gratifyingly different in others. But you realize that part of your reason for wanting the promotion is to please *him*. Firmly, you remind yourself that plaasing him is not a rational motive at all, and you're faintly amused.

For that matter, loving him is not the most rational thing a girl could do. There will be time to examine that idea later. Tonight, it is enough for you to appreciate the incredibly romantic sky, the intoxicating scent of the *c'avitas* blossoms riding the warm breeze, and the aliveness of the man who invited you to share this part of his world with him. Too soon it will come to an end, you'll leave it behind, leaving also the heady awareness of each other to make room for the total concentration demanded by your respective assignments. You find yourself thinking in one of the major Earth tongues, for your own language contains no single word to express your feelings. The word you want is *poignant*. The poignancy comes from knowing that no matter how hard you might try to bring them back, these moments can never really be reexperienced. Despite the anguished

34

inner voice that says you *must*, and that it would be monstrously unfair if you *couldn't*, you and he have no chance at all of sharing each other's total lives. Isolated segments, maybe, but that's all. This holiday is probably the only time you'll ever be as close as you are right now—each hour is a precious, fragile blend of awesome beauty and heartbreaking transience. Any moment you might wake up and discover it was all a *xanthe*-dream fantasy, that you had imagined your love for this man who long ago chose the code name Hannibal Fortune.

As if in answer to your thoughts, his arm tightens around you and you feel his eyes studying your face.

"Still pondering the imponderable?" he asks.

"I suppose so," you murmur.

"I've given up on that," he tells you airily. "It's impossible but it's real. There probably won't ever again be two people who feel so right together. I've given up trying to figure it out. The odds against it are fantastic."

Laughing, you turn your head so you're looking directly into his eyes. "That," you inform him, "was not the imponderable I was working on."

"What were you thinking, then?"

"I love you. And we only have two more months together."

"If you think I'm going to let you get away that easily—"

You silence his mouth with your lips. "Darling Drajne," you whisper. "We can't spend the rest of our lives tagging around after each other on all forty-seven time-lines."

"We've already proved we can work together," he reminds you. "And back then we didn't even like each other."

You know better than to contradict the man. Wild,

impractical plans for the "happy ever after" are as much a part of Being In Love as is the wordless communion lovers share each time they touch. It's all part of the pretending, part of the eloquent exaggeration that transforms the commonplace into lyric poetry and insists on gilding honest passion with the gingerbread lie of "forever." Drajne has studied the cultural myths of Earth in even more detail than you have, and you know perfectly well he's aware of the fatuousness of Cupid's glittering foreverafters. But the sky and the *c'avitas* blossoms seem to demand flowery, all-embracing gestures. You'd be disappointed in him if he failed to honor the picturesque traditions of knight-errantry.

After all, no girl wants to hear her sweetheart whisper, "My love for you will last for the next two months."

If nothing else, it would offend the poets, who have unanimously decreed that Love *Ought* to be Eternal.

Still, the practical side of you insists on being heard, and your lover did ask you to share your thoughts. But your thoughts, at that moment, had been gloomy ones. Voicing them would shatter the romantic mood, so instead you rely on the rapport you've built together to bridge the gap between stark fact and wistful longing. You sigh—you squeeze his hand—gently, you kiss his nose. And you say, "Actually, what can you ever take with you?"

He has no answer. His silence seems to confirm your feeling that parting is something you simply won't talk about.

A minute later you continue:

"Just your experience."

"Yes," he agrees. "And your ability."

His reply annoys you, because it shoots off in a direction you didn't have in mind. Unwilling to travel down that particular path, you drag the misty dialogue back to the point you wanted to make in the first place:

"Now is what counts. It keeps turning into yesterday and blowing away."

There, that ought to please the poets. And somehow it seems at the time to make magnificent sense.

The black-bearded Operations Chief scowled, considering her answer. Yes, he decided, putting the best interests of T.E.R.R.A. above her own preferences was not only commendable, but entirely congruent with her zeal to win the Residency which had put her in Mohenjo-daro and would next see her—unless he reassigned her to Special Agent status—living watchfully in the early days of the Shang Dynasty.

Pohl Tausig made up his mind.

"Luise," he said, "I appreciate your devotion to the goals and interests of this organization; we can never have enough people like you. I doubt that there's a job category in the entire agency that isn't absolutely vital. Properly assessing all of my people, making sure they're given the duties that best fit their abilities, is a constant headache. Finding people with the peculiar qualities that go into being a successful Special Agent is perhaps the toughest part of my job. Whether Resident or Special, though, the agent in the field is our front line of defense."

"I'm aware of that," Luise replied.

"Forgive me if I seem harsh, but I can't afford mistakes. I've reviewed your work quite carefully and I don't regret having given you the Residency you requested. I don't think I'll regret the decision I'm making now, to send you back to finish out that Residency."

An expression of relief appeared on her face as she let her breath out in a long sigh. "Thank you," she said.

Tausig smiled. "I hope you have a quiet, uneventful tour of duty, with no further interruption from Empire."

"So do I," she agreed. "But if anything happens, I'll report it immediately."

Tausig nodded. "I expect your usual standard of excellence, Miss Little. In fact," he added, "I'll tolerate nothing less."

History, someone else had said, is a jotting down of how historians think past events ought to have happened.

Or, histories are written when annalists attempt to become analysts. All of which helped produce one of the most galling aspects of any restructure assignment: the inherent uncertainty of whether the mission was necessary. That "glaring discrepancy" observed by a Resident Team could quite easily be a deviation, not from what really happened, but from a stupid, prejudiced or outright insane reporting job done by a presumably conscientious native historian.

Experience had taught Fortune that most of the wars fought on G.F. Planet 38 had been abysmally reported. Since hatred is almost indispensable in a people-against-people conflict, the winners too often tend to destroy the losers' best records of what actually happened, such as at Carthage in 146 B.C., when they leveled the entire city. The best account of the action he and Webley were supposed to unscramble was that penned by the Greek historian Polybius better than fifty years after it had taken place. Polybius had been attached, as a sort of war correspondent, to the Roman army which had razed Carthage in 146 B.C., and his sources were largely the recollections (already highly distorted, no doubt, in the interests of herosim) of the family of Scipio Africanus. Thus it was entirely possible that the aberration noted by the Resident Team in 203 B.C. merely indicated a flaw in record-keeping, rather than a departure from events-as-they-happened. But T.E.R.R.A. Control couldn't afford to take that chance. Fortune had to proceed on the assumption that the discrepancy was being produced by outside intervention (presumably some action on the part of Empire, despite the fact that Empire's chief, Gregor Malik, was surely dead or at least hopelessly lost in the twisting maze of time) and that such intervention, if not stopped and the time-line repaired, would eventually threaten the temporal substructure of base-time reality.

To make the assignment doubly annoying, one could neither examine the resultant time-line in detail to see how far forward the deviation would extend nor go back before the deviation occurred and actually do anything to prevent its happening. The rules of temporal safety dictated that any restructuring attempt must begin no earlier than the moment a deviation report was filed.

Fortune reminded himself, as he watched the slowly moving sheet of micronite crawl up the wall, that the information it contained was only an outline of the best available data cross-checked by the computer for internal consistency. As maps go, it was an excellent one. But the map, Fortune knew, is never the territory. Finally satisfied that he'd ordered all the sources he could possibly need, Fortune returned the vococall unit to the reference desk and proceeded to Cubicle B.

Fitting the induction helmet to his head, he settled more comfortably in the fatigue-proof chair and touched the activating stud. The cerebrofield playback unit's polymodulated energy probes invaded his brain . . . .

Although already proficient in Greek, he'd included it among the language tapes, along with Latin, Phoenician, Ligurian, Hebrew, Aramaic, an assortment of related Semitic dialects and, for good measure, Etruscan. The high-speed cerebrocircuits added almost a dozen tongues to his arsenal of earth-languages in less than one-tenth of a G.F. Standard Time Unit.*

Before he'd ever heard of the Temporal Entropy Restructure and Repair Agency, Fortune had been familiar with the campaigns of Hannibal of Carthage. The unbridled patriotism of Titus Livius caused him to present Hannibal as a thoroughgoing villain, but the sweep of Livy's narrative and the ringing oratory he invented for his characters made a glorious epic of the Punic Wars. Polybius, writing earlier and without Livy's mania for turning each event into an illustration of a moral precept, was more honest. But it had been a line from the satires of Decimus Junius Juvenalis, written three centuries after the fact, that had triggered Fortune's interest in the Carthaginian general: "Forward, you madman, and hur-

---

*A "day" at T.E.R.R.A. Control (10 G.F. Standard Time Units) is equal to exactly 25.116 Earth hours, or 1507 minutes. Thus, one STU equals 150.7 minutes (2 hrs., 30 min., 42 sec.); and .1 STU equals 15 min., 4.2 sec. For rough computations, the reader is invited to consider one STU equal to 2 ½ hours.

ry across those horrid Alps so that you may become the delight of schoolboys." Surely, those ancient chroniclers never dreamed that translations of their works would survive to delight a schoolboy more than twenty-six centuries away in time and almost two hundred quadrillion miles away in space, or that that boy, grown to manhood and hardened by battles more spectacular than the venerable Livy could imagine, would bridge time and space to witness events Livy had merely heard of.

Now, for the first time, Hannibal Fortune read Livy in the original Latin, and Polybius in Greek. In French, English, German and Italian he absorbed a stack of speculative commentary that would have taken a conventional scholar years of effort to master.

Even with the cerebrofield, making sense of it all was no easy job, as the majority of the available sources were enormously cluttered with the writers' opinions and prejudices and further muddied by whatever style of "objectivity" happened to be fashionable at the time each was written.

Hannibal Fortune absorbed it all, storing every scrap of data, from the trivial to the unquestionably significant, in order to have it at his mental fingertips. Sorting it out would have to wait until he got there. Mainly, it was his peculiar talent for considering all of the data and using it to make the right decisions ninety-eight percent of the time which had earned him his License to Tamper.

By mid-afternoon he was finished with it—and exhausted. He sat motionless for several minutes, staring blindly at the wall of Cubicle B. Across his shoulders, Webley's featureless protoplasm rippled quietly as the symbiote inserted a mind-probe into his partner's consciousness and found the expected reactions. With skills developed over many years, Webley began the therapeutic gentling. Within an hour Fortune was feeling good enough to go looking for Luise Little.

"He *what?*"

"He's sending me back to finish out my Residency," Luise repeated patiently.

A muscle pulsed in Fortune's cheek. "You'll be gone for four years," he said.

"No, darling," she corrected him. "I'll be right back here in a little over sixteen days. Are you afraid I'll forget you in that time?"

"As far as *here* is concerned you'll be back in sixteen days," he said. "But you'll spend four years there. A lot can happen. . . ."

Luise hushed him with a kiss, then whispered, "The only thing we have any right to predict is that I'll be four years older when you see me again. Maybe you're afraid I'll be too old to appeal to you," she chided. "Don't worry, darling, my people age almost as slowly as yours."

"It's unfair of Tausig to do this to us," Fortune declared. "I'll see if I can get him to reconsider."

"He won't," she said quickly. "Not until I finish up my Residency. We'll see what happens when I get back, all right?"

Reluctantly, Fortune agreed. "I love you," he added somewhat superfluously.

She kissed him again, quickly. "I have to hurry," she said, "or I'll be late for surgery. Dinner tomorrow night?"

"Surgery?" Fortune frowned.

"Cosmetic restructuring," she explained breezily. "By Earth standards, I'm too Nordic to pass as an Oriental. Don't look at me that way—they won't do anything drastic, I'm sure. Mostly facial."

"I like your face."

Luise laughed. "I looked quite a bit different when you met me in Mohenjo-daro, remember? It'll still be me inside."

"You said *mostly* facial. What else?"

She shrugged eloquently. "Let's face it, Drajne, they'll have to take a few tucks here and there. I'm really not built like a typical Chinese female."

Fortune's eyes took quick inventory of the girl he'd known so well at *Time Out*. "All right," he murmured, acknowledging but not endorsing the notion. "When do you come out of surgery?"

"Probably about eight seventy-five. But I won't be in any shape to be sociable."

"I don't care," he said, brushing his lips across the soft gold of her hair. "Now go."

The face under the semi-rigid bandage T.E.R.R.A.'s surgical technicians had sprayed over their handiwork was that of a stranger. Luise was asleep, heavily sedated. Fortune stood silently at her bedside, fighting the impulse to hold her in his arms. Feelings of pity, concern and anger formed a palpable lump of sadness in his chest, despite his forcibly reminding himself that she *wasn't* the pain-racked victim of sadistic violence. It was as if he'd been abruptly robbed of something indescribably precious through the arbitrary, unfeeling monomania of a man Fortune had respected until now.

He supposed he'd known from the start, academically,

43

that it wasn't merely her mind that he loved. Her smile, gestures, skin texture, the way her nose crinkled in laughter, the taste of her mouth and the firm proportions of her body—all these were important, too, all these were definitive parts of the Luise he loved. But much of that had been changed. In a few days she'd emerge from her sterile cocoon with her features rearranged, her body restructured, even her skin tone and texture biochemically altered to conform to the Shang Dynasty somatotype. He wondered how much of her personality had been trimmed away by the technicians' bloodless dialoops.

Quietly, he let himself out of her room and walked through the short hallway to the acceleramp. For an hour he rode aimlessly along the swiftly-moving corridors, until at last he found himself at the door of his own quarters. Tomorrow, he knew, would be another demanding day in his pre-mission schedule. Sleep eluded him; almost half of his scheduled sleep-time was filled with annoying, resentful wakefulness.

It was the following night before he had another opportunity to visit Luise. Her facial bandage was still in place and her swollen lips made conversation impossible, but she was conscious and she seemed to appreciate his coming by to hold her hand.

Fortune's intensive training continued; he forced himself to concentrate on the task at hand. At last, d'Kaamp was satisfied that his pupil had an excellent chance of surviving all predictable combat situations, the chief technologist in the Special Weaponry section had completed revising his personal armament. Now, only three days remained before the lipless mutant, Wi'in, would be free for empathy.

The schedule Tausig had mapped out for him allowed little time for personal affairs; thus, Fortune missed the unveiling of the new Luise. Her own briefing for the balance of her Residency was a much shorter process than what Fortune was going through, and her departure for duty was slated for a full day before his.

Conflicts in their respective schedules prevented them from seeing each other until the night before her departure day. The door of her room opened quickly in response to his signal.

Hannibal Fortune kept his face carefully impassive as his eyes examined the strange woman who stood in the center of the room. Although he'd expected her to look different, the transformation came as a shock. The first word to leap to his mind was *mutilated*.

"Luise?"

She laughed and walked toward him. "Drajne, darling, you look ill." At least her voice was the same. But the body which flowed into his arms was completely alien.

They'd even restructured her lips; it was like kissing a stranger.

"Is it really as bad as all that?" she asked.

"I wish I had time to get used to it, but you're leaving tomorrow."

Tomorrow arrived with astonishing rapidity.

They met again, briefly, the following day, when Fortune violated his crowded schedule to make room for a hurried farewell moments before she left.

"Come back to me," he whispered, wrapping his arms around her.

"In sixteen days," she promised.

"That's a long time away," he murmured, his lips brushing her ear. They held each other tightly in eloquent silence, painfully conscious of the gulf of subjective time that was soon to separate them. The moment begged for memorable phrases, but neither of them seemed able to think of any.

"Take care," he said, releasing her.

"You too." Her eyes searched his face, as if to etch it on her memory. Then, wordlessly, she turned away, stepped onto the acceleramp and let it whisk her down the long curving corridor leading to the departure area.

Fortune watched until she disappeared from view. He hardly felt his symbiotic partner's speech tendril crawl into his left ear. "A pint or two of *xanthe* might be appropriate," Webley hissed.

I agree, Fortune replied in loud-think. *You feel the same way about Ronel, don't you?*

"I've grown accustomed to her presence," the Torg growled. "Given time, I'll probably get used to the lack of it."

Wi'in knew about the situation in Carthage, Fortune discovered moments after their chess game got underway. Judging from the uncharacteristic hesitation in his tentacle as he reached for a pawn, the mutant didn't like Vango's report at all. "There iss a renote kossigility, uff course," he mused aloud, "that thiss diskrekancy iss insignifficant."

"About one chance in twenty thousand," Fortune demurred, watching the lipless one nudge the pawn forward.

"And kerhaks it iss not eeffen the work uff Enkire."

"Perhaps," Fortune agreed. "But not likely. It would help if we knew who'd taken over after Malik's death."

"Yess," Wi'in murmured. "Your nuve."

Fortune took the pawn with his king's bishop.

The chess game might seem a curious response to the report from Carthage, but T.E.R.R.A. Control was taking no chances. An hour with the empathic Wi'in could mean the difference between success or failure, for the lipless one identified so completely with Hannibal Fortune that throughout the assignment he'd function as a living analogue to the agent's thought processes. How will Fortune react to a given stimulus? Ask Wi'in.

There were only two more like him in the galaxy— each of them an unintentional mutation, the product of a genetic engineering experiment gone wrong. In a more primitive ecology they'd have been unfit for survival, for their sole talent was their knack for psychological mimicry. Misfits extraordinaire, Wi'in and his two others held T.E.R.R.A.'s highest rating, Double-A.

Think of the brain as an organic computer busily processing all the data it encounters, sifting, evaluating, comparing it with previously acquired information and rejecting that which fails to meet its pre-programmed standards of validity. But all data, at the point of entry, is "true." If the computer has a false concept in its validation circuits, the way all subsequent data is processed can be dangerously affected. In short, Wi'in's function was to absorb the agent's total mental pattern, including any subtle irrationalities which might have escaped challenge by the Psych Section. He couldn't identify which false concepts were present, but in solving problems he could be relied on to use them in the same proportion as Hannibal Fortune would use them.

"Skalenake," the mutant announced, waving a tentacle at the chessboard. As always, the game had ended in a draw. As always, it had taken exactly one hour. Hannibal Fortune was ready for the year 203 B.C.

FOUR: "I UNDERSTAND SHE
DANCES WELL, TOO."

Two-oh-three B.C. turned out to be singularly unready for Hannibal Fortune. The gleaming, twenty-four foot long temporal transporter winked out of otherwhen a few minutes after Vango filed his discrepancy report. The fertile tongue of land on which ancient Phoenician explorers had established the beginnings of Carthage hundreds of years earlier was barely visible on the southern horizon. Directly beneath the time-craft lay the incredibly blue Mediterranean, with Sicily to the north and the toe of Italy behind it.

Fortune phased the transporter into the observation module, making it invisible to outsiders, and approached the three hundred foot high mountain of red sandstone which stood between the walled city and the open sea.

Traces of winter lay strewn about on the higher slopes like forgotten toys, as spring, with classic lack of originality, joyously started the whole cycle over again.

Webley, sensing his partner's tingle of anticipation, built a pair of eyes and looked through the transparent bubble forming one end of the silvery ship. Fortune swung the craft to the left, bringing into view the vertical sea wall protecting Carthage from amphibious attack. A range of lesser peaks curved west and south to shield the northern third of the city and ended in an imposing hill capped with massive structures which towered commandingly over the rest of the settlement.

"The Byrsa," Fortune murmured, pointing.

"That's where they keep their money?"

The agent grinned. "True, the treasury and the mint are both up there, but the big attraction is said to be the temple in the middle, to the great god Eshmun."

"They're ambitious builders," observed the symbiote.

"It's a beautiful city," Fortune agreed, "as cities go."

They were directly east of the city now, with the mid-morning sun behind them, its rays glinting off the burnished rooftops and white and pink marble walls of the larger buildings. Swarming up the near side of the hill supporting the Byrsa were hundreds of closely-packed wooden buildings, some as many as six stories high, their overhanging balconies all but obscuring the three narrow streets leading up from the marketplace below to the fortressed structures at the top. Tens of thousands of Carthaginians, the cerebrotapes had taught him, lived in those many-level tenements. The marketplace was a tangle of winding Oriental streets faced with a thousand shops. Closer to the sea were the business offices of the shipping combines, and then the forum, a huge colonnaded square containing marble-faced administrative buildings, ornately decorated commercial offices, law courts and another dozen temples, their grounds lavishly furnished with Greek sculpture. Here the streets were a vast mosaic of black, pink and green stone worn smooth by the sandaled feet of the great city's quarter of a million inhabitants.

A broad avenue extended south from the forum for more than half a mile, ending on a small, fortified island in the middle of a perfectly circular, man-made harbor, the first of two landlocked harbors serving the commercial and military needs of the city. Two hundred Phoenician-style warships were berthed around the perimeter of the military harbor; almost that many merchant ships were visible at anchor in the rectangular commercial harbor adjoining it.

Fortune eased the invisible ship lower and glided across the seawall for a closer look at the Carthaginian navy. Compared to the colossal floating fortresses later Earthmen would build, these Punic warships seemed tiny. Indeed, few of them were much larger than the time-craft itself; all were powered by banks of oarsmen. Fortune was eager to see them in action; he imagined they'd behave like corks, their crowded decks swarming with sword-wielding warriors.

Beyond the harbors were row upon row of military barracks, parade grounds and permanent command posts stretching back to the great triple wall enclosing three sides of the thousand-acre city. Beneath one section of the wall, he knew, were stabling facilities for three hundred elephants while at ground level were accommodations for up to six thousand horses. The wall itself consisted of three steep-sided wedges, one inside the other, each rising forty-five feet from the ground and six feet thick at the top. The outer wall bristled with a multitude of watchtowers stretching up another twenty feet. Remnants of that three-mile-long triple wall would remain for the next two thousand years, long after Carthage was nothing but a historical curiosity.

Still out of phase with the objective *now*, Fortune piloted the transporter north, swinging in for a close look at the Temple of Eshmun, then continued almost a mile past the Byrsa to the area where Vango and Arrik maintained their Residency headquarters. As had happened before, at the much more ancient city of Mohenjo-daro, he was thankful that the local architecture featured walled and roofless courtyards. Skillfully, he set the time-craft down on Vango's lawn.

"Are you ready to get on with it, Web?" he asked.

"*I* am," the symbiote replied archly, "but don't you want to get into costume first?"

"As soon as you get off my back I will," the agent retorted.

Fortune's hair had been closely cropped over most of his head, leaving only enough forelock to arrange in a stylish neo-Grecian bang. Pigmentation pills had given his skin a sun-bronzed appearance while another chemical had changed his eye color from slate gray to walnut brown. His nose had been left alone on the grounds that it would be a versatile asset—straight enough to imply Greek ancestry, prominent enough to pass as Phoenician or Roman and with just enough aquilinity to validate an extemporaneous claim to Hebrew bloodlines.

From a storage cabinet, Fortune withdrew the garb of a typical upper-class Carthaginian and began to put it on. Over a soft beige-colored tunic of fine-spun cotton he skillfully draped a voluminous purple toga. The toga, all eighteen feet of it, had been woven in one piece from a purple-hued yarn guaranteed by T.E.R.R.A.'s technologists to fool even a wool-merchant —unless he tried to cut it. Both sleeves of the tunic and the lower edge of the toga were fringed with gold and silver ornaments. Next, on a bronze chain around his neck, he hung a fist-sized amulet, its silver surface bearing the bas-relief likeness of Baal-Moloch, the Saint Christopher of the pre-Christian world. Lightweight sandals in the Greek style and gold and silver rings on three fingers and the thumb of his right hand completed the costume.

"You look lovely," Webley murmured as Fortune checked his appearance in a mirror. "But doesn't a beard go with this one?"

"Patience," retorted the agent, unwrapping the beard. Moments later it was in place, its micron-thin dermoidal foundation molecularly bonded to his lower face, leaving the upper lip bare. Nothing less than a reversal of the binding field would remove it. "Better?" he asked.

"Perfect," agreed the Torg, resuming his yoke-like vantage point underneath his partner's tunic.

Fortune adjusted the time-craft's controls to warp it into the objective *now*, then strode to the exit and slapped the hatch control. With a mildly plosive wheeze of mismatched pressures, the sterile air in the transporter mixed with the spring-scented atmosphere of ancient Carthage.

Fortune stood in the open hatch and inhaled deeply, savoring Earth's peculiar green smells. "*Shalom!*" he called loudly, fully aware that the already ancient greeting would survive, unchanged, until his own time.

The ebony head of a servant boy peeked hesitantly from the edge of a doorway. Spotting him, Fortune laughed and continued in the Punic tongue, "Fear not— I am a friend of your master. Tell him Hannibal Fortune is here in answer to his message."

Eagerly, the head vanished. Fortune leaped to the ground and fished the silver amulet from the folds of his toga. It opened at a touch, revealing the remote phase-out controls for the temporal transporter. As the agent twisted one of two unmarked dials the hatch swung silently shut. Unhurriedly, he detached the body of the charm from its bronze chain, adjusted the other dial and carefully placed the amulet on the grass at his feet. This innocent-appearing device was one of the most sophisticated doorknobs ever built, and while fantastically easy to operate, it could kill you if you were careless with it. He touched the activating stud and prudently withdrew his hand.

Less than a second passed before both the amulet and the time-ship vanished, creating a tiny thunderclap which bounced off the veined marble façade of Vango's courtyard. Five seconds later the amulet reappeared, pulverizing several blades of grass in the process. The transporter remained safely tucked ninety degrees around the temporal corner from the objective *now*.

Fortune restored the amulet to its chain and dropped it out of sight inside his toga.

Vango, similarly attired but with more ostentatious rings glittering on his right hand, emerged from the doorway. For a moment he viewed his visitor with suspicion, then grinned broadly and strode across the barbered turf to extend his hand in welcome. Fortune had forgotten how tall the man was.

"Drajne, you devil!" the Resident exclaimed. "I thought you had a Residency of your own."

"That was a long time ago," Fortune replied, bridling at the unexpected use of his long-forgotten name.

"Seventeen years, that's all, Draj. For me, anyway. When'd you make Special Agent?"

"About forty years ago. My name now is Hannibal Fortune."

"Of course! You'd hardly have chosen any other. What's happened since last we saw each other?"

"I'm here to find out what's happened at this end."

"Naturally. Come on in and I'll give you all the information I have." Vango shook his massive head. "Hannibal Fortune," he repeated. "At least it's a shorter handle than you started out with."

"By one syllable," Fortune agreed, remembering that Vango had come from a culture where the shorter an individual's name the higher his social status.

"No hard feelings left, are there?" Vango asked, ushering them through an archway.

Fortune regarded him coldly. "Why should there be?"

The other shrugged. "Well, I mean, we both applied for this time period."

"I've had a fairly interesting life since then," Fortune replied dryly, reminding himself that he'd have to shelve his dislike for this man at least for the duration of the mission. The tendril of protoplasm in his ear agreed. "Now fill me in. According to your message, Syphax has joined forces with Hasdrubal. How'd this happen?"

"I don't know, but right now the two of them seem to have Scipio and his legionaries bottled up on a point of land several miles to the east of Utica." The Resident pulled out a large map from under a table and unrolled it. "Here's Utica—and here's Scipio. I didn't get wind of the development until about a week ago. As soon as I'd checked it out—you wouldn't believe the wild rumors that circulate in a place like this!—I put in a call to T.E.R.R.A. Control. That was early this morning. You boys on the fixit squad don't waste much time, do you?"

"We've learned not to." Fortune studied the map. "The siege of Utica was supposed to have been over in eighteen days. That was almost two months ago. Why didn't you report the discrepancy then?"

"Draj," Vango began, "you know how communications are in a place like this."

"That's one reason you have a partner, to help you keep track of what's going on. And please call me Fortune. The other name is dead; I prefer to stay alive."

"Good point," the Resident conceded. "Arrik and I have been rather busy lately, copying some of the better books in the local libraries. There's no point in letting material like that be lost. Most of it's going to be scattered to the barbarians when Rome wipes Carthage out completely."

"That won't happen for another fifty-nine years—if it happens at all."

"What do you mean?"

"If Scipio can't conquer Utica, what's he going to do when Hannibal gets back from Italy?"

"I see. It does present a bit of a puzzle, doesn't it?" *Web, where's Arrik?*

The symbiote's speech tendril pulsed in Fortune's ear. "Under his partner's toga—where else? The tall one's afraid of you."

Why?

"I don't know. That's all I could get. Arrik has him shielded beautifully."

Fortune's one-word reply in loud-think earned a chuckle from the Torg; aloud, the agent inquired: "How many men does Syphax command?"

"About forty thousand, I think. Maybe fifty."

"And Hasdrubal?"

Vango pulled thoughtfully at his lower lip, apparently thinking it made him look profound. To Fortune it was obvious the man was stalling while Arrik fed him information. "He claims thirty thousand infantry and about three thousand horse."

"No elephants?"

Another pause for silent prompting. "Arrik says Hasdrubal hasn't had very good luck with elephants."

"*Arrik* says?"

"I don't have much opportunity to move around among the military crowd," the Resident explained. The look of apology seemed grotesque on Vango's strong, angular face.

Fortune smiled crookedly. "All right," he said. "On the side of Carthage we have seventy to eighty thousand foot soldiers and at least three thousand cavalry troops."

"Thirteen thousand," Vango amended, "counting the ones Syphax brought in with him."

"And Scipio?"

"I don't know. Perhaps twenty thousand men all told, but probably not that many."

"How about Masinissa?"

Vango looked blank.

"Scipio's other ally, the hot-headed young Numidian prince. He's the nephew of King Syphax, I believe."

The Resident stood silently for a moment, listening to the voice of his symbiotic partner. "There was a rumor well over a year ago, Arrik says, that he was killed in a skirmish with some of Syphax' troops."

Fortune looked sharply at the taller man. "And you didn't report it?"

Vango's shoulders lifted in an eloquent gesture of futility. "Rumors, rumors, rumors," he whined. "You hear all kinds of rumors in a place like this. Why are you . . . ?" nervously, his voice trailed off into nothing.

"Vango," Fortune said evenly, "that young prince, fifty-nine years from now, was supposed to be a key figure in the destruction of Carthage. My License to Tamper gives me a lot of leeway, but I am not empowered to restore dead men to life."

"What are you going to do?"

"I have no choice," the agent replied. "I'll have to take a tour of the last two or three years and see what else you overlooked."

The taller man cringed as if he'd been slapped. A moment later he asked, too eagerly, "What can I do to help?"

"As a start," Fortune said, "you can have your cook fix us something for lunch. While we're eating you can give me a detailed account of everything you've done since your Residency began."

Vango looked quickly at his visitor, then as quickly away. "I—I don't think I'd know where to begin."

"I will," Fortune assured him.

The squat, lumpy body of Bahrs Tolunem wheezed from the effort of breathing the foul air of this accursed planet, but for the moment Bahrs was unmindful of his discomfort. His vision cones focused greedily on the multicolored ribbon feeding slowly from the monitor between his primary manipulators. If his blotchy face had been built for it, Bahrs Tolunem might have accomplished a triumphant smile; instead, the flexible orange vascules fringing the sides of his head rippled and stood erect. Shifting his glistening foot under him, he rocked forward to better peer at the encouraging readout. If all went well, he'd be back aboard the mother ship in a few days. His facial fringe pulsed with growing excitement as he reached for his communicator and curled it close to the florid vertical slit in his lower face.

"The hunter has arrived," he whispered.

From the doorway to his courtyard, Vango watched Hannibal Fortune unfasten the silver amulet from his neck and place it on the ground. He saw it vanish and flinched five seconds later at the loud pop when the cylindrical time-craft appeared.

"I messed things up nicely, didn't I?" he whispered bitterly.

The thin tendril of protoplasm which extended from his right ear and continued skin-clingingly down his neck to disappear under his tunic murmured reassuringly: "It's never the end of the world."

"Not until now, Arrik."

Thirty paces away, Fortune put the doorknob away and swung himself up through the open hatch into the transporter. Only when the hatch was closed again behind him did he break his angry silence.

"Webley, what do you think?"

The Torg lumped himself, made legs and jumped to the time-ship's deck. "It's not his fault," he said. "He's a collector."

"So's Luise," Fortune snapped. "But she does her job."

Webley assumed the shape of a furry four-footed creature, extruded a magnificently plumed tail and began pacing about the ship. "That's because she considers gathering data a part of her job. Vando sees the Residency as an excuse for collecting. He's interested in the books simply because they're books; he's not really concerned about what's in them."

Fortune, at the controls phased the craft again into

the observation module before taking off. "I hope we don't need his help—I'd hate to have to depend on him. How long will it take you to make a complete tour of the city?" As he spoke, the transporter leaped two thousand feet into the sky; its inertia-free field nullified all sensation of movement.

"Looking for Empire?" inquired the Torg.

"Of course."

"Maybe three hours."

"All right. Three hours from now, meet me"—Fortune looked out at the landscape spread out below him and decided upon a rendezvous point—"on top of that hill over there."

"Good hunting," Webley said, scampering to the exit hatch and revising his physical shape into that of a large bird.

After releasing the symbiote, Fortune piloted the capsule quickly to the hill they'd selected and flew several times around it, then headed west.

A single outer wall, some three miles long, ran across the narrowest point of the isthmus, making the peninsula on which Carthage was built seem like a five-sided figure, with the wall on the west, the Mediterranean on the two northernmost sides, Carthage proper occupying the southeast side and the Lake of Tunis lying mirrorsmooth on the southwest. Beyond the outer wall spread a great sandy plain through which the River Bagradas meandered northward to the sea. A few miles west of the river Fortune could see the hills on which the city of Utica sat stubbornly resisting Scipio's well-planned but abortive siege.

"Just east of Utica," Vango had said. Yes, there it

was, a smaller promontory which Scipio had appropriated for his winter quarters. Apparently anticipating a wet spring, he'd picked the driest and most easily defensible spot he could find and turned it into a garrison. With sublime faith in their destiny, Roman engineers invariably built things to last forever; they'd fortified the campsite until it resembled a permanent settlement, but despite the rocky nature of the landscape, mud was still a factor to be reckoned with. Earth's poets, the agent recalled, had written many an ode to spring, but to his knowledge none had ever penned a rhapsody to mud.

After three perfunctory passes over Scipio's temporary garrison—undeniably Roman with its precisely parallel streets, orderly rows of barracks and sturdy administrative buildings—Fortune began searching for the armies of King Syphax and the Carthaginian general Hasdrubal. As a rule, armies camp near sources of fresh water. Those of Syphax and Hasdrubal were no exception; Fortune followed the river for less than twenty miles before he came upon two separate encampments no more than a mile from each other.

The smaller of the two (assuming Vango was correct about their relative troop strength) should belong to Hasdrubal. In contrast to the harsh Latin linearity of the Roman outpost, the Carthaginian camp seemed unkempt and tawdry, lacking even the echoes of elegance that haunt the meanest slum. Here, mud was more than a nuisance; narrow wooden walkways laid on beds of twigs and branches spanned pools of ooze; hundreds of small tents and lean-tos sheltered Hasdrubal's troops while the officer corps apparently was housed in flimsy wooden barracks obviously not intended to last much longer than through the winter—by Roman standards most of them were sorely in need of repair.

A mile upriver was a larger, more untidy sprawl of multihued tents, plus a few temporary wooden shacks and extensive, rambling corrals; the land for several miles back from the river had been denuded by men and horses foraging for food. Even to Fortune's anti-spit'n'polish eye, the obviously Oriental encampment reflected an abysmal lack of organization which the spring mud magnified. A wall of sorts encircled the splendiferous chaos. Approximately in the middle of all rose an immense, gaudily striped tent with myriad pennants fluttering above it. Here, he guessed, was the headquarters of the aged Numidian monarch. Fortune frowned with disgust at Vango's failure to discover the elderly king's defection earlier in the game; the age and proximity of their campsites indicated the alliance between Syphax and Hasdrubal had come into being much sooner than "about a week ago." For the hundredth time he asked himself what possible profit Empire could derive from such a move, and for the hundredth time he reminded himself that finding out *how* Empire had accomplished it was the logical first step in determining *why*.

He let the transporter hover invisibly over the Numidian camp for several minutes while he looked for a starting place. When measuring a circle, start anywhere. Vango would be no help—his interview with the Resident had established that beyond doubt. Sending Webley to telepathically search the city admittedly was a shot in the dark; Fortune didn't expect positive results. And below him, he saw nothing bearing the convenient label, "clue."

Impatiently, he reached for the trolling lever and pulled it back a few notches. Outside the world changed color, as if a red filter had been placed between it and the time-craft. A gentle breeze he hadn't noticed before announced itself by changing direction, while the people inside the encompassing wall walked rapidly backward. As Fortune continued to watch, shadows lengthened perceptibly and the sun sank toward the eastern horizon, sucking the dawn along with it until starstrewn blackness prevailed above and the embers of a thousand small campfires glowed on the ground below. As the night grew progressively younger, flames feebly licked up from the coals. Fortune nudged the lever, causing the stars to wheel, and watched as cooks in quicktime hung blackened, food-encrusted pots over the fires, and milling troops emptied their plates and bowls into them; then he turned his eyes to the west to watch the rapid rise of a spectacular sunset.

A week flickered past in reverse. Fortune adjusted the controls and touched the jump switch. The transparent end of the capsule clouded and cleared; below, the Numidian camp lay swathed in snow, which the trolling effect turned pink. Another jump deepened the snow; the next swept it away to reveal windblown, frozen ground. The sun continued its leaps and plunges. Fortune pushed the lever forward when half the tents collapsed, and watched the troops tear the camp apart.

In the ensuing half hour, Fortune observed two skirmishes with the Romans, saw the fantastic Numidian horsemen in battle—every bit as exciting as d'Kaamp had described it—and witnessed the arrival of this disorderly army. By means of small samples, Fortune managed to keep track of all three armies in the field,

Syphax', Hasdrubal's and Scipio's, and to get a remarkably clear idea of their fighting styles. He regretted that the observation module limited him to visual monitoring only—something like silent movies—but even so, watching it was highly instructive.

He tracked Syphax' forces to their headquarters at Cirta, some two hundred miles west of the great plain where most of the maneuvering took place. Although built of stone instead of tents, Cirta seemed as haphazardly constructed as the Numidian winter encampment. The army itself was camped around two sides of the small city, completely enclosing an ostentatious assortment of buildings which could only be Syphax' palace. Fortune grinned. Sumptuousness seemed a keynote of the venerable ruler. Every luxury known to early Earthmen was in evidence—including what looked suspiciously like a harem. The king might be old, but apparently he still liked his dancing girls. Hovering closer to examine the palace grounds, Fortune lingered musingly near the half-dozen spangled young women in the walled gardens of the palace. They were adequate, he decided, as was the palace by the standards of its time, but he'd enjoyed greater luxury and a far more beautiful girl at *Time Out*.

Thinking of Luise brought a pang of emptiness; in all his years he'd had little experience at being lonely, particularly for one specific woman.

Webley had started at the extreme northeast corner of the city, where the municipal water supply was kept in huge cisterns. He'd flown slowly along the waterfront, combing an area fifty feet wide with his telepathic probe. Reaching the end of the seawall some two miles to the southwest, he turned abruptly right and followed the triple wall which protected Carthage from attack by land. Made of stone slabs and mortar, the outer wall was six feet thick and forty-five feet high. About ten feet behind it stood a second wall, identical to the first, and a third ten feet behind that.

The triple wall ran in a straight line for almost a mile paralleling the Lake of Tunis, then turned again at right angles—so did Webley, noting that the foundation here was thicker and heavier, and hollow. His probe detected elephants beneath the walls, but no alien life-forms. He followed the walls northeast for another mile and a half, where they bulged outward slightly to curve around the Byrsa. At the end of an hour he'd made two complete circuits of the city, the second smaller than the first, and was well into the third. Humans, pack animals, elephants—but still no aliens. Patiently he continued, his great brown wings flapping lazily as he searched in ever-tightening circles.

Thinking about Luise would not get the job done. Annoyed, Fortune manipulated the time-craft through a series of jumps to monitor the preceding six months, pausing here and there to troll at quick speed, but still without turning up anything of value. He was about to abandon further search along this line when a random jump revealed a scene of pomp and pageantry with feasting, games and precision riding by the cream of Syphax' horsemen. The climax was a solemn ritual which puzzled the agent until he realized it was a wedding ceremony. The bride was a delicious looking bit of dusky pastry, probably still in her teens—but the bridgeroom was the aged warrior himself. Fortune grinned and settled down to watch.

And to wonder.

Clearly this was no simple affiliation between desert tribes—the crowd was too formal for that. Here and there among the gaudy tribal costumes were the civilized purple togas of upper-class Carthaginans. Was the bride herself, then, a daughter of Carthage?

He recalled no mention of a state wedding in the annals of either Polybius or Livy, yet this was far too impressive an event to go unrecorded. Syphax was in his eighties, decidedly old by Earthly standards. Might his head have been turned by a temptress not yet out of her teens? Fortune trained a scope on the royal couple. A blissful expression adorned the bearded bantam's lined and sun-etched face. And there was something disturbingly familiar about the girl. . . .

Mentally, Fortune sifted through the file of known Empire faces, drawing a blank. He recalled how his own side had altered the face of Luise Little; it was reasonable to assume Empire might have perfected comparable techniques of cosmetic surgery. Again, it might be a wild-goose chase, but if he failed to check it out he'd be guilty of the same sort of negligence Vango had committed.

He trolled several days into the past, watching the quicktime world below. At last he found the bride's arrival. In the red-tinted world of backwardness, it looked like a stately departure with people and horses solemnly proceeding hind part foremost, magically erasing their own footprints. Fortune kept the time-craft directly above them for a while, then edged ahead, following their trail into the desert until he came to an oasis where the tracks abruptly vanished.

Hmmm. Had the tiny caravan spent the night here, while the desert wind erased their tracks of yesterday? If so, the same wind had erased all evidence of camp-fires and the litter human companies invariably leave behind. Discreetly, he piloted the invisible capsule to a knoll a hundred yards away and settled back to see what had happened.

Before the morning sun had dropped much lower in the sky his answer burst swiftly over the top of a dune. It was a custom-styled IntraSystem luxury skimmer, not over four years old, its pyroceramic finish gleaming smartly. As it pancaked toward the oasis a small dust-storm swirled around it and then settled quickly under-neath. A moment later the backward caravan galloped into sight. A ramp swung open and the five horses and their riders clattered tail-first into the skimmer, taking their hoofprints with them. The ramp scissored shut and the sleek craft departed, this time without any ac-companying dust cloud.

"I wonder who she is?" Hannibal Fortune murmured, nodding in satisfaction. Canceling the trolling effect, he matched entropy with realtime. Obediently, the Intra-System skimmer returned, gaped open and the caravan trotted down the metallic incline. As the horses and riders departed, the ramp swung shut again and the skimmer took off in a cloud of dust. Fortune followed the skimmer.

As long as he stayed in the secondary or observation module, warped a few degrees out of phase with ob-jective reality, his craft was invisible to human eye and electronic sensors alike. Thus there was no way for the

Empire ship to detect his presence. Unsuspectingly it led him straight to the enemy stronghold. Fortune grinned—once again his opponents had sought the security of a cave. This one was about two-thirds up the side of a sheer rock facing which rose a good two hundred feet out of the water about five miles north of Carthage. Inaccessible . . . to anything short of a skimmer.

Feeling far better about the assignment, Fortune went back to the wedding.

An hour later, by dint of patient trolling back and forth through the doddering monarch's wedding day, Fortune had found him a spy. At least that seemed a likely category—the label could be changed later, if necessary. The spy attended the wedding as an old man, obviously crippled with arthritis, then hobbled painfully away from the banquet and faded quietly into the sunset. Once out of sight of the town, his gait became astonishingly springy. A quarter of a mile into the desert he was joined by a horse. Stripping off some of his rags, he tied them into a bundle and leaped lightly to the bare back of his steed. He sped off to the north, then headed northeast.

Delighted, Fortune tagged along overhead.

Keeping the mystery rider in sight was no problem until well after sundown. Fortune tried using the trolling lever and promptly lost him; the red-filter effect made the night seem even blacker. Irritably, the agent reconciled himself to a long trip, matching the speed of his transporter to the twenty-mile-per-hour gait of the unidentified rider. Four discouragingly uneventful hours later they reached Hippo Regius, a small fishing village on the Mediterranean.

When he'd told Webley to meet him in three hours he hadn't realized it might take him a week to find where the deviation began. He checked the lapse-time indicator and discovered why he felt not only tired but hungry—it had been better than ten hours since lunch. Curiosity tempted him to stay with it at least until the mystery rider made contact with someone, but that might still be a long way off. Decades of training warned him he'd function better with food and rest. The beauty of using the temporal transporter was that you could leave any given action line at any time, go somewhen else and rest up for as long as you needed, only to re-join the events-in-progress a fraction of a second after you'd left them. This leisurely approach had given him the edge he needed to win many a battle. He might be "away" for a month—or a year—and still be able to make his scheduled rendezvous with Webley "three hours from now."

Yawning, Fortune punched an address into the ship's computer, read the coordinates and set the controls accordingly. The twin clocks above his control panel continued their synchronized movement for another few seconds. Then a chime sounded, the observation bubble clouded over and the lock on the left stopped. Three seconds later the bubble cleared, the chime spoke softly again and the clock resumed its movement.

Physically, he was still hovering over the fishing village. Temporally, he was a full century earlier on the time-line. From the stores he took a field-rations package, crushed its heat button, waited the requisite ten seconds and then unzipped it from its plastic container. Smiling at the way T.E.R.R.A.'s chefs had tailored the repast to his gourmet taste, he spent the next half hour thoroughly enjoying the meal. When he'd finished, he chucked the remains into the disposal tube, activated the sleepframe and climbed in. The wakealarm would rouse him when he'd had sufficient rest.

Drowsily, he thought how nice it would be if only Luise could have been there to keep him company.

And how rotten it was that she wasn't.

Webley enlarged his wing muscles to take the strain off—two hours of telepathic searching had produced nothing but an ache in his protoplasmic shoulders. Almost a quarter of a million people were crowded into Carthage's roughly thirteen hundred acres—at least a hundred thousand more lived in the suburbs to the west, either working their own small parcels of land or tilling the plantations and estates of the nobility. But there was still no trace of any alien presence. He had less than an hour to complete his survey, then hurry northward for his appointment atop the sandstone bluff which jutted out over the Mediterranean.

Shelving his impatience, Webley began another circuit of the city, flying now through the shadow of the Byrsa, soaring slowly to keep from missing any sign of extraterrestrials lurking in the teeming tenements below.

Refreshed by sufficient sleep, Fortune resumed the chase. He saw the unidentified Numidian rider in conference with a Roman officer, then followed the Roman to the small fleet anchored offshore. Almost immediately the fleet cast off, sailing toward Sicily. Fortune used the trolling lever to speed things up, and soon witnessed the fleet's arrival at the port of Lilybaeum, on Sicily's western tip, where a much larger force of legionaries was waiting. This, he realized, was the army Scipio was preparing for next spring's invasion of Africa. He felt at last that he was on the right track—the news of Syphax' marriage to a sexy young Carthaginian would surely have some discernible effect on the Roman commander's plans.

Yes, there was Scipio himself, resplendently out of uniform, striding down to the docks. Fortune piloted the invisible transporter as close to the Romans as possible. He could see their lips move, and he knew they were speaking Latin, one of the tongues taught him by the cerebrofield unit back at T.E.R.R.A. Control; but without sound, he discovered, his knowledge of the dialect did him no good at all. He could speak it, but he'd never *seen* anyone else speak it. In such circumstances lipreading is impossible. There are a few disadvantages, he realized ruefully, in acquiring a strange language by cerebrofield.

The rules of time travel, learned through the costly method of trial and error, prevented him from warping into the objective *now* to hear what was going on. The slightest participation at this point could easily snowball into a first-class catastrophe later. Light was the only form of energy which could penetrate the out-of-phase time-craft, and light, he was sure, would be all T.E.R.R.A.'s technologists would need. They could easily link an audio pickup to a laser communications unit, which in frozentime he could then plant somewhere in the area—perhaps on Scipio himself, if it was small enough—to monitor the Romans' conversations. But he didn't have such a unit, and going back to T.E.R.R.A. Control at this stage of the game was out of the question. If . . .

But he had something almost as good.

"All right," he said, chuckling softly. It took him but a moment to find it in the supply locker. He grinned happily, turning d'Kaamp's miniaturized recorder over in his hand. Hardly larger than a pea, it was obviously too small (to Roman eyes) to accomplish anything, yet Fortune knew its molecular modulation memory core had room for nearly two G.F. Standard Years' worth of continuous recording. "Gentlemen," he said quietly, "If you'll just be good enough to hold still for a few milliseconds . . ."

The Federation's top theoretical temporalists held that, in theory anyway, the frozentime approach was impossible. Undaunted, T.E.R.R.A.'s techs had found a way to make it work. Fortune didn't pretend to understand *why* it worked, but he was an old hand at working *with* it. Donning an air mask, he assembled his equipment and pushed a button.

Outside, all motion ceased. The breakers seemed to turn to lead—even the spray hung suspended. Scipio, one of the greatest military minds of the age, was caught with his mouth open. The one reporting to him—Laelius, Fortune remembered from the cerebrofield session—was crystallized in mid-gesture.

Fortune opened the hatch and went out into the time-frozen world. It wasn't really motionless; if he watched long enough he'd see movement. Depending on which time-line you chose as a reference point, either the Romans were enormously slowed down or Hannibal Fortune was moving at super-speed. From the agent's side of the temporal mismatch, he had several minutes in which to accomplish his task, while to Scipio and Laelius it would all be over in a fraction of a second, much too quickly for any of it to register on their consciousness or be admitted into their view of reality.

Since he planned to retrieve the gadget in a few days at most, he decided against implanting it in one of the general's teeth and settled for the hemmed edge of Scipio's tunic, near the throat. Merely walking through the slowed-down air molecules to reach the man was like wading through neck-deep mud. The soft fabric of Scipio's tunic couldn't have been harder to manipulate had it been made of sheet steel; Fortune had to pry the hem apart even after severing the threads holding it together. Once the device was in place, a tiny spot of glue repaired the damage; he felt confident that Scipio would never notice the alteration.

He waded back through the heavy atmosphere and sealed the transporter's hatch behind him, then pushed the button that turned the world on again. The entire operation had taken less than a fiftieth of a second.

He wondered what Luise would think of d'Kaamp's micro-miniaturized audio snoop. It couldn't compare, of course, with the portable cerebrofield unit she was accustomed to—it lacked the eight other channels needed to make full-sensory documents. Designed for sound only, it was clearly an instrument of intrigue and espionage, but remembering her communications background he felt it might appeal to her passion for gadgetry.

He wondered what she was doing now. Deceptive question, when "now" was any point he might decide to visit. He frowned. An unscheduled side-trip to the Shang Dynasty was decidedly not a part of his assignment. But on the other hand he could remember no specific rule against it. Why not? She was more than a thousand years away on a part of the planet which had nothing to do with any event even remotely connected with the Punic Wars, so there'd be no breach of temporal safety. And perhaps seeing her again would keep him from thinking about her all the time. In a sense, he told himself, such a visit could prove beneficial if it increased his efficiency on the job. She might even have a useful idea to contribute. And it wasn't as if he was stealing time from the task at hand . . .

The only difficulty was a minor one: without map coordinates he'd have to work from memory to establish her temporal placement and then mix luck with logic to locate her geographical whereabouts. The adventure at Mohenjo-daro, he recalled, had occupied less than a week of the Earth-year 1481 B.C., Mark 4054 on T.E.R.R.A.'s calendar. That week had been in midsummer, but he couldn't remember exactly when. Luise and Ronel's Residency in China was to have begun only a day or so after their departure from Mohenjo-daro. For his own safety, he elected to avoid the entire year of Mark 4054. Considering the feverish maneuvering everyone had done to keep him from violating the Double Occupancy Rule* during *that* escapade, blundering

---

*T.E.R.R.A. had learned the hard way that Time won't tolerate a double. Once you occupy a given segment of a time-line, any attempt to occupy it again—so that two of you would exist at the same time—constitutes a violation of basic temporal dynamics and results in your instant annihilation. The resultant entropy vortex could cause dangerous ripples for centuries to come. Apparently, the Double Occupancy Rule applies equally to all physically coherent objects with appreciable mass. Presumably, grains of sand,

(*Footnote continued on next page*)

into *Doubletime* now would be most unseemly, in addition to being decidedly fatal.

The Shang Dynasty Residency spanned four years, from Mark 4054 to 4050. The middle of 4053, he decided at last, would be as good a time as any. Luise would have had a year in which to get her work underway, and might well be hungry for a familiar face. He admired her for taking so gracefully Pohl Tausig's stubborn refusal to promote her to Special Agent status, but Fortune suspected that underneath the cool façade she was bitterly disappointed. Tausig, he realized now, might even have insisted on her finishing out the Residency as a way to enforce a separation. Yes, Pohl was not above pulling a trick like that, particularly if for some reason he thought it would be beneficial to the Agency to break up a "dangerous alliance." Fortune had known Tausig long enough to recognize his quirks, one of which was his doctrine that no good agent could afford a lasting personal involvement with anyone but his symbiotic teammate. Perhaps Tausig himself wasn't man enough to handle such a thing, but he had no right

(Footnot continued)

specks of dust, air molecules and chemically processed substances such as the food you're digesting are not significantly affected by violations of doubletime. Thus far, the research and development team headed by Linz Lipnig, co-inventor of the temporal transporter, had perfected a number of ways to "cheat" the so-called Laws of Temporal Displacement—the time-craft's capability to navigate both in the primary and secondary modules was one, and the frozentime phenomenon was another—but as yet they hadn't found a way to violate doubletime and live. Technically inclined readers are referred to the previous three Agent of T.E.R.R.A. books.

to assume that his own shortcomings were shared by every member of the Agency. Now that he thought of it, Fortune seriously doubted that the Operations Chief was really capable of a meaningful involvement with another human being. If so, he wasn't the first brilliant administrator with such a defect. Fortune marveled that he'd overlooked Tausig's peculiarity for so long.

FIVE: "YOU WERE EXPECTING
GREGOR MALIK?"

IN THE BEGINNING was chaos, with sky and earth like the white and yolk of an egg. Into the chaos was born P'an-ku, who gave form to the sky from bright and clear elements, and to the earth from dark, impure elements. Each day the sky became ten feet higher and the earth ten feet thicker, while P'an-ku himself grew ten feet taller. He lived exactly eighteen thousand years, by which time the sky was very high, the earth was quite thick and P'an-ku rather tall.

His tears became the mighty Huang-ho and Yangtzu Rivers, and upon his death P'an-ku's body fell apart to form the Five Sacred Mountains; his eyes soared heavenward to become the sun and the moon, his fat ran down to fill the seas and his hairs covered the earth with growing things.

Four hundred thousand wonderous years passed while mighty personages walked the earth.

At long last the Yellow Emperor, Huang-ti, ruled the entire world, from the mountainous headwaters of the Yellow River to where it empties into the Yellow Sea. In 2697 B.C., Huang-ti established the First Dynasty, whereupon his beautiful Empress, the Lady of Si-ling, invented the silkworm, the reel and the loom so that her people might practice the arts of sericulture and weaving.

Eleven hundred years after *that*, the Emperor Chung-ting built the City of Ao a few miles south of the sluggish, silt-laden Huang-ho, making it the capital of the Shang Dynasty.

The city had been flourishing for eighty years when Luise Little arrived. The data she'd absorbed in the course of her cerebrofield sessions had been remarkably accurate, considering the limitations of the survey which had garnered them.

Inasmuch as the mainstream of Earth history—that part of it which had made the greatest contributions to the planet's eventual membership in the Galactic Federation, at any rate—had been centered around the Mediterranean, spreading to northern Europe and hence to the Americas, all of T.E.R.R.A.'s continuous Residencies were in those areas. The earliest Resident Team had been based in Egypt in 1800 B.C. By 1550 B.C the headquarters had shifted to the island of Crete. With the destruction of the Minoan civilization it was moved to Greece and a second permanent Residency was established in Phoenicia, to keep tabs on the shipbuilding and mercantile centers of Tyre and Sidon as well as to monitor the emerging Hebrew culture during Solomon's heyday. In the ensuing two dozen centuries there were times when as many as five continuous Residencies were operating at once on various parts of the planet, but Luise knew that China would not have one until the days of Gengis Khan, in the thirteenth century A.D., some twenty-six hundred years after her own assignment on the banks of the Huang-ho.

Thus, instead of stepping smoothly into an established niche prepared by a team whose tour of duty had expired, Luise and Ronel had to start from scratch, as

78

they had done before at Mohenjo-daro, with a minimum of equipment and no prearranged cover story. The survey team had buried the computer, dynamo, transmitter and directional broadcast grid for the sub-spatial communicator some four miles from the City of Ao. Among her portable effects was a remote control unit which could cause the buried equipment to hurl a tight-beam, four megawatt distress call halfway across the galaxy. With luck, she'd never have to use it.

Of more interest to Luise were the pair of portable cerebrofield recorders and the stack of blank tapes upon which she hoped to collect a wealth of full-sensory data for T.E.R.R.A.'s History Section. Imbedded in her skull were hundreds of tiny cerebrofield sensors which transferred to the recorder whatever she saw, heard, smelled or otherwise experienced. The bulk of her tapes, along with an assortment of other gadgets, were concealed at the transmitter site; once she'd established herself in Shang society her shapechanging partner could bring them, a few at a time, to the Residency Headquarters. But to start, she carried only a small, ornately decorated trunk such as would logically be owned by an upper-class Chinese beauty in 1481 B.C.

The chances against Empire's interfering during the time of her Residency were astronomical. And the odds were even greater, she firmly believed, against Drajne Wokajeni showing up. Only an extremely stupid sentimentalist would make herself needlessly miserable by continually rehashing the cherished memories of her great love affair; Luise may have been somewhat of a sentimentalist but she was far from stupid. Quite sensibly, she determined to hurl herself wholeheartedly into her assignment, and to allow the year at *Time Out* to fade quietly into her past. It might be interesting, she reasoned, to begin a new love affair with him at the end of her four-year absence, but to make definite plans for it until that time actually arrived would be pointless.

Meanwhile, she and Ronel had a job to do, in a culture whose social structure gave little freedom of action to females. The success of her assignment, she knew, depended upon learning the rules of the game being played by the Shang Dynasty's inhabitants and then using those rules to her own best advantage. It had been impossible for the survey team's cerebrosnoops to gather more than an outline of the customs and significant mores she'd have to contend with, and although the Chinese themselves were already developing a written language, it would be another thousand years before the celebrated social philosopher Confucius would record the first references to Shang traditions and value systems. The opinions of subsequent Chinese historians, she knew, could no more be trusted than could the guesswork of any other culture's ancient history buffs. Learning the game, and developing a practical proficiency at playing it, would be enough to keep her thoroughly occupied for the first several months, without the extraneous burden of worrying about yesterday's love affair.

When she found that in order to conduct her Residency with any degree of efficiency the Shang game required her to attach herself to an influential male member of the ruling class, she discussed the problem with Ronel at some length. The symbiote then spent the next week in various guises snooping about the households of a score of the city's most influential families.

With the Torg's telepathic talents, it was relatively easy to find several likely candidates and then probe their attitudes, beliefs, appetites and temperaments thoroughly enough for Luise to decide which one of them would be the most potentially useful to her. After carefully weighing all the factors, she made her choice and devised a plan of action.

Thus, Cheng Te-k'un, eldest son of Cheng Tso-pin, who owned the bronze factory half a mile to the south of the city, one day set off in pursuit of an exotically plumaged bird and found instead, to his astonishment and delight, a lovely princess from a far-off dynasty. Her caravan, she told him, had been set upon by marauding bandits who had killed or kidnapped her entire company. Accompanied by her pet monkey, the terrified girl had miraculously escaped with only a small, exquisitely lacquered trunk containing a few of her personal possessions. Young Cheng was familiar with the periodic raids conducted by the savage Tartars who infested the hills to the north, and he was completely captivated by the aristocratic but quite helpless girl before him. Not only was she young and physically attractive but she seemed to share so many of his tastes and opinions that it was hours before he remembered that the gaudy bird which had accidentally led him to her hiding place had vanished completely.

For a young nobleman such as Cheng Te-k'un, the name of the game was "finders keepers." The girl's claim to noble blood merely enhanced her value as a prize. Concepts of ownership applied as much to people as to things in those days, which made Luise Little the uncontested property of Cheng Te-k'un, a trophy with which he had every right to do as he pleased.

China, Hannibal Fortune soon discovered, covers a lot of ground. To complicate his search, he wasn't sure which of the many rivers the Shang Dynasty had been established upon. As a result, he wasted a day exploring the 3,400 mile length of the Yangtzu before remembering a reference Luise had made to the Central China Plain. He found small settlements along every river he encountered—and he was well aware that flying over a village is not the most efficient way to locate a specific individual, particularly when she'd been surgically altered to look like a typical native.

Still, Luise had one peculiarity which would set her apart from every other individual in China: like all Resident Agents, she carried in her skull hundreds of miniature transmitters keyed to the frequencies of a full-sensory cerebrofield recorder. And the time-craft contained instruments whose specific purpose was to detect those faint radiations.

Leaving the mountainous headwaters of the Yangtzu, Fortune traveled north and east, flying over snow-encrusted peaks and finding beyond them a vast alluvial plain that stretched for hundreds of miles. Then more rivers, more villages. But nothing that even vaguely resembled a city.

She'd known before leaving T.E.R.R.A. Control that the Shang dynasty was inconsequential as far as the planet's political history was concerned. Furthermore, from a standpoint of monitoring cultural development it was equally unimportant, because the Dynamic Theory of History* made it immaterial which specific individual

*See *Agent of T.E.R.R.A. #1, The Flying Saucer Gambit.*

did what in a given time-period; advances in a civilization tended to take place only when the culture was ready for them, never earlier, never much later. An innovator "fifty years before his time" was invariably handicapped by the lack of supportive technology to make his ideas work—or else he found himself derided as a crackpot.

From a technological standpoint, one rather thin excuse for her mission could be made, and that was to find out how Shang bronze manufacture had progressed from the pottery level to an advanced degree of metalcraft without leaving traces of intermediate stages. Prior to the Shang Dynasty, established in 1766 B.C. by King T'ien-yi, Chinese bronzes had not existed. Under the House of Shang, however, extremely sophisticated bronzeware had displaced the proto-Chinese neolithic gray pottery, duplicating the pottery forms in metal, often with considerable improvement. All other Bronze Age cultures had come about gradually, but here it had been an abrupt (and to countless generations of archeologists, a puzzling) technological breakthrough.

Becoming the property of Cheng Te-k'un gave Luise an ideal opportunity to learn how it had happened.

Invisibly, Fortune hovered over the ancient City of Ao. Covering less than a third of the area of Carthage, this early Chinese metropolis seemed to be almost a perfect square, approximately a mile on each side, and was completely enclosed by a high wall some sixty to sixty-five feet thick. Although its streets were arranged with all the rectilinear precision Fortune had observed at the Roman camp, somehow it avoided looking starkly functional—as though these early Chinese already had a glimmer of the beauty inherent in simplicity which Zen artists would bring to a later age.

At a distance the most predominant feature was the cluster of bright yellow rooftops approximately in the center of the city. Yellow, Fortune remembered, was the imperial color. Most of the rest of the buildings were roofed in gray, with a few blues and greens topping the larger ones. Somewhere in this city, the ship's detector circuits told him, was Luise Little. It took but a few minutes for him to pinpoint the structure from which her cerebrofield radiations originated. Keeping to the observation module, invisibly out of phase with the objective *now*, he piloted the time-craft closer.

Her strategy had worked out rather well, Luise reflected, although she admitted it hadn't been entirely without problems. Despite the limitations Shang society imposed upon her because of her sex, and the concomitant role she had to play in her dealings with young Cheng Te-k'un, she was allowed a full retinue of slaves and almost complete freedom to come and go as she pleased. She could hardly have chosen a better protector. Not only was he affectionate, but he had the capacity for great understanding, if only his culture would allow it.

Now and again she thought about Drajne Wokajeni, but not often. The interlude with Drajne had been educational: it had taught her the folly of becoming too deeply involved with anyone else. If their positions had been reversed she was sure Draj would have done the same thing, because diligence was too strong a part of his life pattern for anyone to rationally expect anything else of him.

The telltale radiation was coming from one of seven small structures clustered in a U around a much larger one. All eight houses obviously belonged together, judging from the relative elegance of the architecture. Could Luise, Fortune wondered, have acquired in only a year enough local economic strength to afford such a mansion? He remembered what she'd accomplished at Mohenjo-daro—the thriving toy shop—and decided it was entirely possible. Still, elementary caution dictated a circuitous approach; Fortune was keenly aware of how helpful Webley's telepathic talents would have been in determining the exact situation below. Lacking the Torg's assistance, he hovered close to the buildings and used the trolling mode to help gather information.

The experiment proved peculiarly unsuccessful. Although there were considerable comings and goings in the red-lit world below, none of them made particular sense. At the end of the speeded-up day, Fortune knew little more than he had at the outset. And now, as dusk quick-stepped across the countryside it brought with it a platoon of roiling storm-clouds striding swiftly on spindly stilts of lightning.

The storm wrapped the small city in howling sheets of darkness, vomiting tons of water on the yellow, blue, green and gray roofs. The pop of the materializing time-craft was lost among ferocious thunderclaps. Hannibal Fortune was throughly drenched by the time he reached the shelter of the broad eaves over the window from behind which came Luise Little's cerebrosensor radiations. The lightweight frame slid easily aside.

From the darkness came a voice in Unispeak:

"Come in and close the window, please, Drajne. I do hope you didn't let anyone see you arrive."

"Luise?"

The girl laughed. "You were expecting Gregor Malik?" Unshielding a lamp, she held it high to look at him.

Drenched, bearded, shivering in his indestructible toga, Hannibal Fortune sneezed. Rainwater dripped from his Grecian bangs and trickled down his nose.

"At least," Luise said, suppressing a giggle, "you no longer look like a Professional Hero. Where's Webley?"

"Carthage."

"Oh?"

"He doesn't know I'm gone. I came to see you."

"You shouldn't have." Her manner was suddenly serious; her voice carried a note of dismay as she continued: "If anyone sees you it could wreck everything I've worked a year to accomplish. . . ."

"Nobody saw me," he assured her quickly. "I'm not a newcomer to this game."

"You're acting like one."

"What sort of welcome is that?"

"What did you expect? Do you want me to pat you on the head and tell you what a clever boy you are?"

Conscious of the puddle that was growing at his feet, Fortune stared at her. The sense of alienation he'd felt when he'd first seen her restructured face at T.E.R.R.A. Control returned, augmented by her present obvious hostility. Hannibal Fortune, hero, reduced to soggy, sneezing Drajne Wokajeni, like a movie extra who's blundered onto the wrong sound stage; a Don Quixote

86

disappointingly insignificant in his role, his aspirations, his hungers and his importance—even to the windmill. "You've managed to turn it all off, haven't you?"

"I'm sorry," she said. "That was cruel of me. I'd forgotten how it was for me the first few weeks. I loved you."

"Loved," he repeated, giving her a chance to amend her statement.

Luise nodded. "I can't afford it any more," she said firmly. "And neither can you."

He breathed deeply, his mind auditioning several responses and rejecting them all. Hannibal Fortune opened his mouth to speak but Drajne Wokajeni had nothing to say.

Sensing his discomfort, Luise made her voice softer. "I've had the good feelings and the bad. I finally decided it would be stupid to go on making myself miserable with it."

"I've missed you," Fortune said, trying to sound casual.

"I've missed you, too," she assured him patiently. "At first. But I lived through it."

"Thanks."

"Darling Drajne, I've been away from you for over a year. For you it's only been—what?—two days? Three days? Believe me, love, you'll get over it. It just takes time, that's all."

"You're right," he agreed unconvincingly. "Foolish of me to expect anything else, I guess."

"Everybody has a right to be foolish sometime." She smiled, remembering something. "I wrote a poem several months ago. A silly thing, I suppose."

"I'd like to see it." Anything, now, to prolong the encounter.

She found it in a discouragingly short time.
He unfolded the paper and read—too quickly:

Doe soft eyes
   Watching, gently
Lips that show a faint inviting smile.
Lowered lashes veil the momentary fright
   Of a smallest doubt
All answered.
   Both know somehow, somewhere
Two hearts must share a touch.

Lips meet briefly
   In the softness of the sweet protecting night.
Sharing, loving
   Two bodies press in passion-filled embrace.
Two souls
       blending
          are one.
Love fulfilled, and time has run her length
The hour of parting
         hesitant
            reluctant
              is done.
Remember,
   And in remembering leave no regret
Tender thoughts
   That what has passed
         though gone
           was good.

Fortune refolded the paper and tucked it inside his toga. "You wrote that when?"

Luise shrugged. "Six, seven months ago."

"I see. You write well." Inwardly, he winced at the banality of his words.

"It's not great poetry. I wasn't at all satisfied with the ending."

"I'm not either." An awkward pause. "I still want you, Luise."

"I know. But really, it's over. It's all gone; don't try to bring it back. It's never any good when you try to bring it back."

"Who told you that?"

She smiled. "We knew when we started it that people like us can't afford to fall in love. I know how you feel, Drajne, but there's nothing I can do to help."

"I don't think you do."

"Maybe not," she agreed, shrugging. "But that doesn't change things. You're here and you shouldn't be."

"Is that all that bothers you?"

"Isn't it enough? I have a job to do here. I think I have a right to be annoyed at anything that endangers my Residency."

Fortune laughed harshly. "If there'd been any danger I certainly wouldn't have come."

"I don't believe that."

He reached for her but she turned quickly away.

"Do you still want me to leave?"

"Yes."

"Luise."

"I want you to get out of here," she insisted. "Go back to whenever it is you're supposed to be, and leave me alone."

"All right," Fortune said slowly. "If that's what you want."

"That's what I want," she assured him. "And try not to be seen leaving. This is a culture that doesn't take kindly to strangers messing with other men's women." She hooded the lamp.

Wordlessly, Hannibal Fortune stared at the darkness, then let himself out into the storm.

SIX: DIGRESSION IS THE
BITTER PART OF VALOR.

ONCE INSIDE THE the time-craft, he disgustedly stripped off his sodden toga and hurled all eighteen feet of it against the rear bulkhead. The tunic underneath was relatively dry—his beard, however, was soaked. He cursed the overconscientious technician who'd developed the molecular bonding that held it to his face. Puddles of rainwater made the deck slippery underfoot.

Outside, the storm still raged, shattering the dark with lightnings, flogging the City of Ao with angry winds. The storm's violence seemed almost an echo of Hannibal Fortune's mood as he viciously worked the transporter's controls to return the ship to invisibility.

It is a numbing experience for a man to discover he's no longer wanted by the woman to whom he thinks he's been Number One, particularly if he's assigned to her a similar status in his own life. The experience is a threatening one, usually interpreted by the organism as a surprise hostile attack, and calls for the instant erection of ego-defenses which invariably involve a strong impulse for revenge. Hannibal Fortune, however, was in no mood to philosophize upon what happens when a high-intensity interpersonal relationship falls apart . . . nor was he in a position to launch an effective counterattack.

Another culture, every bit as curious as the one he'd just left, would say that he had blown his cool. Critics of later civilizations would have rightly blamed an overdose of romanticism. Strict logicians would have sagely observed that when a social researcher immerses himself too long in the values of a given culture he can't avoid being contaminated by the social diseases which shape that culture.

Fortune glared angrily at the storm outside, watching the ripples across the transparent end of the capsule. After several minutes he realized that although the timecraft itself was invisible, the water running down its outer surface was giving the ship a distinct outline. Muttering, he took the transporter up into the storm, then cursed eloquently as it was hurled sideways by the wind. For several moments his attention was focused exclusively on the task of piloting the craft. At last the ship burst free of the clouds, accelerating steadily.

Loneliness was a sudden invasion of moonlight.

And he was cold. He hadn't realized just how cold, but now he hugged himself and shivered. Then he remembered the case of *xanthe* he'd put aboard for Webley—that would warm him. "Much more reliable than people," he observed aloud to nobody in particular.

His hands still trembled as he eased the transporter into a stationary orbit more than a thousand miles above the puny storm which obscured all he'd just left behind. For what seemed a long time he stared at the dials and indicators on the control panel, forgetting momentarily how to read them, then forcing himself to concentrate until he was satisfied that he'd done everything properly. Numbly, he moved to the supply locker, got out a bottle of the amber liquid that was his partner's favorite fuel, and opened it. The taste of it on his tongue was at once friendly and forgiving. A moment later, as it began to tiptoe through his blood, he underwent a brief paroxysm of guilt in which he viewed his action as a cowardly evasion of a problem he was afraid to face head-on. Still, it was warming, and that was the primary consideration.

Wasn't it?

Having made that decision, he tilted the bottle again to his lips and drank deeply. The contempt he'd felt a moment ago refused to go away. All right. Analyze it. Explore it. Exorcise it.

Fortified by the *xanthe,* he realized that a large part of his emotional reaction was disgust that he'd been so humanly vulnerable, while at the same time he was genuinely shocked to find he'd clung to so many erroneous ideas. Decades of training as a Very Rational Man had kept him from physically striking back at Luise or spitefully sabotaging her mission, but it could not save him from wanting to smash *something.*

Even as he clenched his fists and jaw in seething anger he recognized his rage as childish, but the realization merely intensified his disgust with himself.

The only good thing about the entire episode was that Webley hadn't been there to witness his humiliation. Even so, that temporary advantage would be lost once the symbiotic weld had been reestablished, for when your partner is a telepath there can be no secrets. Fortune was aware that the Torg had been amused time and again by the relationships his human partner had entered into with various human females, for to a creature such as Webley with no fixed physical form the ideas of sex, gender and the mating instinct were nothing but entertaining abstractions. But to Hannibal Fortune it was certainly not an abstraction, and it was anything but entertaining.

To say he was annoyed by Luise's change in attitude would be like calling mutilation an inconvenience.

Perhaps the most infuriating aspect was her patronizing assurance that he'd get over it, combined with his frustration at not being able to "get over it" instantly. And that silly poem she'd written—what had prompted him to tell her it was any good? He rescued it from a puddle and read it over again. It stank. Still, instead of flipping it into the disposal tube he refolded it and placed it safely inside the time-craft's logbook.

It was almost impossible to reconcile her present attitude with the things that had happened at *Time Out*. Fortune knew the psychological mechanism that keeps ordinary enthusiasms alive, but the feelings they'd had for each other, he was sure, were no ordinary enthusiasms. Even if he'd been willing to admit, intellectually, that such opinions *might* function according to the same rules—and thus require continual self-propagandization —the more basic part of him would find the notion too repugnant to embrace.

Still, her conduct was a clear indication that her feelings toward him had undergone as drastic a change as had her face and figure. For a brief, bitter moment he considered the possibility that he'd been had, that her former declarations of love were nothing more than insincere pretenses as part of a game played by a charming opportunist, but this, too, was difficult to believe— although he'd played the same game himself countless times before he met Luise. No, he assured himself, he was too adept at that gambit to be taken in by it. Which left only one alternative: her rejection of him was a sham.

He asked himself why, and could find no satisfactory answer.

Frowning, he finished the bottle of *xanthe*.

The wakealarm roused him several hours later. Restored by sufficient sleep to put his physical system in good running order, he glared ruefully around the cabin and surveyed the traces of his *xanthe* binge. Although grateful that the stuff never produced a hangover, he nevertheless viewed the need to pick up the mess with an echo of disgust. The indestructible purple toga was still a soggy mass and a few muddy puddles remained in the corners. Methodically, he cleaned the cabin, then fixed himself a breakfast. While eating, he attempted to look at the problem again. His rage had burned out, but despite the colder light in which he viewed it, the same wrong answers emerged. He couldn't tell why the answers were wrong—lack of data seemed as reasonable a hypothesis as any other. Resolutely, he shelved the problem for later.

One advantage of having a temporal transporter is the flexibility it affords for digressing from one problem in favor of another. He'd already strayed from his official objective by running off to visit Luise; he could as easily digress from the problem of Luise to return to his appointed mission. Along the way, hopefully, some of the missing data would turn up.

In the meantime, there remained several pieces of Vango's story to be substantiated. Accordingly, Fortune reset the temporal coordinates for 203 B.C. and, following a faint hunch, returned to the African coastal city of Hippo Regius. It took him but a few minutes to relocate the anonymous horseman who'd brought Laelius the news of Syphax' perplexing marriage.

The hunch saved him several days of time-trolling and led him to the rebel Numidian prince, Masinissa. From there, it was but a short distance (as the time-craft flies) to the ambush which had produced the rumor of Masinissa's death. Actually, the wily Numidian had narrowly escaped the planned murder, but had let the story of his demise circulate freely. Feeling considerably better about the mission, Hannibal Fortune adjusted his course for Carthage, leaped forward to the day he'd first arrived and zeroed in on the time appointed for his rendezvous with Webley.

On the way, he wondered again how much more of Vango's report consisted of unverified rumors. Fortune had as little patience for incompetence as he had for outright treachery. Even more disturbing, Vango's blowing the Residency indicated a weakness that might extend throughout the chain of command, all the way up to Pohl Tausig himself. Fortune doubted that such gross inefficiency was characteristic of every organization of T.E.R.R.A.'s size—the dynamics of group interaction had been systematized to a point where built-in bungling could be virtually eliminated. With ten thousand Resident Teams in the field, there was no room for incompetence. Wi'in and his others were insurance against disaster from a Special Agent's goofing, but there were only three of *them* and no way to recruit any more, so the solution to ineptitude among the Resident Agents had to lie elsewhere. Mentally, Fortune was already composing a scathing report to present when he got back to T.E.R.R.A. Control.

Ahead of him loomed the sandstone bluff. Five miles

beyond it lay Carthage. The twin clocks on the control panel showed that his three hours were up.

Webley was a cat, sure-footed and sleek-eared.

As the time-craft popped into objective reality, the symbiote sauntered over to it, then vaulted lightly through the entrance hatch. "This is not the most judicious spot we could have chosen for a meeting," he observed. "Empire is right underfoot."

Fortune had already begun cycling the ship back into invisibility. "I discovered that myself," he replied. "Find anything in the city?"

"Nothing. If they do have another headquarters it isn't in Carthage."

"There seems to be a minor outpost in Cirta," Fortune said, describing in detail the curious arrival of King Syphax' teenage bride and the subsequent drama in the old monarch's desert stronghold.

"You've been busy," Webley observed. "Where else did you go?"

Fortune told him about the courier who'd led him eventually to Scipio himself, and of the way he'd managed to plant d'Kaamp's tiny recorder on the Roman general.

"That should help us fill in the gaps," the Torg agreed.

"I filled in a big one already, Web. Remember Vango's story that Masinissa'd been murdered?"

"The old king's nephew?"

"The same. His uncle apparently arranged the ambush, but it didn't quite come off as planned. The lad got away—which means he'll probably still be around to help out in the final destruction of Carthage. But if his uncle believes he's dead, that takes some of the pressure off. The situation is messy, but it's not impossible. I think we know enough now to concentrate on our friends from Empire, don't you?"

"You're the strategist in this outfit," Webley reminded him. "Do you want me to sneak in and look around?"

"While I wait up here? Don't be silly. If we take them by surprise we might be able to destroy the whole nest at once."

"Lead on, O Mighty Worldsaver."

Fortune grinned, happy to be back with his fifteen-pound partner.

From its somewhat knobby top two hundred feet above the Mediterranean, the hill sloped sharply down to waterlevel—by no means the "sheer cliff" he'd thought it earlier, but still not the sort of territory often explored by an ordinary citizen out for a stroll. Most of its lower half was deeply undercut, hiding the entrance to the Empire cave in the shadow of a sharp overhang. But since Fortune had seen a skimmer vanish into that hole, he knew it would be roomy enough to accommodate the twenty-four foot long temporal transporter.

What else waited inside could only be learned by going there.

Keeping the gleaming time-craft invisibly out of phase with the objective *now*, Fortune maneuvered slowly under the overhang, alert for any flicker of movement. Webley had resumed his customary position across his partner's shoulders, with one slim protoplasmic tendril inserted in Fortune's left ear. "There are at least six of them in there," the Torg reported. "All different species. None of them up front."

"Keep your feelers out," Fortune said unnecessarily, inching the ship forward.

Beyond its well-concealed mouth, the cavern was darkly illuminated with reddish light which revealed an area easily twenty-five feet high, extending back into the cliff a good fifty or sixty feet. The roof was festooned with stalactites. Cautiously, Fortune nudged the invisible craft deeper, soon finding a sheer drop which apparently led down into a bigger cave.

"That's where they are," the symbiote confirmed.

Fortune eased the transporter through a ninety degree turn to keep it from brushing against the rock walls during their slow descent. The main cavern proved to be a near-duplicate of the outer vestibule, except that it was twice as long and twice as high and the back half of its floor was covered with a mirror-smooth expanse of water.

Parked at one side of the cave was the skimmer he'd seen before, while ranged around the walls were several enigmatic pieces of equipment, two of which supported what looked like primitive radar antennae.

He was swinging the craft around for a better look when the stillness was shattered by a blast of sound, so intense he could hear it with his skin, so penetrating it made his bones hum. In the same moment, the temporal transporter was wrenched from the observation module into the objective *now*, becoming suddenly visible to any watchers in the cave. Even as he tried to reach the controls the exit hatch behind him began to cycle open and the intruding sound changed pitch, resonating with his nerves to produce violent trembling in every muscle.

Webley!

Even as his mind screamed he knew that the Torg was no longer there.

Paralyzed, Hannibal Fortune stared through the clear

bubble as the ship continued its slow revolution on its own axis.

Awareness faded smoothly to zero.

DAY 103: There is no down, just loud, and you're a shimmering ripple of orange feathers racing away from yourself then collapsing, your bubble-thin surface alternately swelling and receding, each implosion triggering another ripple, faster, bouncing in and out, fantastically huge one instant, microscopic the next. Your ears have become disconnected so you're spared having to endure the disgusting stench, but even with your eyes closed you can see the strident

PING-ga-PING-ga-PING
aaaaaaaaaaaaaaah
ga-PING-ga-PING
ssssssssssh

which you suspect is the sound of your own heartbeat and breathing.

Good. Even with the accompanying pain, the fact of awareness bolsters your faith in the only thing you've ever found worth believing:

You still exist.

SEVEN: "BUT DARE A PAIR WITH
PARANOIA SCARE?"

THE REALIZATION THAT he was still alive came as no great comfort. He wondered, fleetingly, if it would be possible for anyone to wake up and be surprised at his own continued existence. He couldn't recall, in any of his previous seventeen missions as a Special Agent, ever being particularly astonished at having lived through a potentially lethal episode. His experience so far had taught him that there's a way out of every trap, once you work at it enough. Being Caught, he reflected is One of the Risks You Take. It followed that one of the knacks you must develop is Being Clever Enough to Escape. It did not occur to him that a more helpful lesson to learn about traps would be how to avoid falling into them in the first place.

This time, however, was clearly different from ever before. In the past he'd been chained to walls, imprisoned in jail cells, sealed into various enclosures and worked over by experts from a dozen different planets, but this was the first time he'd ever been unsure about what sort of restraint, if any, held him prisoner. He could neither see nor feel the presence of his arms or legs, and moving his head was an impossibility. It seemed to take an enormous effort merely to operate his eyelids.

No more than two feet in front of him was a concave wall of some smooth plastic or metal, in the center of which was a square aperture barely large enough to crawl through. Outside he could see a narrow corridor with an almost rectangular door at the far end.

In contrast to the information his eyes gave him was a persistent feeling that "down" was behind his head. Intrigued, he worked some saliva to the front of his mouth and shoved it with his tongue to the edge of his lower lip. It flowed back into his mouth. All right. That put the door at the top of a shaft, with him at its bottom. He tried again to locate his arms and legs, without success.

Still, he was alive. And breathing, too, he realized belatedly. That was encouraging. Experimentally, he tried holding his breath. It was an effort, but it worked. He couldn't feel his chest expanding or contracting, but he could control it. It seemed reasonable now to assume that the rest of his body was still attached. Sensation might return, in time; until it did all he could do was try to analyze his predicament.

The most annoying part of it, he realized, was that he'd been captured so early in the game. If he'd been a novice at this sort of work it wouldn't have been so bad, but to be one of the nine agents recognized by T.E.R.R.A. Control as resourceful enough to hold the coveted License to Tamper and *still* fall flat on your face at the outset of an assignment was a bit disturbing. Hannibal Fortune simply didn't do things like that. Minor goofs, yes—Webley had seen enough of those in their sixty years together, but—

Webley?

Fortune looked carefully at the wall and into the corridor beyond.

Web? he repeated.

Nothing in sight bore any resemblance to anything Webley might choose to look like. He forced himself not to leap to the conclusion that the Torg had somehow

en destroyed—he'd made that error too often in the
ast only to have the crusty symbiote turn up at the last
oment alive and well, armed with all manner of jibes
bout the folly of leaping to conclusions. No, Webley
as still around somewhere. Fortune felt sure that once
gain his shapechanging sidekick had managed to sur-
ve whatever the baddies had thrown at them and was
robably at this moment plotting his rescue. If what had
aralyzed him in the time-craft was some sort of force
eam—and Fortune was fairly sure it was—the same non-
thal energy had hit Webley. The symbiote probably
adn't even been slowed down; nothing much short
instant vaporization could stop a creature whose re-
exive response to all physical injuries was Consolidate,
epair, Run. In all likelihood Webley'd scampered out
sight before their assailants had time to realize he'd
en there in the first place. With any sort of luck, he'd
ave darted into an obscure corner of the ship and
ight even now be back at T.E.R.R.A. Control rounding
reinforcements. Hannibal Fortune decided that wor-
ing about Webley would be a massive waste of time.
That settled, he returned his attention to his own pre-
cament.

By the time his protoplasm had followed the mind-
ss mandate of his species and had accomplished suf-
ient internal repairs for Webley once more to ex-
rience conscious thought, both Hannibal Fortune and
e temporal transporter were gone. Painfully, the sym-
ote focused his energies into a mental probe and ex-
ored his environs for some trace of his partner. Find-
g none, he puddled himself in the shadow behind a
assive stalagmite and finished the restructuring proc-

ess. Satisfied that his injury had been minimal, he snake
a flexible eye-stalk to the top of the stalagmite an
peered all around the cave.

The reddish light showed that several pieces of equip
ment remained, but the Empire skimmer was gone. Th
two parabolic antennae were still focused on an area jus
below the cave entrance; there was no way for the Tor
to be sure whether they'd been turned off or left operat
ing. Cautiously, like a bizarre cross between a vine an
a centipede, Webley began to move up the wall of th
cave, growing legs or tendrils as needed, performin
inverted slaloms among the stalactites overhead. Find
ing a small hole near the top through which air was escap
ing, he flowed into it and up a long, twisting natura
chimney until at last he encountered sunlight. He spen
several minutes of concerted effort dragging all of hi
fifteen pounds up through the crevice and out onto th
dry ground above. As soon as he'd accomplished thi
he extruded a set of protoplasmic wings, feathered ther
and launched himself into the air. Sure now of his orien
tation he flew swiftly to the mansion of Vango and Arrik

The Residency was deserted.

Sensibly deciding that his value to Fortune woul
be enhanced if he was operating on a full energy leve
Webley discarded the bird shape in favor of a simia
structure. Finding Arrik's private cache of *xanthe* took bu
a few moments. Webley poured himself a generous cu
of the golden nutrient and settled down to wait for th
Resident Team to return.

"Hannibal Fortune."

It was a wheeze, a rasping, dusty whisper penetratin
his skull. Fortune opened his eyes. Standing just insid

the open door at the end of the corridor/shaft was an orange-fringed purplish lumpiness half as tall as a man. Whatever species it was, Fortune had never encountered it before. Automatically, he noted the mottled network of magenta and blue visible just under its translucent surface, but what interested him more was the fact that it was standing on the "floor" of the corridor, which his sense of balance told him was above him.

Four of the longer orange fringes were gesticulating; beneath the creature's bloated body glistened a green tongue analogous to the muscular foot of an Earth-snail.

"I can't really say your face is familiar," the agent replied. "Of course, it might not be your face I'm looking at."

The bloated one's expression remained static, although its upper vascules hesitated in mid-ripple. "I am Bahrs Tolunem," it said in Unispeak.

Fortune smiled. "I feel rather that way myself. Do you mind telling me what you've done to me?"

Without answering, the creature moved slowly forward, apparently to get a better look through the square window. Although his facial muscles had begun to ache, Fortune kept a noncommittal smile on his lips. At last the lumpy one turned and moved ponderously away.

"Despite your beauty," the agent murmured, "you're certainly not the world's most sparkling conversationalist."

Leaving a trail of slime in his wake, Bahrs Tolunem crawled slowly through the open door, pulling it shut behind him.

Drowsily, Fortune closed his eyes and tried to extract some useful data from the encounter. The expression "taciturnip" was no help at all. He slept.

Until he actually began explaining the problem, it did not seem to Webley at all ironic to be asking help from Vango and Arrik, whom Hannibal Fortune had treated so highhandedly earlier in the day, in order to get Fortune out of a jam the Special Agent should probably have been able to avoid in the first place. Vango pointed out the humor in it, almost triumphantly. Overcoming his reflexive desire to top the Resident Agent's sarcasm, Webley chose instead to inquire into the events behind the animosity the two humans felt toward each other.

Immediately, the cumbersomeness of verbal communication became obvious to both symbiotes. Vango was nervously inclined to gloss over any details that might reflect badly on his record. Consequently, Arrik tried to protect his partner—which was perfectly understandable to Webley, for when a Torg is involved in a symbiotic weld with another creature, his opinion about his partner is necessarily a favorable one.

"I request a Sharing," Webley said.

Still yoked across Vango's shoulders, Arrik reacted with waves of outrage. Adroitly, Webley thrust a telepathic feeler between the interstices in the other's mental shield and quickly explained his reasons, adding that he, too, found the suggestion personally distasteful but could see no other way to do it.

Arrik reluctantly agreed. Detaching his protoplasm, he dropped to the floor. His hesitancy reminded Webley of Ronel's nervousness when they'd first met in the treetops near Mohenjo-daro. But thinking about Ronel would not help, Webley told himself firmly.

Part of what makes a Torg a Torg is his desire to avoid intimate contact with other members of his own species. Among sex-based organisms such an antisocial characteristic would have had extremely low survival value, but in the evolutionary history of the Torg it had been a prime factor in the development of strong individuals.

Leaving Vango where he was, the two symbiotes retired to another room to begin the complex Ritual of First Encounter.

The prickly pain of returning sensation roused Hannibal Fortune from sleep. Every muscle ached, every joint protested, but at least he was now sure that he was all in one piece. His mouth was dry and his eyelids seemed crusted over. The corridor/shaft was still visible through the square window in "front" of him, but his suspicion that he was looking "up" was confirmed by the pull of gravity on his body; quite plainly he was lying on his back looking obliquely into a mirror.

He tried to flex his arms and legs but they refused to cooperate.

The door opened and Gregor Malik stepped nimbly into the corridor.

Fortune blinked. At least it *looked* like Gregor Malik—the same ugly green face, the same spiderish appendages ending in leathery, tridactyl pincers—but Gregor Malik was dead.

Correction. *Presumed* dead. Presumed lost in the twisting labyrinth of time, a victim of the Double Occupancy Rule, his evil genius obliterated from every known space-time continuum.

"We meet again," said the Tyrant of Borius.

Fortune winced. "Surely you can think of a more original opening line than that," he said, and then smiled.

"No, I suppose if you could you wouldn't be Gregor Malik. Congratulations on your survival, Greg. How'd you manage it?"

"Through what you would probably call luck, my good Fortune—although some credit should be given my colleague, Rimaud Rudnl. He developed some way or other to quadrangulate my distress signals. Technologically, we're not as far behind your organization as some of you would like to believe."

"I'm happy for you, of course," the agent replied. "I assume I have no hope of escaping you."

"You are correct."

"So would you mind clearing up a minor point that's puzzled me for some time?"

The Tyrant's chuckle was like dry leaves in a sudden wind. "You want to know why Empire has involved itself in this war between Rome and Carthage, eh?"

"Exactly. Where's the profit?"

"Profit?"

"What gain do you hope for if Carthage wins?"

"None at all. Our interference in this quaint conflict has already served its purpose. It was intended solely to bring you, my dear *Hannibal*, into my net. I trust you won't resent my saying it was a clever trap."

"Diabolical," Fortune agreed. "I'm flattered that you consider me so important that you'd go to all this trouble. It would have been a pity if some other Special Agent had been assigned to straighten things out."

"Your vanity would never let that happen. You have been an annoyance to us in the past, but what you did to me at Mohenjo-daro is unforgivable."

"Sorry if I offended you, Greg. Can't we talk it over?"

The arachnoid face gazed coldly at him. "Before you

die, I intend to play with you. Not only will I have my revenge, but in the process I shall extract every bit of useful information you possess."

"More Solupsine?" Fortune inquired.

"Not this time," Malike said tonelessly. "You have far too much to divulge for me to waste you like that. There are other forms of torture which will keep you alive much longer."

"Generous of you."

"We are already in possession of your time-craft. I am told it is yielding one secret after another."

Webley retracted his pseudopods and sucked his protoplasmic fur into himself until he was as featureless as a large round loaf of bread, then extruded a central vertical shaft which grew quickly to a height of about three feet before exploding in a spray of jeweled branches that flowed out and down like a decorative fountain.

Arrik answered with a bouquet of rather waxy petals and the mental apology that he was out of practice.

Webley relaxed into a tumble of carefully faceted crystals, each with a pulsating, phosphorescent core. Although it was an extremely difficult form, he accomplished it with such ease that it served as a gesture of contempt.

Arrik puddled himself into a flat, circular disk, deepened his color to resemble burgundy wine and began flicking ripples out from his center. Abruptly the ripples turned to expanding squares and then to a rainbow-hued burst of flowers, finishing with a dull black velvet upon which grew several varieties of toadstool.

Clouding his crystals, Webley coalesced into an inverted teardrop, balanced himself nonchalantly on his pointed end and began to spin like a top. Varicolored tendrils extended out and fell to the floor, forming a beehive shape that quickly rose up to enclose the teardrop, then melted away to reveal a grinning lizardthing with iridescent scales.

Conceding defeat, Arrik reverted to his previous monkey shape.

Courteously, Webley duplicated the shape. "Now the Sharing," he said aloud.

Arrik nodded. "Now the Sharing."

Pohl Tausig scowled thoughtfully at the computer readout. It was a burdensome job, trying to keep abreast of all the suspected deviations along forty-seven planetary time-lines. It called for teamwork of a high order just to correlate all the data in order to know the most useful questions to ask. The last thing the bulky Operations Chief wanted was a conflict between members of the same team.

He should have seen this one coming. But he'd thought all the possibilities had been covered. Shaking his head, Tausig activated the communicator and ordered certain documents to be delivered to him at once.

He had slept without resting; he had no idea for how long.

The huge spiderish one was in his cell again. "I trust you spent a comfortable night, my dear Fortune."

It was agony to turn his head. Even his face ached from the prolonged muscular effort, but Hannibal Fortune's grin was as mocking as ever. "I'll be all right."

"I am so happy to hear you say that," the green one replied silkily. "I want you in condition to appreciate

110

the pastimes I've devised for you. I give you fair warning, these little games will eventually kill you, but it will take a while."

"You told me that already."

"Since last we met I've made an exhaustive study of your species, giving particular attention to the nervous system. My, ah, associates and I have come up with some rather interesting ideas about inflicting pain upon members of your species. Until now, unfortunately, our approach has been largely hypothetical. It was good of you to deliver yourself here so that we might put our theories into practice."

Any lingering doubts Fortune might have had about Gregor Malik's authenticity vanished; only the real Tyrant of Borius could be quite so diabolical. Remembering the events at Mohenjo-daro, he knew Malik was not merely mouthing an empty threat. But he allowed no trace of fear to show on his smiling face. "You mean you want to try it out and get the bugs out of it."

"You might say that."

"I don't think it's possible to get all the bugs out of it, Gregor, as long as you're involved."

If the spider thought Fortune's remark humorous, he gave no indication of it. "We have no choice but to try. You should find it quite fascinating, particularly as it's your nervous system we'll be toying with."

"Of course," Fortune agreed amiably. "Tell me, Greg, am I expected to cringe at the prospect of torture?"

"Cringe if you like. You might even cry out from time to time, but it won't really be necessary. Our equipment, I assure you, is quite sophisticated. Your neural reactions will be automatically monitored throughout the experiment. In short, my dear Fortune, it will do you no good at all to feign unconsciousness."

"Clever of you," the agent allowed.

"I think so, too," Malik agreed. "Are you at all interested in psychology?"

"Enough so I can recognize a sick mind when I see one. I spotted yours right off."

"It may amuse you to know that the experiments will also be guided by my studies of pride and vanity in the human male. You might think about that. I won't be seeing you again until the experiments actually begin."

The Tyrant moved toward the door.

"And when will that be?"

"My dear Fortune," Malik chuckled reprovingly, "you don't seriously expect me to tell you *that*, do you? It would take all the suspense out of it."

One of the cultural values instilled in each Torg soon after budding is the sanctity of an individual's private opinions. The young Torg is taught that if he *must* exchange information with another, he shields his opinions and transmits raw data only. Thus, Webley and Arrik invaded each other's minds, sharing fully their experiences but not their individual conclusions about Hannibal Fortune and Vango. Even with the privacy safeguards, the Sharing was an almost traumatic experience. At the end of it, Webley knew everything Arrik knew about Vango, and Arrik knew everything Webley knew about Fortune.

Trembling, they moved apart; each seemed to huddle into himself, sorting, digesting, processing the new information. They stayed that way for a long time.

Hungry, he was unable to recall when he had last eaten. He couldn't even remember going to sleep. His body ached. Moving was an effort, and still his movements seemed curiously slow, dreamlike. Weak from lack of nourishment? Or merely sluggish from disconsciously administered drugs?

His environment had rearranged itself into an irregularly shaped room with twelve distinct surfaces, no two alike in shape, color or texture. The floor had five unequal sides. Some of the wall and ceiling surfaces glowed faintly, their light intensity constantly varying. He moved painfully around the room, examining it; then, exhausted, he sat in the middle of the floor and watched the slowly shifting lights. The surface under him was abrasive, like coarse sandpaper. The air was chilly and carried an odor which seemed an uneasy compromise between stale sweat and rotting flesh. He breathed it deeply to desensitize his nose; within minutes the stench faded.

When next he woke, the room was uncomfortably hot and the air reeked of fish. The light panels flickered distractingly. Ugly bruises glared at him under the film of sweat on his naked flesh. His head ached, probably from hunger, perhaps from something else.

There was no way to keep track of time except by monitoring his own body functions. Examining himself carefully, Fortune found a small abrasion on his left ankle and picked at it until it began to bleed. When unconsciousness came again, he reasoned, he'd be able to estimate its duration by observing the degree of healing that had taken place. It might well be useless data, but at least it was a start. Hunger and thirst, he knew, were less reliable indicators, being far more subjective in their intensity.

. . . less reliable indicators, being far more subjective in their intensity.

. . . indicators, being far more subjective in their intensity.

. . . far more subjective in their insanity.

. . . subjunctive in their insanity?

. . . in their inanity.

Warm, and deep it breathely, without resistance. Sleep the gentle warm, more subjective than your propensity. Be your hungers less reliable . . . inhale the subjunctive insanity. Pohl Tausig? A bulbous bureaucrat too blind to appreciate real ability even if he could recognize it. Yes, the nine of us, for there are only three of the others. I am thou, quoth the lipless one, but only for a while, for when thee is not, I will be another.

Your bees and fleas Luise foresees in breezy seasons wheezing pleas of freezing keys to ease my tree's disease. The cheese agrees that pleasing teasing frees appeasing seas of these decrees. If she's to seize her knees and squeeze the fees by three cerise degrees, displeasing treason eases reason wheezing pleas appeases sneezing sprees.

The Torg? The morgue. Or smorgasbord.

Luise? Chinese!

There's no one I can count on but myself.

Ten. Nine. Eight. Seven. Five. Four. Six. Three. Two. One.

ZeroQueeroNeroHero.

Although his eyes were open he saw nothing that made any sense. Two shadowy figures wavered in front of him, refusing to get in focus. He was dimly aware that his

114

hypno-block had taken over, ready to deliver a meaningless garble in response to any direct questioning—and he was equally sure it wouldn't work.

There's no one I can count on but myself.

OneTwoThreeFourFiveSick. Sorry, fellas.

One of the figures spoke, uttering twelve syllables. Twelve syllables, Fortune discovered, stubbornly refused to make sense because somehow he couldn't keep track of more than three syllables at a time. By the time his questioner got to syllable number four, Fortune had forgotten number one.

"You stare at where the sparrow flies in air," he replied earnestly.

The other shadowy something interrupted with a sharp demand for—what?

"Aware that blare will paralyze the square," he added promptly.

The hazy shapes held a brief conference, then rephrased their question. Fortune tried his best to follow what they were saying, but it slipped away from him again.

"A rare affair is terrible to bear," he informed them.

Time passed. Eventually they pried from him the disturbing intelligence that they'd best "prepare to share impairable despair."

Another conference. Another question. Another answer:

"I swear the T.E.R.R.A. era will repair—"

They seemed to be urging him to finish it, so he did his best: "—to scare the pair in there beyond compare."

Fortune sensed, hazily, that that wasn't quite the answer they were looking for.

"Take care!" he warned. "Beware!"

They seemed grossly dissatisfied, so he countered with a question of his own. "Will glare," he asked reasonably, "annoy a bear?" He could tell at once that he wasn't getting through to them, but it seemed important that he finish the thought. "But dare a pair with paranoia scare?"

And that, he felt, was all he wanted to divulge, considering the circumstances.

EIGHT: "IF YOU DON'T DO IT RIGHT
YOU'RE DEAD."

VOMITING ACCOMPLISHED NOTHING but to intensify his headache and leave a bitter taste in his mouth.

Either he'd been moved to a different cell or the one he was in had shrunk since last he'd looked at it. Although there seemed to be less area around him, there were more and bigger bruises on his body. Painfully, Hannibal Fortune checked himself over. Nothing missing —yet. Still, from the tenderness of his various hurts, there might well have been. Given the opportunity, he'd have bet even money that more than one rib was cracked, judging from the pain flashes that accompanied every breath. His Carthaginian beard itched, probably from the growth of his own facial hair underneath the microbond of the false beard, but that was a piddling discomfort compared to some of his other hurts. Apparently they'd really worked him over after failing to pry loose any useful information, but he couldn't recall any of it.

Not remembering bothered him, for it seriously limited the amount of data he'd have to work with if he intended to escape. As there was clearly no point in beating him while he was unconscious, it seemed obvious that they'd inflicted his injuries in hopes of breaking his resistance; ergo, he must have been conscious when it happened. Either that, or Gregor Malik had ceased being a coldly practical opponent, which was a hypothesis Fortune wasn't prepared to accept.

Remembering the impromptu "clock" on his left ankle,

he located the scab and toyed with the edge of it. No more than two days had elapsed since he'd made it bleed. The stubble on his upper lip confirmed the two-day estimate. His belly, however, told him it had been much longer than that. Another few days of fasting would probably make him too weak to escape, even if he found an opportunity.

Painfully, he examined his prison with its flickering lights and apparently shifting dimensions. Although the surfaces varied in texture, each was sturdily constructed, even the translucent ones, and each was firmly fastened in place, as prison walls ought to be. However, with a few tools . . .

Wishful thinking never helped anyone but a Torg.

Tired, he sat down on the floor again to conserve his strength, then focused his energies into a penetrating mind-scream to his partner. It might have been a waste of time, but then again it cost him nothing. The scream delivered, he sat back and waited, running over the elements of his predicament once again, sharpening their definitions, alert for relationships he might not have recognized before.

In another part of the subterranean complex, Gregor Malik crouched at an observation screen and conferred with his purple-hued underling, Bahrs Tolunem. On the screen was a view of Hannibal Fortune, sitting cross-legged in apparent dejection, virtually motionless. The Tyrant reached forward and cranked up an audio monitor; over the speakers came the sound of the captured agent's breathing.

"He looks almost comfortable," Tolunem observed.

"Correct it."

Obediently, the lumpy one extended a prime vascule and increased the heat supply to the cell. Malik made a small sign of approval and inquired:

"How long before Rudnl will be ready?"

"With luck, tomorrow," the orange-fringed one wheezed.

"Excellent. We will begin phase two tonight.

Relishing his captive's discomfort, Gregor Malik stayed at the observation screen until Hannibal Fortune collapsed from the relentless heat.

When next he woke, the room had changed again. New hurts competed with the old ones, attesting to another beating. Even his fingernails seemed thirsty. As before, he had no memory of the beating, and no idea of its duration. Gingerly, he began the painful process of working the stiffness out of his body.

"My dear Fortune." Malik's voice intruded over a concealed speaker. "Life would be so much easier for you if you would cease these childish attempts to escape. I would admire your persistence were it not for the fact that you have forced us to redesign your quarters three times in the past week."

Hannibal Fortune tried an insolent grin but quickly canceled it when his lips cracked.

There were no more messages from Malik. Some time later the cell filled with a fine, foul-smelling mist, and unconsciousness came once again.

Pinpoints of light flickered in the blackness, outlining shadowy approximations of things and people, while voices faded in and out, overlapping each other.

"*At least*," said the Chinese girl disgustingly, "*you no longer look like a Professional Hero.*"

From another direction, a voice with vaguely academic overtones rumbled, *"I wonder, however, if your view of her is entirely objective."*

"No hard feelings, are there, Draj?" Vango asked.

"This is a culture," Luise continued, *"that doesn't take kindly to strangers messing with other men's women."*

"Cease these childish attempts to escape," Gregor Malik added.

From somewhere on the edge of his left ear a symbiotic whisper dripped sarcastic: *"Your bravery continues to astonish me."*

"She's not really your type, Hannibal," Pohl Tausig proclaimed.

Before he could reply, the Chinese girl asked him, *"Do you want me to pat you on the head and tell you what a clever boy you are?"*

"Lead on, O Mighty Worldsaver," Webley hissed, dissolving into a wisp of smoke.

The fog turned unbearably red as d'Kaamp said crisply, *"You're dead."*

The hunger, the headache, the bodily hurts and the refusal of his memory to recall any attempts to escape were joined now by alternating chills and fevers and intermittent muscular convulsions—all of which added up to massive exhaustion. A lesser man would have welcomed the escape of unconsciousness; Hannibal Fortune resented it. Although there was no evidence to indicate that help would ever be forthcoming, and although Fortune knew that hoping for miracles was a waste of energy, he clung to the only thing he was absoutely sure of: he still existed. And he'd been in far too many tight places to discount his own ability to find a way out.

He examined his data and gingerly extracted a few posits. One, he was unquestionably Empire's prisoner. Two, Gregor Malik's personal hatred for him was painfully obvious. Three, despite the fact that he couldn't remember the incidents, he'd probably been of very little use to the Empire chief, assuming that his hypnoconditioning hadn't broken down—it forced him to respond with meaningless garble to all direct questioning under duress. Four, his own teammates, from Pohl Tausig and Webley on down, were either dead or unaware of his predicament. Five, if he didn't find a way to thwart Malik's forces, Earth's time-line would shortly develop a lethal warp. Six, all other considerations, including Empire's capture of his temporal transporter, were relatively inconsequential compared to the total annihilation of significant portions of base-time reality. Seven, his course of action thus far had produced no useful results at all.

It was time, Fortune decided, to take the initiative away from Gregor Malik. Obviously, nobody else was going to do it for him.

Holding pain blocks on all of his hurts was taking too much effort, so instead of fighting them he accepted them, relaxed into them, redefined them, allowed them to surge over him and into him for an excruciating eternity/instant. It was as if the pain itself, previously an impenetrable sheet of pain, had suddenly opened up, gaped emptily and sucked him through to the other side, popping noiselessly as it turned itself inside out, returning his welcome with a million little screams of ecstasy as it shifted into his cellular embrace. After the first agonizing instant it was almost comfortable.

121

It was decidedly educational—this discovery of how it was done. It was a surrender to reality, he suddenly knew, a surrender of What Is and a simultaneous rejection of What Ought To Be as a useless frame of reference, a lie, a seductive fantasy which no longer fit the real world. Perhaps it never had.

The trick, he discovered, was to exist in harmony with the bubble of pain, not in opposition to it. Smiling, he willed his tortured muscles to relax. Once he admitted that running from the agony would be impossible, it was easy. It was like inching along a very narrow ledge in pitch darkness; your chances were better if you kept moving.

"Fortune," a familiar voice whispered behind him. Hannibal Fortune turned to confront the speaker—and froze.

Facing him was an exact duplicate of Hannibal Fortune, complete with all of his bruises, lacerations and swellings.

Beautiful, Fortune thought. *I'm hallucinating.*

"We have less than forty seconds," the second Hannibal Fortune said curtly. "Through this doorway, quick. Listen to me, because I can't tell it to you twice. I found a way to get around the Double Occupancy Rule. The ship is at the end of this corridor, controls pre-set; just slap the switch on your way in. You'll go through the continuum sideways, in frozentime. Follow me?"

Numbly, Fortune nodded agreement. "It might work," he murmured.

"It *does* work," the other Hannibal Fortune assured him, hurrying him toward the end of the corridor. "They haven't been able to learn much from it, but you've got to take it out of here before they have another crack at it. I'll take your place in the cell. I don't know how many of us there'll be by the time the oscillations damp out, but I'm counting on at least one of you to come back with reinforcements." The newcomer threw the door open and darted inside, where Fortune could see his temporal transporter centered in a circle of technical equipment. The room was a tall one, with a cavernous natural ceiling and a synthetic floor.

"Hurry! That hatch takes five seconds all by itself!"

"Sideways, huh? How does it work?"

"How should I know? *Move!*"

That was an entirely reasonable answer, mused Hannibal Fortune as he swung toward the time-craft's open hatch. He could see no cause to distrust his own reasoning just because in his drugged condition he couldn't follow the gist of it; obviously he knew what he was doing and had done it successfully or he wouldn't have rescued himself. After a while, you get to know just who you can trust. Satisfied, he reached for the boarding handle—

—and was hurled violently backward by a fast-moving something that caromed off his head and shoulders and vanished inside the time-craft. Losing his balance, Fortune tumbled inelegantly to the floor. Everything seemed to be happening at once, the hatch cover cycling swiftly shut, the other Hannibal Fortune similarly afflicted except that the swift-moving something didn't bounce off like the first one had. There was a ripping, cracking, eggshell-crunching sound and the other Hannibal Fortune's head flew off; seconds later his plastic torso split down the middle, revealing a tangle of laminated circuitry. From the severed neck oozed a small amount of thin yellow fluid.

The shapeless blob responsible for his double's abrupt dismantling extemporized a lump of vocal apparatus. "Malik planned the whole thing," the symbiote said briefly. "Rudnl built the robot. The ship's controls are set for *Doubletime* violation. We tuned in on the plot and figured this was our best opportunity to rescue both you and the transporter. . . ."

The captured time-craft winked implosively into otherwhen. Wincing, the Torg hissed, "I hoped he'd be able to reset the controls in time."

"Then you *can't* slide through *Doubletime* sideways," the agent whispered.

"No."

Fortune took a deep breath in the sudden silence, realizing how close he'd come to being his own excutioner. "Thanks, Web," he said softly. "Vango may be an idiot, but Arrik proved himself."

"Correction," replied the symbiote, lumping atop the disabled android. "I'm Arrik. Webley was in the transporter. I'm supposed to help you get out of here. What's the matter?—you look—"

Hannibal Fortune felt as if he'd been hit by a giant fist as he realized that Webley's mission had been suicidal. To come so close to freedom, even if his first glimpse of it had been a Malik-made delusion, and then to see his partner snuffed out in a futile gesture, would have been an emotional shock even if he'd been in good shape, but after he didn't know how many days of skillful maltreatment Empire-style, it was too much to cope with. The game was suddenly too fast, the dues too high, and in the last few days he'd grown incredibly old.

He felt his control slipping, unable to either resist or adapt to the expanding wave-fronts of pain; with a cry of alarm, the Torg leaped at him.

NINE: "YOU PLAN TO DO THIS
WITHOUT BREATHING?"

SEMICONSCIOUS, FORTUNE WAS only dimly aware of the alien symbiote leeching itself to him, flowing swiftly over and around his body, spreading over every part of him from his neck down, becoming a second skin which squirmed warmly against him, anchoring itself to every hair, finding a toehold in every pore, spreading its protoplasm so evenly that the initial fifteen pounds seemed to disappear. Fortune relaxed into Arrik's strangely comforting and distracting embrace; he knew it was only a matter of time before Gregor Malik and his cohorts would burst into the subterranean room.

Knowing his limits and being able to project exact probabilities of success or failure was a skill possessed by every Agent of T.E.R.R.A. Hannibal Fortune had reached those limits and, based on the available information, had correctly forecast doom as the outcome of the adventure. He had no doubt that the symbiote had gleaned that information from his mind the moment the computation took place, but he was too tired to care. If Arrik was making no attempt to save himself, it followed that there was no way for either of them to escape. Despite his curiosity about the manner of his own death, Hannibal Fortune had no energy left with which to watch it. Gratefully, he collapsed into unconsciousness—

—and was immediately jerked awake by an excruciating pain which let up at once. His arms and legs were being moved by the envelope of symbiotic tissue,

Arrik's fifteen pounds functioning like a body stocking of amazing strength and muscularity. Held together by the tough membrances of symbiotic protoplasm, he stumbled and lurched, yet somehow remained on his feet. Too weak to inquire what the other had in mind, Fortune contented himself with being led.

They came to a featureless door. Arrik leaned the human against it, then flowed a thin film of protoplasm around the edge of it and into its locking mechanism. A moment later the door swung open, tumbling the compound agent into the corridor beyond. Fortune grunted in pain as his legs were jerked into place under him and the "walking" began again.

He woke up three times on the way to the end of the corridor.

Later he discovered they were in a vertical shaft; somehow, the symbiote had managed to get his hands and feet on the ladderlike cable that ran from top to bottom. Vaguely, Fortune realized they were escaping, and for several microseconds he wondered how they were doing it. Staying conscious long enough to find out was too much work; besides, he suspected the symbiote would have an easier job of it if he merely slept.

Wincing awake another time, he discovered he was being crawled through a low tunnel that sloped gently down, with a faint light at the end. This time he made an effort to stay awake, and only dozed briefly.

Can you hear me, Arrik?

A tendril of protoplasm snaked into his right ear. "Yes. Are you feeling better?"

A little. Do you know where we're going?

"Out," hissed the Torg, in tones poignantly reminis-

127

cent of Webley. "You have to swim underwater for several minutes."

Forget it. I can't hold my breath that long.

"Webley knew that when he figured this out. I'll hold it for you."

They were near the end of the sloping tunnel. Ahead was an underground lake. "Webley and I explored the whole mountain, and the only unguarded way out that's big enough for you to get through is underwater. The tide has already started going out—it should help us. I can carry all the air you'll need until we come up again. But you'll have to stay awake in order to swim."

The pool inside the cave, the Torg explained, was connected to the sea outside by means of an underwater passageway through the rock. All the details of the escape had been worked out in advance; the only weak part of the plan was that no one had had a chance to practice it. Thus, it was Webley's estimate of the volume of air Fortune would need that guided Arrik in sprouting and inflating hundreds of long, snakelike air sacs.

And it was more a hope than a realistic appraisal that caused them to think that both man and Torg would survive the underwater swimaway. "The water is quite cold," warned Arrik as they reached the edge.

That may help me stay awake, Fortune replied. *Let's go!*

"Dive as deep as you can the first time. Then I will direct you."

Fortune gulped a considerable quantity of air and launched himself into the water, bracing himself against the icy onslaught; he entered the pool without much of a splash, in the sort of dive that can take a good swimmer twice his own length beneath the surface, then deeper still with the first powerful stroke of his arms. But instead of slicing into the murky depths, Fortune and the air-carrying symbiote bobbed instantly to the surface.

Imbecile, leave the air up here! We're too buoyant!

"You plan to do this without breathing?" inquired the Torg.

Web—I mean Arrik. Wait until I'm on the bottom, then send part of yourself back up here for air, okay?

Arrik extemporized hundreds of tiny vents and deflated noisily. Feeling better than he had in days, Fortune launched himself cleanly into the water.

This time the dive was everything he hoped for. Arrik directed him to the lip of the underwater tunnel. Reaching it, Fortune got a solid grip and gave rapid loudthink instructions; the symbiote extruded almost half of his putty-like substance in a long tube of pseudo-cartilage which grew swiftly toward the surface, found air and sucked it down to the swimmer. Fortune exhaled, then filled his lungs several times to load his blood with oxygen.

Let's take about two lungfuls with us, the agent suggested, crawling into the mouth of the tunnel. Arrik enlarged the tube fractionally, then began pulling it down, making storage space on Fortune's back and belly where he needed the most insulation. The tide was pulling strongly on them now. *Ready?*

"Proceed," hissed the Torg.

Hannibal Fortune, clad in the most extemporaneous scuba gear ever worn by a diver, climbed down the subaquatic tunnel hand over hand, aided by the outrushing tide. *Air!* he ordered, feeling his escaping breath bubble ticklingly against his face and neck. The Torg formed a breathing tube. Fortune inhaled. *How much further?*

"Almost halfway," said the voice in his ear.

The cold was starting to penetrate now, despite the insulation of Arrik's protoplasm, and his tortured muscles began to complain. Doggedly, the agent crawled on, trying to ignore his near-bursting lungs and the numbness in his hands and feet. *Air!* he commanded again; the symbiote obliged immediately. They moved faster now, deeper, closer every moment to the freedom outside. Fortune could see nothing in the total blackness, but the Torg moved their arms and legs in a purposeful fashion while the tide sucked them on.

Air! he thought sharply, exhaling.

"All gone," said Arrik, the two words conveying the Torg's astonishment that Fortune had lost count. He started to say, "Not much further," but saved the effort as he felt the agent collapse into unconsciousness.

TEN: "FORTUNATELY, THERE SEEMS TO
BE A HOLE IN YOUR THEORY."

PRIMITIVE CIVILIZATIONS in all parts of the galaxy have poetically conceptualized time as a river, imagining it to be a substance which flows, with "now" floating like a leaf in midstream. Picturesque as this notion may be, it was no help in arriving at a temporal technology that would allow mobility along the time-lines. It had taken a team of theoretical correlationists from Bortan III, thinking in terms of perpetually unbalanced energy systems, to develop the necessary mathematics for time travel to become a reality. Arising from it was the temporal transporter (and T.E.R.R.A. and Empire), and around it had grown a protective webwork of rules.

Neither Hannibal Fortune nor Webley fully understood the theory behind it, but both had been checked out in the operation of the time-craft. Each was aware of the rules; each knew, from having lived with those rules since joining T.E.R.R.A., exactly how far he could go in any direction, spatial or temporal.

At Gregor Malik's order, Rimaud Rudnl, who knew the rules every bit as well as Fortune or Webley, had set the ship's controls to violate *Doubletime,* and then had blocked off the control panel with a transparent shield. Merely by entering, Webley had triggered the countdown and there was nothing he could do to stop it. It was the same fate T.E.R.R.A. had earlier engineered for Gregor Malik, only this time the trap was laid with much more precision. According to the rules, it could not go wrong.

131

According to the rules, Webley was dead.

"Dead," however, had suspiciously familiar scenery. As the observation bubble cleared, sunlight splashed over the surprisingly solid interior of the time-craft. It was hovering about half a mile above Carthage; looking down, Webley could see all the territory he had so painstakingly searched a few days before. There was the Byrsa, over there the two artificial harbors, off in this direction sprawled the forum, down there, almost lost in the edge of a residential area, was the Residency Headquarters of Vango and Arrik, and there, in Vango's courtyard—*the unmistakable shape of the temporal transporter!*

He checked the coordinates and phase indicator. It wasn't possible. Every dial showed a clear violation of the Double Occupancy Rule. Obviously, something had gone wrong. A microscopic error, a switching device deep within the guts of the machine, a circuit that had flopped when it should have flipped, a speck of dust holding a microrelay open. Any second it might correct itself, the switch would close, current would surge through the errant circuit. . . . Webley worked in a frenzy, ripping, prying, forcing the baffle away from the control panel, laying bare the function monitor section, checking the telltales for the location of the malfunction.

Everything was working perfectly. Primary Module. Impossible.

Gingerly, he touched the control that would twist the transporter ninety degrees out of phase with the timeline, and nudged it forward. The instruments registered the shift to the Secondary Module.

The immediate danger past, Webley reset the co-

ordinates for T.E.R.R.A. Control, cross-checked his figures twice with the onboard computer and finally
pressed the activating stud. The computer chuckled to
itself, lights blinked, a chime spoke softly, the clock on
the left became a blur and the puzzled symbiote settled
back to wait.

There was no hurry. The nature of time travel pre-
cluded most of the impending catastrophes that make
suspenseful adventure stories. A delay of several days in
one mode of operation, Webley knew, produced but a
few seconds' lag in another. Hungry, he found and
opened a container of *xanthe,* noting that the locker held
one less than he thought it should.

A little under four hours later the temporal transporter
warped out of otherwhen a scant 7.6 million miles from
the exact center of the galaxy. Webley was still puzzled, but by now he'd reconciled himself to the notion
that figuring it out was a task best left to those who
were better equipped to examine the technical dis-
crepancies. With elaborate care he made the required
course correction, which brought the gleaming, twenty-
four foot long craft within talk-back distance of
T.E.R.R.A. Control. Gratefully, he relinquished control
of the ship and turned his attention to the remaining
container of *xanthe.*

It is a peculiarity of Torg metabolism that it is completely immune to the intoxicating effects most species
experience during and immediately after ingesting *xanthe.* The Torg, however, did not consider themselves
unfortunate in this respect; on the contrary, most of them
felt that everybody else was unfortunate for, without
having to drink, chew, smoke or otherwise absorb any
outside chemicals at all, each Torg could *think* himself

to whatever psychedelic state he desired and maintain it for as long as he wanted.

Thus, by the time he reached T.E.R.R.A. Control, Webley was thoroughly inside his head. It was a nice place to be, all things considered.

He turned the ship over for servicing and took the most direct route through the hollow artificial planet to Pohl Tausig's office. The Operations Chief was not there. "He's in Emergency Session," Tausig's aide, a blunt-winged Kabobra, stridulated importantly.

"I must see him," Webley repeated.

"No one interrupts an Emergency Session."

"Except for an emergency," Webley added.

"Not even for an emergency," he was told. Like so many insectoids, the Kabobra relished well-defined regulations, and would not be put off by mere logic.

"This one is serious."

"Aren't they all. If you'll just leave your name, team number and location I'll have him contact you the moment he's free," the aide recited, then added conversationally, "Unusual for a Torg to come in here alone. Where's your partner?"

"That's the emergency."

"How strange!" exclaimed the Kabobra. "Most unusual, in fact. A true coincidence—same sort of situation the Emergency Session's about. Would you believe it, Control lost track of a whole Special Team in one of the Rim systems! Remarkable, don't you think, that a situation like that should happen twice during the same shift? I mean, it isn't often that we misplace *anyone*, much less a Special Team. . . ." The aide rattled on, but Webley had disconnected himself to sweep the administrative area with a telepathic probe tuned to

Pohl Tausig's characteristic *alpha*-modulation. Finding the Operations Chief took about three seconds; Webley listened for another half minute before reactivating his audio sensors. The Kabobra was still talking.

"I belong in that meeting," Webley said. "It's my partner they're talking about."

"Well, simmering supernovas!" exploded the Kabobra. "Why didn't you say so earlier?"

There were a dozen beings assembled in the conference chamber. When Webley sauntered in and identified himself, Pohl Tausig expressed only mild surprise, which annoyed the symbiote as he felt his entrance warranted reactions of shock and hysterics.

"I didn't expect you back so soon," the Operations Chief rumbled. "Where's Fortune?"

"Carthage."

"*How* is he?" a worried soprano voice inquired.

"Half dead," Webley responded before he identified the speaker as the Chinese girl at Tausig's left.

Serves him right, came a Torgish thought from the same direction.

Ronel?

Only Hannibal Fortune could screw up two assignments at the same time.

What happened?

Ronel hesitated while Webley's probe nuzzled the edge of her consciousness, then she flooded him with data, sensory impressions, even the dialogue between Fortune and Luise during his unscheduled side-trip to the City of Ao.

I see, Webley mused. *Who blew the whistle?*

Luise, of course.

Of course.

"I asked you a question," Tausig said, somewhat testily.

"Sorry. Just catching up. What do you want to know?"

"Why you are here."

Webley chuckled as he mentally auditioned his answer. "As my missing partner might say, if Linz Lipnig were to ask him that question, it's because, fortunately, there seems to be a hole in your theory."

"I don't understand you."

"You will. Now do you want to play word games or shall I begin my report?"

From somewhere in the assembly came an instant mental blast of outrage at the Torg's flippancy, but Pohl Tausig silenced the protest before it could be voiced. "Proceed," the bulky Operations Chief said dryly.

Forewarned by Ronel's capsulization of what had happened so far in the Emergency Session, Webley proceeded.

They paid close attention, all twelve of them. Pohl Tausig toyed with his beard, his deceptively bland eyes monitoring all of the others as Webley began his narrative. Linz Lipnig, co-inventor of the temporal transporter, sat as still as a trideo image, apparently unaware that he was in an uncomfortable position. Luise and Ronel radiated anger and righteousness, which Webley thought entirely unwarranted but their privilege if they chose to feel that way about it. Purple-Fin, the prideful weapons technologist whose creations had helped save many an assignment, followed every word with bright-eyed excitement in contrast to d'Kaamp, the wiry, white-bearded combat instructor, who pretended boredom. In one corner, watching everything but seeming to doze, was a cylindrical, cone-headed PsychSecRep named Alelis. Webley suspected that if he'd done his job right in the first place there'd have been no need to call the meeting, but he knew if he said anything like that he'd only get a lecture on the childishness of blame-placing, so he held his tongue. Scattered about the chamber was a quartet of minor lights, none of whom looked at all important; a quick mind-scan revealed three of them to be aides while the fourth represented the acting head librarian in T.E.R.R.A.'s History Section.

Sprawled over one entire end of the conference area was the tentacled Double-A empath, Wi'in, who was listening most intently of all, for it was to him that the 93rd Emergency Staff Session would eventually turn for tactical answers.

The Torg's story was simple and succinct—as straightforward, anyway, as so complex a narrative could be. From time to time he was interrupted, usually with a pertinent question, each of which he answered with a minimum of fuss.

He told them of their arrival in Carthage and the initial attempts to locate an Empire force; he told of the first encounter between Fortune and Vango, and of Fortune's disgust with the Resident's slipshod performance of his duties. He told of his partner's Observation Module trip into the past to try to discover the events leading up to the reported discrepancy, and of Fortune's witnessing the marriage of the venerable Syphax to an unidentified "Carthaginian" who arrived at the old king's headquarters in an Empire skimmer.

"And just what," asked the PsychSecRep, "was your partner's reaction to this unscheduled wedding? How did he seem to feel about it?"

"He was angry."

"I suspected as much. It's a typical Earthian attitude, the refusal of the male to grant competence to females in what they persist in thinking of as 'man's work,'" Alelis explained.

"Correction," Webley objected. "He doesn't hold that opinion at all." The Torg related Fortune's views on male supremacy as expressed during the Manukronis incident.[*]

"I agree with Webley's interpretation," Tausig rumbled. "Fortune seemed angry with me when I didn't promote Miss Little to Special Agent status."

"He was very disappointed," Luise confirmed.

"Let's not forget that individuals change their ideas," Alelis said smoothly. "We're not born with our neuroses; we develop them as we go, and keep them active as long as they're useful to us in some respect. This fixation on Agent Little, which she reported to us earlier, for instance, seems entirely out of character with the man as we have known him prior to this assignment. His reactions have all the earmarks of paranoid grandiosity."

Pohl Tausig's eyebrows lifted fractionally. The cylindrical PsychSecRep bowed toward the Operations Chief and amplified his statement. "Paranoid in that he seems to be imagining that his friends are letting him down, conspiring against him, or acting deliberately stupid; and grandiose, of course, because he seems to think that it really shouldn't be this way at all."

"I think your diagnosis may be premature," Tausig said, turning once more to Webley. "Continue with your story."

[*]See *Agent of T.E.R.R.A. #2, The Golden Goddess Gambit.*

The Torg told of Fortune's tracing the Empire skimmer back to the cliffs northwest of Carthage, and their subsequent discovery of the enemy headquarters inside the rock. "Some sort of force beam hit us then, and when I regained consciousness Fortune and the timecraft were both gone. I returned to Residency Headquarters and conferred with Vango and Arrik."

Webley told them of the search he and the other symbiote made of the seaside mountain and the vicinity around it—a search conducted visually and telepathically. He told of his surprise on the second day when, instead of finding his partner they detected the mental matrix of Gregor Malik, along with the information that Fortune was still alive. He told of finding the renegade inventor, Rimaud Rudnl. ("Motherfuck!" exclaimed Linz Lipnig, drawing a brief smile from d'Kaamp, who had taught him the archaic Earthian battlecry without telling him what it meant.) Curiously, though, there was no telepresence which Webley could positively identify as Hannibal Fortune for almost another full day. ("Sedation?" asked Tausig. "Obviously," Alelis confirmed.) The two Torgs invaded the mountain, constantly monitoring the Empire crew, gradually piecing together the Tyrant's diabolical plan and trying to find a way to get in to help the captured Special Agent. Despite their best efforts, they could find no chink in the security of Fortune's cell. They elected to maintain surveillance and take advantage of whatever break came their way.

Although they knew exactly where Fortune was, the symbiote emphasized, better than half the time there was no telepathic evidence of his presence there. From monitoring his jailors they discovered the seemingly senseless pattern of drugging him into insensibility and

then very carefully beating him while he was unconscious, apparently so Fortune would conclude that his
memory was failing.

"Malik's intention," Webley amplified, "was to overcome Fortune's resistance through drugs and environment control, and convince him that his case was hopeless. And to question him about T.E.R.R.A., of course."

"He was hypno-conditioned against that sort of thing,
wasn't he?" Tausig asked rhetorically.

Alelis nodded. "Gibberish implant."

"It didn't work," Webley said.

"It had to work," the PsychSecRep responded.

Webley told them about the android—the duplicate
Hannibal Fortune—and the story the android told Fortune about slipping into *Doubletime* sideways. "How
else," Webley asked the PsychSecRep, "could they have
learned the terminology?"

Linz Lipnig snorted. "My ex-partner is not stupid."

"Since you are here, instead of Fortune," Tausig said,
"I assume you managed somehow to abort Gregor Malik's
trap. Tell us about it, please."

Webley described the placement of rooms and corridors in Malik's underground complex, including the wa-
tery escape route, and traced the movements of the real
and the bogus Hannibal Fortune from the impregnable
cell to the less well guarded chamber where Rimaud
Rudnl had been working on the captured time-craft.
"The controls were pre-set and tied to a triggering circuit that would activate them the instant anyone went
through the hatch. It would have been certain death for
Fortune."

"For anyone," Tausig said.

"I thought I might be able to deflect the setting enough

to avoid violating the Double Occupancy Rule if I reached the controls quickly enough."

"All of us are grateful that you succeeded," Tausig rumbled.

"I didn't," the symbiote said. "Rudnl had enclosed the control panel in a transparent baffle—I could see it but I couldn't touch it. Once the ship entered the vectoral transit mode I expected it to be destroyed at the moment of Double Occupancy. But it wasn't. I don't know if Fortune and Arrik made good their escape or not, but if they did we have one advantage: Malik thinks his trap worked."

"Does he?" Tausig challenged. "I can't imagine Gregor Malik setting all that up and then not being on hand to watch it happen—at least by remote pickup."

"We thought of that," Webley told them. "I disabled the pickup myself, both the video and audio circuits, just a few seconds before the android brought him in where the transporter was. Arrik attacked the android while I knocked Fortune away and took over the transporter myself."

"This," protested the PsychSecRep, "I find hard to understand. I'd think you would have elected to disable the android and have Arrik take the transporter. After all, Fortune *is* your symbiotic partner."

"Arrik wouldn't know what to do with it," Webley snapped, not bothering to conceal his contempt for PsychSec.

"What were the control settings?" Linz Lipnig asked breathlessly.

Webley recited the coordinates. Lipnig looked puzzled. "Are you sure?" he demanded. The symbiote assured him he was. The inventor's gaze drifted thoughtfully for a moment. "That cannot be. It coincides with your arrival time, and we know you didn't violate the Double Occupancy Rule yourself, or you would not be here to testify, correct? Of course it's correct, or else we've made a major error in our definition of *Double-time.*"

"Ridiculous!" exclaimed one of the aides.

"I know," Lipnig mused, nodding more in fascination than in agreement. "The Bortaneans do not make such mistakes. But there is an error somewhere. It causes me to wonder just what special circumstance might be involved to allow this—what is his name?—Webby?"

"Webley."

"This Webley to survive violation of the Double Occupancy Rule. It opens up some rather interesting areas of speculation which should be delved into immediately. For instance—"

Impatiently, Pohl Tausig cut the inventor off. "Director Lipnig, I'm sure that's very interesting, but it's not our primary concern right now. Our job is to figure out what Hannibal Fortune will do next." He turned to the cylindrical one and asked, "Is PsychSec ready to begin testing?"

Alelis shook his conical head. "We'll need more testimony for the Double-A's update. I'd like to ask Agent Little some more questions."

"Go ahead," Tausig agreed.

"I'm particularly interested in the relationship you established at Fortune's vacation retreat. Am I to understand you spent a full G.F. year together there?"

During the next several minutes, Luise Little described events at *Time Out* in unblushing detail, holding back nothing from the other members of the Emergency

142

Session. As her testimony progressed, both Linz Lipnig and d'Kaamp were impatient to get on to more pertinent data, each with his own concept of what "more pertinent" would be. Purple-Fin sat, enraptured, through the whole thing, although Webley was sure that an account of human romantic entanglements would make no more sense to a Narcturnean than it did to a Torg. Webley concluded that the weaponry technologist would be enthralled by *anything* complicated.

Suddenly Linz Lipnig heard something he deemed "pertinent" and asked Luise to back up a few sentences. She told about Fortune's teaching her to operate a temporal transporter and his unexpectedly returning from somewhen else during a time-gap in which he didn't already exist on *Time Out*. Although the episode was news to Webley, he didn't see anything particularly significant about it until Lipnig excitedly asked her, "Did he seem to be aware that it was a different transporter than he'd started out in?"

Luise frowned. "No . . . at least if he was he didn't give any indication of it. Not that I could see, anyway. Is it important? He said it was important that I never mention it to him."

The PsychSecRep seemed to expand in size as he asked, "Luise, are you still 'In Love' with Hannibal Fortune?"

"Why do you ask me that?"

"I've been monitoring your emotional indices as you talked; you seem quite agitated whenever you mention his name."

"You think I shouldn't be?" she snapped. "When his stupidity can cost all of us our lives?"

The PsychSecRep subsided.

Despite the annoyance potential of some of the questions, all of them were answered, for each participant in the Emergency Session recognized that his colleagues represented the best qualified minds in the galaxy. The testimony went on and on, with first one department and then another digging for more details. Official records were sent for, brought in and pored over. Linz Lipnig discovered a partial answer to the technological puzzle: the Servicing and Maintainence Division had found it necessary to switch time-craft shortly after Fortune's assignment had begun, calling back the original to correct an oversight in component rotation. It had been an almost routine substitution; *almost* because of a technician's boast that he could swap transporters and the team involved wouldn't know the difference. Zeroing in on its locater chip (a fragment of negative entropy trace material) they'd had no trouble finding the transporter during the early hours of the assignment; Fortune and Webley had been conferring with the Resident Team at the time the exchange took place. That covered part of the anomaly: since it wasn't the same transporter, it didn't violate *Doubletime*.

But Webley did.

Lipnig looked at him as if he wished the symbiote were lying. A quick mind scan showed that the physicist also wished Webley would violate *Doubletime* again, with Lipnig watching.

Hours after the Emergency Staff Session had begun, its end finally came in sight. Each of the experts signified that he was satisfied. It was time now to put the next question to the one creature who could be counted on to respond with a close approximation of the missing agent's thought patterns.

"Shall I?" the cylindrical PsychSecRep inquired of Pohl Tausig, "Or do you wish to ask him?"

Tausig turned toward the tentacled empath, Wi'in, who had said nothing throughout the entire session. "Assuming you and Arrik managed to escape from the Empire cave," Tausig rumbled, "what do you plan to do next?"

The lipless one laughed derisively and countered with a question of his own:

"What nakes you think any uff you iss qualiffied to ask? Your conceit, ny dear Kohl Taussig, gets nore insufferagle effery day!"

There was a thoughtful silence which was broken a moment later by d'Kaamp, who smiled humorlessly as he said, "I do believe we're in trouble."

The PsychSecRep spelled it out. "It would seem," Alelis drawled, "that the fate of the Galactic Federation lies in the hands of a seriously disturbed Special Agent."

"All right," Tausig snorted, "let's find him. Without a temporal transporter he can't have gone far. At least we know what year he's in."

"If he's still alive," murmured Webley.

ELEVEN: ONLY THE BEST SECRET AGENT
IN THE HISTORY OF SECRET AGENTING

WHEN THE COMPOUND agent finally bobbed to the surface, the symbiotic part of him calmly built a bladder, sucked it full of fresh air and pumped it into Fortune's empty lungs. The agent stayed limp; his heartbeat was random and almost imperceptible. Arrik fed him more air, squeezed it out, filled him up again. For a long time there was no change, and then the Special Agent started breathing for himself.

Indulging in the Torgish equivalent of a sigh of relief, Arrik puffed up a flotation collar to keep Fortune's head clear of the water, then let down a network of filaments which slowly sieved the seawater for its complement of single-celled lunch. He wished there was a way his own cells could process such food into a form Hannibal Fortune could use, but no such process existed short of voluntarily amputating some portion of himself and trying to force the unconscious agent to eat it. Arrik's self-preservation reflexes shuddered at the thought every bit as much as Fortune would shudder at the taste. Arrik knew without thinking exactly how Fortune would react to that idea, for since the moment of the Sharing his memory-field held a duplicate of Webley's experience with Fortune. Arrik could not help comparing the two men. In sixteen years as Vango's partner, he'd not had one-half the adventure that had come his way in the past few days. In retrospect, Arrik felt vaguely cheated. He'd never suspected that such men as Hannibal Fortune actually existed, much less that he'd ever

146

have a chance to work in symbiosis with one. He was furiously proud that they'd come this far together already. Eagerly, he waited for his new partner to wake up and take command of the situation.

Like every other Torg who ever lived, Arrik was an accomplished telepath. Thus, the instant Fortune regained consciousness Arrik was fully aware of what he was thinking, fully aware that he was mentally and physically exhausted, and fully cognizant that in his near-delirium his new partner thought that he, Arrik, was Webley.

No matter.

If Hannibal Fortune wanted to think of him as Webley, he'd be Webley. What's a name, anyway?

Especially once you've been through a Sharing.

And with Webley heroically dead, who would ever challenge him? Identity, he suspected, depended as much on the opinion of others as on your own notion of who you happened to be. And there clearly was more potential for adventure in being Webley than there'd ever been in being Arrik. Fortune himself, for that matter, had led a far more fascinating life than Drajne Wokajeni had ever managed, so there was ample precedent.

Arrik/Webley had no way of knowing that he was not the first other Torg ever to ask himself what Webley would do in similar circumstances.

Your name is Hannibal Fortune and you are probably the best, most highly trained secret agent in the entire history of secret agenting. You are alive and considerably smarter than you were before you realized that

147

T.E.R.R.A. was riddled with incompetents and traitors.

The time-line must be repaired.

Rome must win this Second Punic War.

Carthage must eventually be destroyed.

If you have to do it alone, you'll simply have to do it alone.

It is your job because you are good at it and it is your duty because you are what you are—considerably more intelligent than either your enemies, who are blinded by their own greed and lust for vengeance, or your so-called friends, who are disgustingly incompetent and would only get in the way if you relied on them for anything, or your once upon a long time ago love affair. . . .

You wonder what it was you ever thought was there.

You were sick and she was nearby and there wasn't anybody else around to compare her to so why shouldn't you have the right to think she was wonderful and it was so good for a while—while it lasted—but she didn't really mean the things she said and it's your tough luck if you took them at face value and thought it was really happening for her, too—and you're probably better off without her, except . . .

You can still remember what it felt like to hold her; you remember the texture of her skin before they changed her face and voice and the shape of her eyes and her opinion of Hannibal Fortune or Drajne Woka-jeni and you wonder if she remembers any of those things; you wonder if it meant anything to her in the first place.

Maybe it was just an amusing way to spend a vacation.

Funny.

That used to be all you were looking for, too.

An amusing way to spend a vacation.

But then you found what you wanted, didn't you?

At least you thought you did because she let you think so and it was fun but something much more than fun—a meaning—a meaningful cul-de-sac in the busy life of Hannibal Fortune. At least you thought it was meaningful while it was happening but it turned out empty. And she turned sarcastic. You have to give her credit for a fine sharp turn of tongue—if only her head worked as well! But then she'd be in a class with Webley, who had died to save you. No, she would never be in a class with Webley.

Why does the world have to fall apart all at once as if somebody had plotted it that way?

Your name is Hannibal Fortune and you are (1) resourceful (2) highly trained (3) the most competent choice for the job (4) the hope of the world (5) in all probability the best secret agent in the history of secret agenting (pick two of the above).

Only two because that's the way the rules are, arbitrary, and you're a pretty good arbitrator when it comes down to basics Empire is the reason you're here and putting a ruptured time-line back together is the only problem you've really got time for since you discovered you were on your own

just you and me, Web, we're on our own

the two of us against the world

and what has the world

ever done for us

secret agents don't have time for all that other stuff and you can't count on anything even the quality of your information it's like trying to paint a

picture in the dark for an eyeless entity who doesn't
know you're doing it anyway and your partner probably isn't Webley although he'd like you to think he is
so play along since it doesn't cost you anything taking
inventory your name is Hannibal Fortune and you're a
very capable secret agent even if the others are inept so
you look at the problem and you take a certain cold
fierce pride in knowing that without help at all you can
put the damage straight and make it all come out the
way it ought to be there is sharp pleasure in driving
the thing that calls itself Webley to take on tasks it
never thought it could do before and to do them the
same sharp pleasure in forcing your own body to keep
on and on and on you tell him how to do it and he does
it and you send him for food and he gets it and as your
body repairs itself you wrap it in the clothing the symbiote steals for you and you make your plans relying on
your own mind and your own abilities to see all the
variables and come up with consistent right answer
they tried to convince you this was just a quirk you had
like perfect pitch or blue eyes but they really chose you
for this job because they recognized that you were
superior but they didn't want you to know it because
then you wouldn't need them so you let your mind play
with it and the plan builds with some areas of it figured
out twenty or thirty chessgame moves in advance and
others left open because you know you're in command
no matter what happens the feeling is good it's what
you were created honed born destined to do putting the
time-line back together again because it's what you do
best and all the time you are drilling your symbiotic
partner in fighting techniques swooping ramming bouncing spearing strangling whipping suffocating skimming

along an inch above the sand and scooping loose sand up inside himself then blowing it into the eyes of the enemy spinning flailing flogging scaring soaring booming scooting darting stinging scratching ripping flipping tripping bruising flinging winging the most versatile weapon ever invented for hand to hand combat a living bludgeon sharp hard fast intelligent instantly responsive functioning like a fifteen pound infinitely maneuverable extension of you fifteen pounds of killer muscle telepathically linked to the most perceptive battle-wise mind in the entire history of secret agenting was a combination guaranteed to turn the tide of any battle ever fought in what later Earthmen called the Ancient World or the Golden Age of the Greco-Roman civilization bloody heroic gutsy and somehow symbolically fitting to test the mettle of a solitary Special Agent of T.E.R.R.A. and his faithful Torgish companion Webley who for some insane reason is pretending to be somebody else entirely pretending to be Webley and that makes it even more of a challenge

odd

isn't

it

that the truly superior individual thrives on challenge the more difficult you make it the more he enjoys it and the better he does it.

Only one in a million, you remind yourself, can do this sort of job at all, much less do it well.

It takes a certain flair.

The 93rd Emergency Staff Meeting of Temporal Entropy Restructure and Repair Agency stood adjourned while assorted specialists considering the problem of

Hannibal Fortune worked relentlessly toward a solution to it. The bureaucratic delays seemed deliberate and consciously malicious as they piled one atop the other until the only members whose professional detachment remained unscathed were Pohl Tausig himself, Alelis the PsychSecRep and of course Wi'in, who was still thoroughly immersed in Being Hannibal Fortune. Tausig conferred privately with each of the others, Luise, Ronel, d'Kaamp, Purple-Fin and the rest, while Alelis concentrated mainly on the surrogate Hannibal Fortune, running test after test on the lipless mutant, describing the absent agent's psychological state ever more exactly, advancing a hypothesis, checking it, building a sturdier construct with each small confirmation, feeding his results into the Central Computer. Meanwhile, Linz Lipnig and his crew of experts went over the time-craft from one end to the other to find out just what Rudnl and *his* experts had done to it.

It all took time—and time was the key factor.

He'd forgotten about the Residency arsenal—the assortment of non-lethal goodies analogous to his own duty kit, but far more limited in scope. Fortune grinned broadly as he checked the contents. "You borrowed this from Vango?"

"Of course," the symbiote replied, attempting a nonchalant pose and not quite making it. "He wouldn't know how to use it anyway, so it would be wasted at the Residency."

Fortune chuckled. "I accept your judgment. Now let's see what's in this little toychest, hmm?"

There were various chemicals which he recalled from his basic orientation courses so many years ago, with

losages written on the capsules in a code he'd all but
orgotten. There were signaling devices, spy nodes, an
ssortment of diversionary gimmicks ranging from smoke
ombs and noisemakers to eye-searing flashers. There
vas a multi-channel rescue beacon which would repeat
s distress call for weeks before its power supply gave
ut.

He would gladly have traded it all for one laser hand-
un. But he knew better than to look for anything like
hat in a Residency kit. Even by accident, it would be
ifficult to kill anyone with anything found in a Resi-
ency kit.

Still, it was better than nothing.

Publius Cornelius Scipio didn't quite know what to
hink of the improbable old man who walked in off the
esert, looking like a Caananite but speaking Latin like
Greek, melodiously. He had the air of a soothsayer but
gleam in his eyes that showed he knew it was all
imflammery and until they were alone he'd keep up
he pretense. Scipio wondered how he would have
eated the stranger if he hadn't needed allies quite so
esperately.

Things had not been going too well for the Roman
onsul. But then, his life had always been an uphill
ruggle, despite the prominence of his family. Part of
he fault lay in the Senate, particularly with old Cato,
or putting so many restrictions upon the army he'd as-
mbled. He'd have been more comfortable if he'd felt
he people were behind him, but he knew better. He
ad too many enemies in the Senate, just waiting to
atch him in a major error so they could withdraw
hat little support he'd managed to acquire.

But it was the aged Numidian king, Syphax, who
really messed things up for him. In the first plac
Syphax was supposed to be his ally. Last summer, ju
as Scipio was about to sail from his Sicilian embarkir
port with some twenty thousand seasoned invasion troop
a message had arrived from Syphax: "Do not invac
Africa."

That from a so-called ally.

Scipio could not afford to release the actual conten
of that note; what few backers he had in the legisl
ture were counting too much on the tribesmen, upwar
of fifty thousand, he'd heard, commanded by Sypha
The fools back in Rome flattered themselves that the
timorousness was "reasonable prudence," but to Scip
it was obviously the cowardice of senility. They'd fo
gotten what every young man who ever made his ma
learns early, that battles are won not by caution but b
daring. Unfortunately, the palsied old men controlle
the treasury. So, instead, he'd pretended that the me
sage had urged him to make haste.

If he'd been a believer in omens, in signs or in portent
as he'd had to pretend to be often enough, Syphax' me
sage would have seemed ominous indeed. He, too, ha
been counting on those desert troops. Scipio's own forc
numbered barely twenty thousand; the best informe
estimates of enemy strength (Hasdrubal Gisco's Ca
thaginian army) ran from forty to sixty thousand. H
was outnumbered even before he'd sailed, by two o
three to one—and his plan was to make Hannibal fo
low him to Carthage, army and all! Now and the
Scipio wondered how many of his own men woul
have sailed with him if they'd known the true conten
of Syphax' message.

At the very least, it would have been bad for morale.

But Publius Cornelius Scipio had been plotting and planning and scheming, making secret deals and playing complicated games for five years to lead up to the invasion of North Africa, and he was in no mood to let the defection of an ally force him to back off from the brilliant exploits that would carve his name into the history books. As Commander of the Roman forces on Sicily he had the option (thanks to a political compromise the year before, just after he'd been elected Consul) of launching an invasion of Africa if in his military judgment it seemed advisable. It was a complicated game the young general was playing; success depended upon his powers of persuasion once his army had set up housekeeping on African soil. That, too, he considered an item of information best kept from the troops.

Thus, ignorant of the odds and eager to distinguish themselves as part of a successful campaign, they'd sailed, making a completely successful crossing and landing near Utica, roughly twenty miles from Carthage itself. His intention, of course, had been to storm Utica, take the ancient city by surprise and thus gain a fortified base within a day's march of the great land wall separating the Carthaginian peninsula from the mainland. But it hadn't worked that way at all. Utica had resisted.

Utica was still resisting even now, almost a year later. He'd tried to get through to Syphax, to change his mind again, but the old fool wouldn't listen. The rules of the game dictated that negotiations in such delicate matters be carried out by the diplomatic corps, with minor envoys from both sides meeting in some supposedly neutral ground to talk about it. Doubtless, this custom had evolved from far earlier days as a way to advertise one's peaceful nature without having to infringe upon the hostilities; Scipio felt confident the practice would continue for thousands of years; its primary advantage, he felt, was that it gave a military man a breather every now and then during which to bring up reinforcements.

Armed to the teeth, commanding a vast force of foot soldiers plus an enviable contingent of cavalry, Syphax was clearly ready for war despite his pressing for peace. Scipio was willing to talk about it and look for an opening at the same time to score a military victory. For much too long, Hasdrubal, the Roman's only rightful enemy, had been strutting his army around in a fashion that could almost be called smug. As long as old Syphax was willing to fight on the side of Carthage, Scipio granted Hasdrubal the right to be smug. He'd probably stay smug, too, the Roman guessed, for Hasdrubal had the old king by the gonads—or at least, from all reports, his daughter had.

Sophonisba was the wench's name, and the seduction of the elderly apparently was her specialty. If Scipio had known what a pushover Syphax would be for a pretty face (or whichever of her other assets triggered the old boy's vital juices) he might have snatched up a talented Tiberian temptress, passed her off as his sister and given Syphax cause to be indebted to Scipio instead of to Hasdrubal, whose daughter she allegedly was. But that sort of maneuver would have scandalized the so-called moral integrity of the prissy old men who controlled military expenditures; it would not have been the virtuous course at all. Scipio had little use for virtue —it only got in one's way—but great respect for style.

Grudgingly, he had to admire Hasdrubal's strategy in giving the girl to the randy old chieftain, whether she really was Hasdrubal's daughter or (as he sometimes suspected) not.

According to Masinissa, Sophonisba was not only a nubile and tempting morsel any man, king or commoner, would be happy to find in his tent, but she'd been tutored by Greeks in music and assorted other beguilements, and the world knew how skilled the Greeks were at that sort of thing. If one were to believe the more outraged critics, most Greeks didn't think a skill worth developing unless it was immoral. In any event, Sophonisba was apparently giving the old fool plenty of reason to keep his alliance with Carthage going strong.

Thus, the tens of thousands of Numidians Scipio had been counting on to help him take Carthage were now allied with the Carthaginian general Hasdrubal Gisco, and both armies were now camped on the banks of the Bagradas, practically within sight of his own encampment on the rocky promontory he'd named Castra Cornelia in honor of his family.

Publius Cornelius Scipio was understandably miffed.

Masinissa had been a disappointment, too. Even if he couldn't have Syphax' Numidians, Scipio had thought it only reasonable that his cavalry should get a few thousand Numidians from Masinissa's branch of the royal family, but the exiled young chieftain had showed up with only two hundred riders and a discouraging story about how his uncle would have hunted him down and killed him if he hadn't spread the rumor of his death after a spectacular ambush. According to Masinissa, he was lucky to have two hundred. But they were the finest, the swarthy desert prince insisted.

And they were, Scipio agreed. They would have been pronounced worthy even by his long-range opponent, Hannibal himself.

Except that there were so few of them. Of what consequence are a handful of mosquitoes to an elephant?

Winter in North Africa, as in Italy, is seldom conducive to full-scale warfare, so the Romans and Carthaginians both had to content themselves with minor skirmishes. The siege lines against Utica were maintained, although not at full strength. Masinissa's two hundred horsemen, fierce tribesmen with fantastic opinions of their own and their chief's prowess, were set to work harassing the enemy encampments, luring the Carthaginian mounted volunteers into ambush so Scipio's somewhat more conventional Roman horsemen could cut them down and scatter the survivors. It didn't compare to taking a city, but it *was* a victory, nonetheless, and as such it was reported to the folks back home. Scipio was well aware that he'd probably be recalled at the first news of a defeat—such was the power of the gutless in the Roman Senate.

Meanwhile, ever since the Romans had landed at Utica, the Carthaginians had been busy building themselves a fleet of warships, the first of which they'd launched in the fall. Until Scipio's arrival, nobody had had the audacity to invade Africa for almost fifty years, and Carthaginian shipbuilding had concentrated on merchant vessels, to maintain mercantile supremacy throughout the civilized world. Now they were building a navy. They'd had all winter to expand that fleet; an attack by sea was all Scipio needed to turn his invasion into a disaster.

And now the enigmatic old Greek had arrived, walking in off the desert, calling himself Sebastian Necropoulis.

TWELVE: THE NIGHTBIRD SCREAMED,
AND SCREAMED AGAIN.

THE PROBLEM FACING Hannibal Fortune was fairly simple when looked at from one end and incredibly complex when viewed from the other. The other Hannibal must be brought home to Carthage. He can be thought of as Hannibal One-Eye, to distinguish him from the *other* other Hannibal, the one built and programmed by Rimaud Rudnl. It is curious, Fortune mused, that nobody'd ever bothered making a note of *which* eye the famous Carthaginian had lost in Italy, much to the amusement, he supposed, of future writers of quasi-historical fiction who set store by so-called "historical accuracy." At any rate, his namesake had been rampaging up and down the Italian countryside for some fifteen years, which is a long time for any tourist to spend in Italy, making monkeys out of one Roman commander after another, doing countless incredibly daring things and probably a few daringly incredible things, moving his entire army, over twenty thousand men and all of their impedimenta, into and out of well-guarded areas as if they were invisible—or the Romans were blind—stinging the Romans in so many places that the rumor, "Hannibal is at the gates!" would strike terror in any part of the peninsula.

Hannibal One-Eye must come home, must be rushed home to defend the very walls of Carthage.

If it hadn't been for Syphax joining his forces with those of Hasdrubal and helping the Carthaginian bottle Scipio up on that rocky outpost, Fortune reasoned, Hannibal One-Eye would be on the way home right now, for Utica surely would have fallen under the Roman siege. That's the way the history charts at T.E.R.R.A. Control went, anyway. After Utica, Carthage —and then Hannibal comes home *after* the collapse of Carthage, and is himself crushed on the plain. But events right now didn't seem to be moving in that direction at all.

Scipio seemed to have been doing his best with what he'd had to work with, but unless the fracas could be managed so that Scipio would win, the whole struggle wouldn't earn a footnote in the record book. It wasn't a question of one side being right and the other being wrong, although both sides tended to think of it in those terms. Each civilization believed itself to be fighting for its life, and thus it was perfectly natural for each to view the other as evil warmongers who ought to be destroyed. Neither side had bothered to figure out that the real losers in any war were the ordinary people who failed to live through it, regardless of which side they fought on.

Most of the complexity of Hannibal Fortune's problem arose from the simple fact that his assistance in the altercation would have to be subtle enough to prevent Gregor Malik from knowing that Hannibal Fortune still existed. It was a job that called for an expert. Perhaps it was fortunate that by this time he'd formed the neurotic conviction that he was the only expert in the universe. At the very least, it gave him confidence, which is a prerequisite to effective swashbuckling.

The events that followed will be easier to stomach if you constantly bear in mind the fact that at all times his motives were Pure. Well, almost always. And, too, the people involved lived and died an awfully long time ago. Some of them weren't even very nice. Of the rest, you can be sure they were no better than they ought to have been.

Simple—and complicated. The problem was for Hannibal Fortune to come up with a way for Scipio to turn the tide of the war and undo the historical damage resulting from Empire's gratuitous meddling, and to do it without tipping Empire off that he was still alive, which meant doing it without the use of a temporal transporter, because the only temporal transporter still around belonged to Empire and Gregor Malik would surely miss it if Fortune was to swipe it.

It could be argued, of course, that there was very little chance of that happening anyway, since the Empire transporter was in orbit several hundred miles up and Hannibal Fortune was on the ground without even a horse, but such arguments would be advanced only by those who have forgotten that there was at least one Empire skimmer still parked in the Empire cave, and that it is a relatively easy job for a skimmer to overtake an orbiting transporter, and that individuals such as Hannibal Fortune and Gregor Malik have no conscience at all when it comes to swiping each other's equipment. Quite often they think of themselves as "subscribing to a higher morality." Since Hannibal Fortune didn't particularly like being limited to three dimensions, one of his first thoughts had been about Malik's orbiting transporter, which he fully intended to commandeer when the time was ripe, but before then there were a few other things to tend to.

With the armies of Syphax and Hasdrubal camped just a few miles away on the banks of the Bagradas, Scipio needed help. Specifically, he need a way to wipe out both of those armies in one daring maneuver which wouldn't cost him too many troops.

It was a large order for one unarmed Special Agent, on foot, and his symbiotic partner.

But it had to be done.

It had been Scipio's present Carthaginian antagonist, Hasdrubal Gisco, who'd said the Roman cammander was "more to be admired for the qualities he displays on a personal interview than for his exploits in war." Thus, we can assume that the Roman either believed what Sebastian Necropoulis had to say or admired the way he said it. What the crafty Greek had said was said to Scipio only—he introduced himself as a master spy seeking gainful employment. As to his motive for this generous offer, he explained that Hannibal One-Eye had grievously offended him on a number of occasions, and that working for Scipio seemed the best way he could think of to gain revenge. Besides which, he was convinced that Roman generalship would eventually prevail, and he could see no harm in aligning himself with the winner. Perhaps, he added modestly, his services might in some small way help change a highly probable victory into a sure thing.

Necropoulis was affably mysterious about his sources of information, and equally well informed about the career and ambitions of Publius Cornelius Scipio, almost as if he'd had a sneak look at Scipio's still unwritten memoirs. Scipio rapidly concluded that Necropoulis not only knew a great deal about the strength and position of the armies of Syphax and Hasdrubal, but that he knew too much about the Roman encampment for Roman comfort.

Verbally, they dickered, fenced, hedged and bar-
gained, all with the supreme confidence of men who
knew and respected their own abilities. In the end, the
two of them made a sort of deal, springing from their
mutual desire to see Carthage brought to her knees and
Hannibal One-Eye defeated in a spectacular battle with
Scipio's legionaries.

"So resounding a victory, if I may suggest it," the one
who called himself Sebastian Necropoulis remarked,
"that there will be no question of awarding you a
triumph when you return to Rome."

Scipio's eyes narrowed cautiously. "Are you some sort
of fortune-teller?"

"Fortune," the Greek laughed, "can seldom be told.
I claim only to be an exceptionally well-informed individual, with services for sale. Have you any objection
to being known as Scipio Africanus?"

Thus, it came to pass that Hannibal Fortune, in the
guise of one Sebastian Necropoulis, gentleman spy, became a Roman secret agent.

At first, the Roman was amused at the master spy's
audacity. Then he became intrigued with what Necropoulis knew of the situation, and flattered by the
effort the Greek had obviously put into learning all he
could about his, Scipio's, past exploits. It was the
normal way a man who's proud of what he's accomplished reacts to the presence of an unexpected admirer. In short, he found Sebastian Necropoulis enjoy-
able and more interesting to talk with than either his
lieutenant, Laelius, who was really too much of a con-
servative for the Scipionic taste, or Masinissa, who was
a bit too bloodthirsty. Furthermore, Necropoulis wanted

no credit or public praise for his contributions to the Roman war effort, an attitude which the ambitious Consul considered an excellent one for an ally to have. In short, they got along quite well together, discussing hastati, triarii, manipules, flying wedges, cavalry placement, single-wing T formations and assorted other niceties of contemporary warfare.

Like Scipio himself, Necropoulis was an admirer of cleverness *per se*, and was familiar with most of the ingenious solutions to battle problems that had already established the existing great generals of the known world. "No man strives for fame and great honor," he told the Roman, "except where a reputation for greatness can be useful in achieving his ends. Your wisdom is evident in your choice of Jupiter Optimus Maximus as your patron. Whatever I can do to enhance the name of Scipio will be, I am sure, to the everlasting glory of Rome."

Scipio smiled crookedly. "An image of invincibility, such as that enjoyed by Hannibal in Rome. And where will you be, Sebastian, at the triumph of Scipio?"

"Cheering you on, with the rest of the crowd. For me, a quiet pension, awarded in private, so that I might live out the rest of my alloted days in satisfaction." Fortune wondered if he might not be laying it on too thick, and abruptly switched subjects. "If we're going to enhance your reputation we'd best get at it. Would you agree that it is an honorable way to prosecute a war if you manage to keep your own casualties to a minimum?"

The Roman thought about it for a moment. "Yes," he agreed. "That's an honorable way to wage war."

"Good!" exclaimed Necropoulis. "If this works it'll help

your reputation no end." He drew a wavering line in the dirt at his feet. "That's the Bagradas. Syphax and Hasdrubal are *here,* while we are *here.* What I propose is *this. . . ."*

Pohl Tausig finally got the peripatetic inventor on the screen. "What do you mean," he demanded, holding aloft a memofax bearing Lipnig's signature, "by this one hundred seventy day quarantine?"

"When we ran test signals through the temporal vector circuits we found an error voltage which gives us a plus or minus one seventy days," Linz Lipnig told him. "Empire's technicians were very clumsy when they attempted to revise the controls—they shorted out enough affiliated circuitry to make pinpointing the exact moment of departure impossible."

"So?"

"So we can't safely intervene during the quarantined period. The chance of destroying our missing Special Agent while we're looking for him is too great to risk . . . unless, of course, you decide otherwise."

There was a long pause as Tausig stared at the screen. Then he tugged at his beard for a moment and cleared his throat. "One hundred seventy days," he said quietly. "I wonder how much trouble Fortune could get into in one hundred seventy days?"

"Answering questions like that is not my department," retorted the inventor, and abruptly signed off.

Tausig shrugged and called PsychSec. "I have a question to put to Wi'in," he told Alelis. "What is Hannibal Fortune likely to do if he gets no support at all from T.E.R.R.A. Control for a period of one hundred seventy days?"

Your name is Hannibal Fortune and you are probably the only secret agent in the entire history of secret agenting who could pull it off. Scipio doesn't know quite what to think of you but he can't afford to ignore you. With practice, he might even learn to think this way himself—he's one of the brightest early Earthmen you've ever dealt with. Too bad he's trapped in this time period. You'd like to see what he'd do in another kind of war, with more advanced technology and an entirely different pace. You suspect that he'd make a good showing in those circumstances, too.

You can see why d'Kaamp admires him so much. A hardness, a precision, the same qualities keep you both going, a singleminded devotion to the task at hand, doing the job, playing the game, without any of the sentimental nonsense ordinary men fall heir to, but getting it done, knowing how many of other men's lives it is going to cost and being willing to pay with as many other men's lives as need be to drive back the enemy, to take the hill, to gain the objective and get the upper hand and damn the fainthearted critics who think the lives of a few thousand pawns amount to anything compared to the glory of winning and you smile as you recall Scipio quoting Cato's poet to you which shows how little Scipio is concerned over the so-called moral justification for the war it was Quintus Ennius who said, "I grant you there are gods but they don't care what men do; else it would go well with the good and ill with the bad—which rarely happens," to which you had answered, "The only moral justification for any war is the triumph they put on for the victor," and Scipio smiled crookedly recalling the triumph they'd denied him two years ago and you hope that later on when the big one comes up after Hannibal One-Eye gets home you'll have a chance to get next to him and see if he considers Scipio a truly worthy opponent and you smile again as you realize that to become a great general a man must forget all the skills of obedience he learned as a soldier and it seems inconceivable that anyone should ever dare criticize a military establishment that produces even one great general in a hundred years. And, you ask rhetorically, for the benefit of the troublesome private citizen who lacks the spirit to see it, is not the honor of being mentioned in the memoirs of a great general a worthy enough cause to die for? The universe may not remember why you fought, but it will never forget how dramatically you died.

Twenty or thirty thousand barbarians will die dramatically tonight because of your help in guiding Scipio's hand. That's half again as many employees as there are in the entire T.E.R.R.A. organization, which you have always thought of as a relatively huge enterprise. It is easier to think of them in the aggregate, which you can call "the enemy" than to regard them as twenty or thirty thousand separate human beings. It is a certainty that none of those killed tonight would ever have amounted to anything, anyway.

Masinissa's small but talented force of Numidian horse is poised, waiting, eager to begin the slaughter, impatient with the diversionary tactic Scipio mounted (a your suggestion) earlier in the day, a feint attack on Utica designed to lull the enemy into a false sense of security.

You have scouted the two camps cleverly and carefully—both Hasdrubal's and Syphax'—and the advance patrols, hand-picked and murderous, have departed in the darkness. This is not the kind of war Scipio's Roman troops are accustomed to fighting; some of the more tradition-bound among them are even grumbling that such stealth and treachery are beneath a legionary's dignity, but most are content to let Scipio and Laelius do the thinking.

The night deepens. Quietly, now. According to the Torg, Syphax and Hasdrubal are both asleep, suspecting nothing. There is no moon; thin clouds obscure even the faint starshine. Ahead, along the outside bank of a long curve in the Bagradas, sprawl the two camps, their campfires dim red glows in the blackness. The mud of two months ago has dried for it is early summer. Insects scratch persistently at the silence. Both camps have a ripe odor about them, but it's not as bad now as during the daytime. Slowly, quietly, the legionaries take their places, ringing every exit. Special squads inch forward to the flimsy walls, ready to make doorways where no doorways were before. Inside the camps, bored sentries chat quietly, keeping each other awake. Outside, neither voice nor clank of furniture betrays the Romans. At a convenient distance, the bareback desert riders silently assemble, waiting for the signal, a thrice-repeated cry of a North African nightbird. A hush saturates the night with brittle breathlessness. At last Scipio himself makes a sign.

The nightbird screams, and screams again, and screams again.

Flames lick at the walls, the tents of the Numidians, the reed-and-wattle huts of the Carthaginians, which you examined from the air two months ago; shouts of alarm are heard, too late. Masinissa's horsemen swoop in upon the unsuspecting sleepers, thunder through the sudden doorways in the walls, dervishes on horseback, flickering death, slashing tent ropes, shaping their victims' panic with bonechilling screams while the legionaries close in upon the exits; as the fear-driven fugitives shrink from the flames they meet the Roman swords. Unarmed, half-dressed, eyes puffed with sleep, they die bleeding screaming burning stumbling cursing falling (Syphax, you later discover, somehow managed to escape along with his lieutenants.) squirting hurting gasping grasping disbelieving clutching moaning touching groaning crawling fighting panting biting dying (So, for that matter, did Hasdrubal and his top officers.) running tripping bleeding jerking stinking dying twitching roasting crying men with juices bubbling out of them black skin shriveling cracking hissing peeling writhing from the heat the dead still moving as their bodies blister and bloat and curl faces burned away charred toes crisp fingers broken off pissing as they die no longer men now smoldering corpses too many to bury thirty-nine thousand two hundred fifty-three of "them" and only fourteen hundred of "us" whatever that adds up to but nobody ever adds the scores together because that would imply that all forty thousand six hundred odd lives were important to anybody.

The victory is yours, Publius Cornelius Scipio.

The victory is yours, Laelius.

The victory is yours, Hannibal Fortune.

You even managed to save some of the horses. They *are* important.

THIRTEEN: "WOULD IT HELP IF
I WROTE ANOTHER POEM?"

MILITARILY, IT WAS a very successful battle, but despite a most favorable (and therefore worthwhile) kill ratio, the incident at Bagradas Bend wasn't as decisive as it might have been if the high command of one or both armies could have been slain along with the forty thousand troops. They weren't all troops, of course, but the remainder were the sort of women who customarily follow armies, so it was no great loss. And the incident clearly had virtue, in that it cost only a relative handful of Roman casualties, although some of the idealists still complained it wasn't a fair victory. Hearing this, Fortune shook his head, reflecting that a little Plato is a pitiable thing, while a lot can be disastrous.

There were rumors, of course, for the next several days, that Syphax or Hasdrubal, or both, had been slain, and squads were dispatched to search through the rotting corpses which still carpeted the charred campsites, fouling the air for miles around, but despite the rewards offered no carcasses could be found which would make convincing dead generals. At last, confirmation of other reports turned up, proving that both the Carthaginian and his desert ally had escaped. Fortune sent out his own reconnaissance force, a fifteen-pound feathered phenomenon, and confirmed the confirmations.

Sophonisba, who was rumored to have been with Syphax that fiery night, was with him now in Cirta, while her alleged father, Hasdrubal, had fled to Carthage, apparently intending to raise another army. Hasdrubal had escaped with about twenty-five hundred men, roughly one-twelfth the force he'd started with, a pathetic remnant of a once-proud army. Syphax had fared considerably better, but seeing that it wasn't his war and he'd still lost almost half his troops, the old king decided to call it quits, go home, and enjoy his declining years in the comforting arms of the lovely Sophonisba. There were no easy answers, Syphax claimed, but it's foolish to die for a hopeless cause.

As for the bad guys (I.e., victims. In any conflict between cultures, the terms are freely interchangeable.), ever since the successful cavalry ambush last winter, Masinissa had been gaining a trickle of recruits; as news that Syphax had withdrawn from the conflict circulated, the trickle turned into a deluge—many of them deserters from Syphax' camp, apparently preferring the way of the sword to the harsh, deadly dull life of a North African desert tribesman.

"The Bedouin," Scipio observed dryly, "cares not for whom he fights."

"In that respect," offered Sebastian Necropoulis, "he is like the Greek. It makes little difference what one does, as long as one does it well."

With the approach of a conscientious craftsman, Scipio turned his attention again to the siege of Utica, throwing seasoned troops into the lines. With Syphax retired and Hasdrubal routed in disgrace, Scipio now merely had to take Utica and he'd be free to march, unhampered, on the triple-walled city.

But, once again, things didn't quite work out that way.

For one thing, Hasdrubal had better luck than he had any right to in raising more volunteers to defend

Carthage. And Hasdrubal's daughter evidently still had more influence over her eighty-year-old husband than a teenaged bride properly ought to, even one skilled in Greek eroticism, because the aging monarch was soon reported on his way back toward Carthage with an estimated thirty thousand fresh troops. This report came first from Sebastian Necropoulis, who had not left Scipio's camp and who, characteristically, refused to divulge the source of his information, and then again, a day and a half later, essentially the same intelligence came in by means of hard-riding lookouts who'd been spotted throughout the hinterlands by Masinissa. The only point of variance was the Numidian lookouts' placing the enemy troop strength at 35,000.

Masinissa flashed an inquiring glance at the Greek.

"Thirty thousand," Fortune/Necropoulis insisted smugly. "My information is more exact."

"Then why," demanded Masinissa, "did you fail to predict the Celtiberians accompanying Syphax?"

"Celtiberians?" Necropoulis blinked innocently.

"A large force of heavy infantry."

In the left ear of Fortune/Necropoulis, the voice of Arrik/Webley hissed: "So that's what they were, Celtiberians! I counted about four thousand."

"Four thousand of them," the master spy added diffidently.

Masinissa looked offended. "Four thousand," he confirmed.

"I'm surprised, Necropoulis," Scipio chided, "that you neglected to mention the Celtiberians. Celtiberian infantry has its own peculiar fighting style, very effective. It always helps to know what you're up against." Fortune was reminded of the way d'Kaamp had analyzed the various armies. Scipio continued, "These, of course, will be the stubborn ones, the ones who refused to surrender when we took Spain. I'm flattered that they'd travel so far to have another chance at me. They'll fight to the death, every one of them—there's a warrant for their heads already, so none would dare surrender now. I predict it will be costly. Eh, Necropoulis?"

"It can be, if we let them get this far north. I'd suggest meeting them on the southern plain, where Masinissa's excellent cavalry can carve them into kabobs."

"I was thinking the same thing," the Roman commander said. "We'll march at dawn. It will take that long to get that excellent cavalry up off their collective pygidia. I'll grant you, astride their mounts they *are* magnificent, but on the ground—" He finished with a colorful Latin obscenity d'Kaamp would have loved to have in his collection, but delivered it with such an air of warm camaraderie the Numidian couldn't possibly be offended.

Luise identified herself, was told to wait one moment please, and less than a minute later was ushered into the cylindrical PsychSecRep's consultation room. "Agent Little." Alelis beamed, bowing slightly from the midsection. "Sit. Be comfortable. Do you write verse?"

"Badly," she replied. "Why?"

" 'Doe soft eyes,' " he quoted. " 'Two hearts must share a touch . . . the hour of parting . . . what has passed though gone was good.' Did you write that?"

"I don't see . . ."

"Linz Lipnig found it in Fortune's logbook." He rummaged briefly among some papers and handed it to her.

Luise glanced at the poem and shrugged. "I wrote it

while I was recovering from my infatuation with him. I thought it might help so I gave it to him."

Alelis nodded. "I read it to Wi'in," he said. "It intensified his feeling of alienation."

"I didn't mean to do *that*," the girl protested.

"Apparently Fortune saw it as one more proof that when you wrote it you loved him and you don't now. Unfortunately, he thinks you ought to."

"I don't see where there's anything I can do about it. Would it help if I wrote another poem?"

The PsychSecRep smiled. "No, but apparently you *are* the key to the puzzle. You're the only person Fortune will trust, even though he feels you betrayed him, assuming my analysis of Wi'in's reactions is correct. I shall ask Tausig to assign you to temporary duty as a Special Agent."

"You're completely mad."

"No. I'm merely making a few token concessions to one who might be."

Scipio drove his two best legions through five days of merciless forced marches, accompanied by his entire strength in horsemen, both Roman and Numidian, until they reached the enemy's mobilization center on the Great Plains.

Once again, what the rank-and-file legionary didn't know would probably have crippled his morale: the fact that he was outnumbered almost two to one. But the element of surprise combined with brilliant use of cavalry to crush the Carthaginian wings, and left the enemy center, with its nucleus of Celtiberians, vulnerable to a tricky enveloping maneuver on the part of Scipio's advancing legions.

As the Roman had predicted, Syphax' four thousand allies from Spain didn't even try to escape, but battled fiercely, apparently determined to do two things: die sword in hand, and take as many Romans as possible with them. This was a battle fought in full daylight, with both sides fully armed, a bizarre, deadly pageant, its inherent beauty of movement made grotesque by blood and butchery, but fascinating nonetheless.

With nothing left to fight for except their honor, which in true heroic fashion the Celtiberians firmly believed in, they fought valiantly against the remorseless Roman war machine, standing ankle-deep in the blood of their own dead and dying comrades, and it is said they fought valiantly to the end. Perhaps some of them thought they could win.

But not old Syphax, or his father-in-law, Hasdrubal Gisco, each of whom could see quite early in the game that it wasn't likely to turn out favorably, so each discreetly ducked out during an early peak in the action.

Masinissa was the first to notice that his uncle Syphax had vanished. Presumably to keep the old boy from recruiting still another army, Masinissa set off in pursuit, hardly pausing long enough to let Scipio know he was leaving.

FOURTEEN: "WE HAVE LITTLE CHOICE
BUT TO GIVE IN TO TEMPTATION."

WITH THE EXCEPTION of the Celtiberians, after the departure of Syphax there was little left of the Carthaginian force save for green troops freshly levied, talented at nothing but dying, which they accomplishd in great numbers. Masinissa had been gone only a few hours when Scipio called Laelius away from the battle still raging on the plain below. "Follow the Numidian," he instructed. "I want Syphax and his bride taken alive . . . Masinissa is apt to slit their throats."

Masinissa and his riders, nearly a thousand strong, swept west and north through these lands where many of them had grown to manhood. It was all Laelius and his legionaries, foreigners all, could do to keep the Numidian cavalry in sight.

As most wars tend to do, the conquest of Carthage dragged on and on—even the pursuit of Syphax took longer than one might expect, largely because both the hunted and both sets of hunters kept stopping to plunder at virtually every opportunity. Such is the nature of armies; indeed, one of the ancient and most honorable privileges of soldiering is the right to live off the land, which means off anybody else who is living off the land, such as farmers.

Syphax was in the lead, with no more than five thousand men and horses, fleeing for the presumed safety of his own borders.

Masinissa was nipping at his heels, his thousand riders insufficient to take on all the retreating army, even though it was composed of quitters. Quitters, the desert prince knew, are not necessarily cowards.

Laelius was marching behind Masinissa, his heavy infantry ready to hup-two-three into the thick of any enemy concentration it encountered.

And the residents of the area, of course, were wondering what they'd done to deserve being plundered by three armies in less than that many days.

If you weigh fifteen pounds, can eat almost anything, need very little rest and enjoy virtually no limitations on physical shape and function—and you are telepathic to boot—you can expect to be exploited. Especially if you're teamed up with Hannibal Fortune. Arrik wondered how Webley had managed for so many years, assignment after assignment, without being some sort of Supertorg. His cells ached from all the flying Fortune was having him do—a trip each day to check on Syphax, Masinissa and Laelius, respectively. And then the great circle route, flying over Tunis, Carthage, Castra Cornelia and Utica in order to keep Fortune current on military deployment in each location. Plus a trip to Cirta every other day or so to make sure Sophonisba was still there. Even at airspeeds of slightly better than a hundred miles an hour, that was a lot of time in the air. And it was a lot of time for thinking, and wondering if teaming up with Fortune had been such a hot idea after all.

Masinissa caught up with Syphax the day after Sebastian Necropoulis informed Scipio that a fleet of warships was putting out from Carthage. The only reasonable targets for a Carthaginian naval strike were Castra Cornelia and the Roman siege lines around Utica, which still

ıadn't capitulated. Scipio left immediately with a small
cavalry force, heading north toward Utica, leaving orders
or his ground troops to follow as quickly as possible.

Fortune/Necropoulis commandeered a horse and left
oon after, traveling northwest. As horses go, it was a
good one, but it was no fit substitute for a temporal transporter. In sixty years as a Special Agent, he'd become
accustomed to such niceties as air conditioning and in-
door plumbing, neither of which are available, even as
optional extras, with a horse.

The days began to blend into one another, like slog-
ing footprints across an endless sand dune. Keeping track
of things for Hannibal Fortune was an exhausting job,
and each time the Torg thought he'd get some rest another emergency cropped up. Like the battle they found
themselves in the day they caught up with Masinissa.
In a desperate maneuver, old King Syphax had laid an-
ther ambush for his nephew and Masinissa had stupid-
ly ridden into it, with less than one-quarter of his
orsemen. They were on the verge of succumbing to
Syphax' superior numbers when Fortune and Arrik ar-
ived. The rigorous training Fortune had imposed upon
he Torg was justified in that encounter as Arrik hurtled
nto the melee, revising his protoplasm as needed to deal
with each momentary threat, flashing here and there,
bludgeoning, blinding, choking, slashing, crashing, trip-
ing, ripping and all the rest, while Fortune observed the
advice given him long ago by d'Kaamp, namely to stay
ut of battle if he could manage it, and directed the
Torg's activities from afar. Presently, before more than
hundred of his desert riders had been fatally unhorsed,
Syphax himself was wounded and captured. Within min-

utes the ambush turned into a rout as word of their chief tain's downfall circulated among the nervous tribesmen. They not only knew the terrain, they knew how to disappear into it and, recognizing the virtue of doing so, did.

It was all over by the time Laelius and his light-footed legionaries* lumbered into view. Syphax had been captured and was being held under double guard, Arrib had flown on ahead under instructions from Fortune and Masinissa was in a victorious frenzy, vastly impressed with himself that he'd finally taken his hated uncle captive. "Build a cage!" he shouted. "We'll put him in a cage and drag him behind us through all his kingdom!"

(Syphax cringed, but he'd have done the same to Masinissa had things gone differently.)

Laelius agreed to caging the old warrior, but suggested delivering him to Scipio as soon as possible, to be paraded through the streets of Rome. Both Laelius and Masinissa, Fortune observed wryly, thought of the aged chieftain only in terms of his value as an exhibit. Both were gratified to learn that Syphax' wounds were superficial and that he could thus be expected to live long enough to be in a parade.

"Actually, Luise," Alelis explained, "the mechanics of Fortune's breakdown are quite simple. Through his entire career he's armed himself against emotional involvement. He learned how to avoid it but not how to

---

*"Light-footed legionaries" is a free translation preserving the irony of the Arabic epithet if not its literal meaning. The expression was a favorite one among Numidian horsemen for describing Roman infantry.

handle it should it take place anyway, which is apparently what happened during your year at *Time Out*."

"We were both recovering from rather severe nerve damage," Luise reminded him.

"You fell in love," the cylindrical one said.

"That's all over now."

"For you. For him, being loved instead of just admired or respected, which as I recall he could handle quite well, was apparently such an alien experience that he was totally unprepared to cope with it. I imagine his mistake was in comparing it with all his other relationships, which were quite satisfactory but lacked the intensity of affection the two of you were experiencing. From there, it was easy for him to slip into the irrational and frightfully grandiose notion that everyone else *ought* to love him, too. Obviously, not everybody else wanted to. Pohl Tausig couldn't, not without sacrificing his usefulness as Operations Chief. Webley did, of course, but not in the same way."

"No," she agreed, thinking of her own relationship with the symbiote Ronel. "It's not the same."

"The point is, Fortune thought it ought to be. It had never mattered before that some of his associates resented him, some feared him, some loathed him; previously, he'd sensibly concluded that other people's feelings toward him were their problems, not his. But he's become a borderline psychotic, and as such he finds the general lack of love for him violently irritating. He now feels that people *ought* to love him, otherwise they're no good."

"What can we do about it?"

"Get him back here for therapy. But in the meantime his mission has to be finished, and from what you and Webley have told us there's nobody else who can do it except Hannibal Fortune. The best we can do i try to find him and give him all the support we can."

"Why me, then? There are more capable agents."

"There aren't any he'll trust. Perhaps making it clea to him that you haven't rejected him will reverse th process that's been happening inside his head."

"I'll try," she said.

Arrik detected another alien presence at Cirta, i addition to Sophonisba, and took it upon himself t investigate. On his first low pass over Syphax' palace h saw the skimmer, parked inside the harem garden wall Apparently it had arrived during the previous night for it hadn't been there the day before. Fortune was stil so far away, riding with Masinissa, that it would tak him the rest of the day and half the night, too, to ge here on horseback.

Finding the skimmer's pilot alone, Arrik overpowered the creature, enveloping its scaly head in loops of proto plasm that tightened instantly to block off sight, sound and air supply, making struggle useless. The Empir agent struggled anyway. Arrik held on until he wa sure the thing was dead.

Sophonisba was in another part of the palace, un aware that her Empire companion had dropped out o play. Arrik decided to leave her in her ignorance and let Fortune deal with her as he saw fit.

Very carefully, he stole the skimmer.

Piloting a custom-styled IntraSystem luxury skimme was not anything he'd been taught in basic training but IntraSystem's designers had tried to outguess th most stupid potential customers and had made allow ances for every conceivable error. It was theoretically impossible even for the rawest outworlder to make enough mistakes at the controls of an IntraSystem product to do much damage to himself or it in the process.

Arrik was lucky. He guessed wrong only four times, and by that time he'd achieved an altitude of better than six miles, which gave him ample room for learning to fly. Within half an hour he became fairly proficient, and thoroughly lost.

The 93rd Emergency Staff Session of T.E.R.R.A. Control reconvened briefly to consider the recommendations of the various section heads. After a minimum of argument, Luise Little, Ronel and Webley were officially charged with the task of rescuing Hannibal Fortune. They were instructed to proceed with extreme caution and to remember at all times to act in a reassuring manner in order to avoid letting the deranged Special Agent feel rejected. A briefing schedule was set up to give Luise an opportunity to absorb the contents of all the historical source-material Fortune had used.

There was a strong sense of urgency connected to this mission, but no hurry at all in T.E.R.R.A. Control, because of Lipnig's quarantine restrictions.

Hannibal Fortune was startled by the flash of something in the late-afternoon sky, and looked around to see if Masinissa had seen it, too. The Numidian prince apparently had been looking in another direction. Empire must be desperate, Fortune thought, if they're willing to show a skimmer in broad daylight, the one glance had been enough to tell him what he'd seen. It was only a question of time before someone else in his party spotted it, too.

As if the Empire pilot could read his thoughts, the skimmer dropped abruptly below the horizon, well to one side of their line of march.

Fortune wished his partner would show up to eavesdrop on the skimmer's occupants, but the Torg was away on his regular recon circuit. He'd been due back over an hour ago.

Thus, it was with relief a few minutes later that he noticed the familiar T.E.R.R.A. recognition symbol done in smoke tree blossoms a short distance ahead. Unobtrusively, he altered his course to bring him in contact with the tree, and before Masinissa had time to notice anything unusual the Torg had flowed up the wide sleeve of Fortune's robe.

I saw a skimmer a few minutes ago, Fortune began in loudthink, but the symbiote's speech tendril was already in his ear.

"I stole it from the palace at Cirta," the Torg explained then hurriedly recounted what had happened.

That's not quite the way I'd planned it, Fortune replied, *but if they're going to leave their equipment lying around like that, we have little choice but to give in to temptation.*

Masinissa made no attempt to conceal his pleasure, a few moments later, when Sebastian Necropoulis complained of stomach cramps and nausea. "I must rest. will catch up with you later." The Numidian's antagonism toward the secretive Greek had grown more pronounced daily; apparently he felt any discomfort Necropoulis might be experiencing was richly deserved

Fortune got the impression that Masinissa was glad to be rid of him.

Ostensibly to get out of the way of the rest of the troops, Fortune moved off at right angles to the line of march and was shortly hidden from sight. Then he doubled back, following the Torg's directions to get to the stolen skimmer, which was hidden in a gully.

It was the same skimmer he'd seen before, prior to Syphax' wedding.

A desert prince neither wins nor keeps the loyalty of several thousand Numidian tribesmen by being soft. Nor does he stay alive by being stupid. Even his most scornful detractors readily admitted that Masinissa was neither. Young, energetic, he was considered an exceptional horseman, a fierce warrior and a capable strategist, suspicious enough of his allies to keep a constant eye on them, thus guaranteeing that they remained his allies. It was this general instinct for caution rather than any specific act on the part of Sebastian Necropoulis that caused the Numidian to suspect the Greek's sudden illness and to follow him into the wild to see for himself what sort of treachery Necropoulis was up to.

The enigmatic Greek had long been on Masinissa's list of Things Worth Looking Into. Perhaps the physical similarity of the two men had something to do with Masinissa's feeling of discomfort: except for their complexions and some minor facial details, the two might have been brothers, so close was the resemblance between them. Masinissa was perhaps more conscious of physical details than another man might be; proud of his own body, which he took pains to keep in excellent shape, he naturally admired any physique which reminded him of his own.

And although he wasn't sure just what he expected to find out, he was decidedly unprepared for the sight of the strange, shiny structure toward which the Greek was riding with no perceptible hesitation. Masinissa shook his head and blinked, thinking the thing was a mirage, but it didn't fade or shimmer into nothingness as he moved to view it from a different angle. He'd never seen anything like it. Fascinated, he moved closer.

A short distance from the smooth, bowl-shaped thing, the Greek reined his horse to a stop. Masinissa hadn't noticed it before, but something that looked at first like a small dog scampered from Necropoulis to the thing. Except that small dogs don't have long, monkey-like arms or the ability to climb smooth, perpendicular surfaces. The not-dog vanished inside.

If Masinissa had been smoking *kif* the things he was seeing wouldn't have particularly surprised him, but such was not the case. A quick glance in all directions confirmed the normalcy of everything else, except what was happening in the gully.

A section of the huge bowl fell slowly out and down, revealing a large doorway.

A not-dog had gone inside; now a not-bird came out.

It flew to Necropoulis, who still sat astride his horse, and landed on the Greek's shoulder.

Then it flew straight up.

Masinissa watched it for a moment, then returned his eyes to the gully. The Greek had turned around and seemed to be looking at him.

There was a sudden loud sound immediately above

him, and before Masinissa could react he was snared in a heavy net that contracted around him as if it were alive. In response to the struggle, the Numidian's horse bolted in panic, but Masinissa stayed aboard. The horse calmed; by the time it came to a stop the cocoon was so complete he couldn't see and could barely breathe.

Something stung his arm.

Drowsiness came swiftly and was swallowed up by sleep.

FIFTEEN: "PROMISE YOU'LL TURN
ME ON LATER?"

FORTUNE BROUGHT Masinissa's mount to a halt before the
ornate palace gates and leaped off in accepted Numidian fashion. There was a Torgish chuckle in his left ear.
"The one who calls herself Sophonisba is waiting for
you inside."

Fortune grinned. He'd parked the skimmer, with Masinissa and a dead Empire flunky aboard, less than a
mile away, and had approached the town slowly, giving the palace lookouts ample time to report his arrogant
approach. Dressed in Masinissa's clothes and on Masinissa's horse merely by having stolen them, and stealing
Masinissa's face as well merely by having Arrik arrange
a thin layer of himself over Fortune's own face so that
it duplicated the desert prince's swarthy features, muscular neck and bulging biceps, he was sure the lookouts
had taken him for Masinissa. The likeness, Fortune knew,
was exact, but to pull it off he also had to mimic Masinissa's voice, vocabulary and mannerisms. Accordingly, he
struck a muscular, swaggering pose and made his chest
muscles ripple to impress the trembling townspeople
covertly watching the gate from the safety of their own
doorways, and replied in loudthink:

*On this planet it's considered impolite to keep a lady
waiting. Does she suspect anything?*

"How could she? She's never seen Masinissa."

A servant appeared and with great ceremony ushered
the conqueror inside. At last they came to a richly-ap-
pointed hall with hanging lamps, braziers of smoldering

incense spotted here and there, tapestried walls and a profusion of pillows strewn seemingly everywhere. Through an arched doorway hung with exquisite brocades stepped Sophonisba, wearing an outfit which gave the impression that the old king's bride had seized upon puberty as her crowning accomplishment.

"Auntie," Fortune breathed appreciatively.

She looked at him sharply.

Fortune laughed. "I'm not surprised that you don't recognize me, Aunt Sophie," he continued in the Numidian tongue. "It's been a long time since we saw each other last. You've put on some weight. But Uncle Sy always did like them plump."

"You must be Masinissa," she said.

"Your loving nephew." His eyes took insolent inventory. "It's been a long, hard ride, Auntie. Why don't we lie down somewhere and get acquainted?"

"If you wish," she said quietly. "Might I ask about my husband?"

Fortune unfastened his cloak and threw it in a corner. "Ornery old son of a cameldriver. He won't be bothering you again."

"You killed him?"

"Carved him up some but he'll live. We packed him off to my friend Scipio. The Skip'll know what to do with him."

There was a moment of silence while the two looked at each other. Then Sophonisba said, "What do you plan to do with me?"

Hannibal Fortune shrugged eloquently. "Maybe I'll leave that up to you. Any ideas?"

Smiling hesitantly as became the teenaged bride of an aging desert monarch, she stepped closer to him and murmured, "As you suggested, perhaps we should, ah, get to know each other better. I'm sure we'll be able to think of something." Turning, she ordered her servants to leave them alone.

It was a pleasure to watch her work, to see the ease with which she adapted to the changing situation. Fortune was tempted to let her go on thinking he was King Syphax' hot-blooded Numidian nephew. It might even be fun for a while, although as an Empire agent she was his sworn enemy. Perhaps if he'd had his temporal transporter and the freedom of movement it afforded, he'd have taken time to toy with her at greater length, but without it there was no room in the equation for such pursuits. The idea that prolonging the masquerade would be taking unfair advantage had nothing to do with it; the fact that the mask of living protoplasm was beginning to get uncomfortable did.

Arrik caught Fortune's loudthink instructions and obeyed instantly, flowing smoothly off his partner's face. "Of course," the T.E.R.R.A. agent said, "if *we* can't think of anything, maybe Gregor Malik can."

Sophonisba stared at him in horror. "Who *are* you?" she demanded.

"Hannibal Fortune. And you?"

"If he was still a Resident, like you, he'd have cerebrosensors in his skull," Pohl Tausig explained, "and you could locate him without much difficulty. But Specials can't afford anything that would show up on Empire's instruments. They were removed years ago."

"How convenient," Luise said. "There are only a quarter of a million people in Carthage."

Tausig smiled blandly. "That's one reason you're taking Webley along. Between Webley and Ronel, they should be able to locate him telepathically. Good luck."

The one calling herself Sophonisba had been born almost as far across the galaxy as had Hannibal Fortune, and had begun her lawless career at a tender age. This was her first assignment as an Empire agent and she was not particularly happy about it. She had the good sense, however, to offer no resistance to capture.

As Fortune had suspected, she wasn't even armed.

Arrik swept the area with a telepathic probe and reported no immediate threats other than a couple of desert-style ladies-in-waiting who were loyal to Sophonisba merely because they thought it was expected of them.

Since the real Masinissa would be needed later (assuming success in restructuring the time-line), he'd have to be stashed somewhere out of the way. And the dead skimmer pilot would have to be disposed of before he started to stink.

"Come on," Fortune said, "we're going for a ride."

"Whatever you say," Sophonisba said meekly.

As a precaution, Fortune tied her hands securely behind her.

They flew north from Cirta, under cover of darkness. Once well out over the Mediterranean, Fortune dumped the pilot overboard, then turned the stolen craft east on a path that would take them about forty miles north of Carthage. Sophonisba watched but said nothing. The unconscious Masinissa slept peacefully all the way, his breathing deep and regular.

They approached from the seaward side, fast, low and showing no lights.

Among the customs Carthaginians shared with other Semitic peoples was a complex system of taboos concerning the dead; they'd put much thought and effort into providing a decent burial ground where members of nobility and perhaps a few distinguished commoners could be properly, respectfully entombed. Cut into the northern slopes of the sandstone bluffs between the city and the sea were hundreds of tunnels which gave access to countless underground rooms, vaults and chambers containing sarcophagi ranging from simple stone boxes to ornate, jewel-encrusted coffins. It was in one of these that Fortune deposited the sleeping prince, after evicting the bones of its rightful occupant.

Carefully, he attached an automated spray-hypo unit to Masinissa's arm, programming it to provide daily sedation for twenty days.

"By that time he'll starve to death," Sophonisba protested.

"He may lose a few pounds, but he won't starve; this stuff slows everything down."

"Is that what you're going to do to me?"

"I'm not sure yet just what I do want to do with you."

She looked thoughtfully at him. "I can probably be of more use to you alive and kicking, than like him. Especially if you untie me."

"We'll talk about it when we get back to the palace."

At T.E.R.R.A. Control, the exploration of Hannibal Fortune's probable neuroses, as proxied in the mutant Wi'in, was not only exhaustive but in the opinion of Alelis was as complete as anyone could ask.

"But what if he's got involved with another woman?"

Luise asked. "One hundred seventy days is a long time for a man like him to be running around loose."

"Involved?" The PsychSecRep laughed. "At this point, impossible. Right now to him women are hardly even people. He views them only as something to be used and discarded. He may even attempt to hurt them, thereby punishing you symbolically."

Luise shook her head. "I don't think I like this Hannibal Fortune at all."

"Like? What in the world has that to do with anything? We need him back."

Masinissa's troops, reaching Cirta during the night and hearing that their leader had already captured the wife of Syphax, amused themselves by looting the desert capital. Laelius, arriving a few hours later, was not so easily satisfied. Fortune and the girl had barely returned before the Roman was pounding at the gates, demanding entrance. Hurriedly Arrik flowed back into position on Fortune's face as the palace flunkie opened up.

Laelius, being a rather straitlaced Roman, immediately drew his own conclusions. "You've had your fun, Masinissa," he said. "Now turn the woman over to me."

"Find your own girl," retorted the bogus Numidian.

"As a former enemy of Rome, she is a captive of Rome."

"I disagree. I claim her as my bride."

"You can't marry this woman!"

"I'm afraid I already have. Sophie and I have been secretly engaged for years."

"You have no authority to marry her."

"You seem awfully upset over it, Laelius old man,

but don't worry, there are two or three other girls in the palace. Take your choice."

"Scipio—" the Roman began, sputtering.

"Pick one out for him, too," Fortune offered expansively. "What's his preference?"

"Boys," Sophonisba said, "if you're going to argue like this I'm going back to bed. It's too early for anyone but a commoner to be awake."

"Good idea, Sophie," Fortune agreed. "We'll talk to Laelius later on this afternoon. He's had a long, hard ride—do you suppose we might put him up in the guest room?"

Laelius, Fortune could see, might easily get to be a pain in the neck. The Roman was staunch, loyal, stodgy, unimaginative and decidedly by-the-book. The sort of man who is incapable of treachery simply because he'd never be able to make it work. The sort of officer who invariably sets a fine example for his men.

After considerable haggling the following day, Fortune/Masinissa agreed to take Sophonisba back to Castra where Scipio could decide what should become of her. It was the sort of compromise, Fortune felt, that the real Masinissa might have made.

As preparations for the rescue mission progressed, Webley felt at loose ends. Without a partner in the usual sense, his part of the procedure was necessarily limited. The obvious answer—multiple symbiosis—had been tried before and had failed consistently. Few human personalities were strong enough to maintain more than one symbiotic relationship at a time—and the vast majority of Torgs were unable to cooperate with each other in more than the most formal and highly

194

ritualized circumstances. To the typical Torg, equality was subversive concept. It is easier for a Torg to accept a member of another species as his better than it is to accept a fellow Torg as his equal. Two Torgs in symbiosis with the same human partner would be too much like that human's hands—far too equal for comfort.

Webley, however, thought the three of them could make it work; Luise was doubtful; Ronel, surprisingly, was willing.

In the end, they settled for a compromise, with Ronel in the middle. It was unconventional, but it worked.

Webley fervently hoped that it would work well enough.

Two human beings, Arrik observed, can get to know quite a bit about each other if they spend six days and nights together on horseback. If they both happen to be professional spies, however, the game is something else again, with each feeding the other large chunks of false information until both realize they're being lied to. Then they begin to realize that it *is* a game.

Each night, Laelius posted a ring of guards around the tent of the newlyweds to keep anyone from bothering them. It was the same ring of guards he would have posted if his intention were to keep the bride and groom from escaping, and it accomplished the same end.

"This marriage ritual that these Earthians have," Sophonisba said at one point, "is an amusing custom, but I still am not convinced of its usefulness."

"You seem to have found it a convenient way to control Syphax."

Sophonisba smiled. "And you," she said, "found it a

useful device for keeping Laelius away from me. If you hadn't insisted on marrying me the moment he showed up—"

"—he would have taken you in chains back to Scipio," Fortune finished for her. "You have no reason to complain."

Sophonisba lay back on a pile of pillows. "The least you could do," she pouted, "is act like a husband."

Discreetly, although not from a sense of prudery but because we're running out of space, we declare Fortune's reaction immaterial to the outcome of the story. At best, it was a different sort of relationship than he'd had with any other human female, no matter what her native planet, and as such was mildly entertaining. Like life itself, it was a diverting way to pass the time on the way to Castra Cornelia. As such it filled six days. It did little to cure him of his delusions and nothing to endanger the mission. On the other hand, it wasn't the sort of thing that would tend to produce additional hangups, because it wasn't particularly important to either Sophonisba or to Hannibal Fortune. The only one to think the relationship at all exceptional was Arrik, but that was because Vango had never wanted to do anything like that.

It wasn't even particularly witty.

When they reached Castra Cornelia, Scipio showed them to the man in the cage. For the real Masinissa it would have been a sweet moment, so Fortune swaggered and smiled mockingly at the old man, while pulling Sophonisba closer to him.

"She is the one responsible for it all!" thundered Syphax, pointing a trembling finger through the bars.

"She beguiled me. She led me into grievous errors. She blinded me to my friends and caused me to turn away from Rome. She is a curse. She will be Masinissa's undoing just as she was mine!" Depending on their politics and their prejudices, historians for centuries thereafter would argue about that statement, some contending that it wasn't what the old king said at all, others accepting the words while disputing Syphax' reasons for saying them, some scoffing at the notion that a seasoned desert warrior would stoop to blaming a woman for his misfortune. A few even held that Livy had gotten carried away while writing it up. In actual fact, Syphax did say it, for a very human, Earth-male reason: he was jealous, miffed, vastly annoyed at seeing a younger man usurp his place, and by indulging in a fit of pique he sought to devalue the object of his recent enthusiastic attention.

Scipio, however, took him seriously.

Which was how Hannibal Fortune, symbiocosmetically disguised as Masinissa, found himself in the middle of a very serious talk with the Roman commander. It was the sort of talk each generation contrives to have with the next in order to impart the delusional structure it thinks of as Eternal Truth.

Scipio could easily have been pompous; instead, he chose a conspiratorial, big-brother air which reminded Fortune of a Rhetagglian used-skimmer dealer.

"I suppose, Masinissa, that it was because you saw in me some good qualities that you first came to me when in Spain for the purpose of forming a friendship with me," the Roman said. "Afterward in Africa you committed yourself and all your hopes to my protection."

Spotting the dramatic pause, Fortune nodded but didn't interrupt.

"But of all those virtues," Scipio continued, "the virtues which made me seem worthy of your regard, there is none of which I am so proud as temperance and control of my passions."

"You want me to get rid of her," Fortune/Masinissa said.

"I can't force you to forsake her," the Roman said smoothly. "That must be your decision alone."

The bogus Numidian glared, obviously not overjoyed at the prospect of having his trophy snatched away.

"When you are king of all Massyleland . . ." Scipio dangled the concept like a carrot.

It was the sort of consolation prize, Fortune concluded, that would appeal to the real Masinissa. What's more, it should help insure a Roman victory over Hannibal One-Eye. "*When?*" he asked sharply.

"King Masinissa," the Roman said slowly, tasting each word.

"How soon?" Fortune persisted.

"Sophonisba?" countered Scipio.

"I will think about it."

Scipio smiled paternally. "I'll expect an answer by morning. Until then, enjoy yourself."

Clearly, the interview was at an end. Fortune was thankful to get back to the privacy of the Numidian command tent where he could dispense with his protoplasmic mask. Arrik extruded some legs and a head and perched on the end of a folding couch while Fortune changed into his Necropoulis costume. Carefully, he selected what he needed from the stolen duty kit.

He'd done all he could for now, nudging Scipio's war

in the historically proper direction. It was time to get back to his own war against Gregor Malik. In Syphax, Scipio had a trophy to show the folks back home. Hannibal Fortune could think of no reason not to take a souvenir to T.E.R.R.A. Control.

Sophonisba would do nicely.

As Sebastian Necropoulis he walked the roughly two hundred yards to the well-guarded living tent she shared with her "husband."

"I have a message for the woman, from Masinissa," he told the guards.

They passed him inside.

"I'm curious," Fortune told her. "What did you do to him?"

"What do you mean?"

"Syphax. He was once a pretty canny warrior. A couple of years ago he was all set to throw in with the Romans."

Sophonisba laughed. "The males on this planet are marvelously easy to control—if you know where to grab on."

"By Earth standards Syphax is an old man."

She arched a perfect eyebrow. "He's no different than a man of any other age. They all like being told what great lovers they are."

DAY 267: The damaged nerve tissue regenerated long ago—now the rest of the year remains to be enjoyed. You look down at the gentle planes of Luise's face, her pale hair made smoke-soft in the *Time Out* twilight. Her smile of a moment ago has moved aside, displaced by a more meaningful expression, a more intense rapport. At this point, words would be extraneous decoration. The important communication is tactile rather than verbal, so you listen with your skin. Without words she tells you you are wonderful. You are the greatest.

And you love it.

"I have no more time for you," Fortune told her. "Take this."

Sophonisba regarded the capsule in his hand with curiosity. "You intend to poison me?"

"It'll turn you off, slow your metabolism to simulate death."

"Like the real Masinissa?"

He nodded affirmation.

"You'll turn me on later?"

"Someone will, sooner or later," he promised.

"All right. Give me the pill."

Sophonisba swallowed the quasi-fatal dosage, lay back gracefully on some cushions, and within minutes was a convincing corpse. Hannibal Fortune looked at her and sighed, then strode from the tent. "Ding dong," he said pleasantly to the two legionaries standing guard at the entrance, "the witch is dead." As Sebastian Necropoulis he hurried to the Numidian command tent, where Arrik/Webley quickly flowed over his face. Then, as Masinissa, he rushed back to the tent of his captured bride, properly shocked at the unexpected news of her death.

Less than an hour later he was explaining to Scipio what had happened:

"I had given her my pledge that whatever happened I would not let her fall alive into the hands of Rome. I sent her a cup of poison—Necropoulis took it to her. She dictated a reply before she drank it down." He pulled a crumpled note from his belt and carefully spread it flat, then read with a voice choking with emotion, "I accept this nuptial present; nor is it an unwelcome one, if my husband can render me. no better service. Tell him however that I should have died with greater satisfaction had I not married so near to my death." It was signed, "Sophonisba."

Scipio understood how it was, and made no protest when the fraudulent Masinissa insisted that his bride's body be spared from the customary Roman cremation.

"It is neither the custom of Carthage, to which she belongs, nor of my own Massyleland, to burn the bodies of the dead. That, friend Scipio, is a custom of Rome. I was your ally in this because I needed you. I grant that Romans are superior to Africans in many things, but not in our respect for the dead."

"What do you propose doing with her?"

"She is of Carthage, where the custom is to bury the dead, as it is with Semites everywhere. It is only right that her body be placed in the catacombs."

"Catcombs?"

"North of Carthage. I know where they are. I will attend to it myself, and return tomorrow."

"You propose to cross the land wall just to observe a funeral custom?" Scipio exclaimed. "They'll kill you!"

Fortune shook his head. "In Africa," he said, "we are not like you Romans. Our respect for the dead includes respect for the mourners. No one will stop a grieving husband returning his dead wife to her family's burial grounds. It might help if you studied our ways, too, as well as those of the Greeks."

Scipio narrowed his eyes. "Remember this, Masinissa:

I can destroy every country in the world and still be honoring one of their common beliefs."

"Which one?"

"The notion that one should be intolerant of foreigners."

As Masinissa, Fortune turned wordlessly away, as even a desert prince should do when verbally bested by a Scipio.

"Leave the body as it is," he instructed, "but wrap it in wet sheets and tie it on a horse. We'll be riding in the hot sun most of the day."

The legionaries looked to Scipio for confirmation of Masinissa's orders.

"Do as he says," the Roman told them.

SIXTEEN: "YOU HAD NO RIGHT
TO DO THAT."

REACHING THE CATACOMBS was more difficult by horse-back than it had been a week earlier by skimmer. Although he left the Roman camp at dawn, it was late afternoon by the time he found the limestone vault where Masinissa was stored. "This," Fortune complained as he unwrapped Sophonisba and carried her inside, "is a lot of work just to start a romantic legend."

"I thought we were doing it so T.E.R.R.A. would have a captive enemy agent to interrogate," the Torg replied.

"That, too," Fortune agreed. "If we make it through this assignment, Tausig will send someone back to pick her up. If we don't, it won't matter." After disconnecting the spray-hypo, he eased Masinissa's body out of the coffin and propped it up against the wall of the cavern, next to the "dead" Sophonisba. "At any rate, it'll give historians something else to bicker about." He looked down at the girl. "Some of them will probably call her evil, and others will say she was noble—both for the wrong reasons. Give me a hand, will you, in getting her in the box?"

Once Sophonisba was safely stashed and her attachments satisfactorily automated, Fortune sent Arrik to Cirta for the skimmer they'd left in the ex-king's back yard. Within moments the Torg had streaked out of sight in the moonlit sky.

Bringing the unconscious Numidian back to life was a ticklish operation which kept Fortune busy for more than an hour with an assortment of hypo-sprays and life process monitors. Masinissa woke up, again in his own clothes, to see Sebastian Necropoulis crouching over him.

"Your strength will return in a little while," the Greek assured him. "For now, just relax and listen—you have no other choice."

Glowering, Masinissa tried to sit up but was instantly overcome by waves of dizziness.

"You've been unconscious for almost ten days," Necropoulis said. "You and I are the only ones who know about it, because during that time I've been impersonating you. I've accomplished a lot on your behalf, *King* Masinissa, so shut up and listen." In short, sharp sentences the Greek related everything Masinissa needed to know about the past ten days—the marriage to Sophonisba, the dispute with Laelius, the accusation of Syphax, the man-to-man talk with Scipio, Sophonisba's suicide and his own trip to bring her body here to the catacombs. "Upon your return to Castra Cornelia, you'll be crowned king of Massyleland. I suggest you say nothing to contradict what I've just told you."

Unexpectedly, Masinissa grinned. "Nobody would believe me, anyway, would they?"

"Good thinking, King. Don't worry. I'm just as anxious as you are to see Carthage destroyed."

Masinissa nodded. "Otherwise you'd have killed me outright. Did you think to bring something to eat?"

Fortune broke out the stores. As they dined together in the moonlight, not really friends but with much less antagonism than might be expected, Fortune answered questions and furnished needed details. He regretted that the Torg was not there to monitor what was going on in Masinissa's mind.

At last, the Numidian mounted his horse for the long trek back to Castra Cornelia. "Necropoulis," he said in surprise when the other made no move to mount up, "aren't you coming, too?"

Fortune shook his head. "You'd better take both horses. I have another means of transportation. Good luck."

Instead of flying directly to Cirta, as Fortune had instructed, Arrik detoured in a wide circle that brought him back over Carthäge and the Residency he'd shared with Vango for sixteen years. He hadn't seen his former partner in months now, and he looked back on those years with a certain nostalgia. The pace of living had been relaxed, dull even, but much easier than the constant activity he'd let himself in for as Hannibal Fortune's partner. Probably the best thing about the relationship with Vango was that it had been undemanding. Arrik felt a lump of homesickness as he glided ever nearer the location of the Residency. Mentally, he cast a tentative probe ahead of him, tuned to Vango's alpha-modulation. Apparently the Resident wasn't home. Perhaps it was just as well, thought Arrik.

Then, suddenly, he was there.

The gutted shell of the building told a story of unexpected attack, intense heat, devastation far too thorough to be anything but deliberate. The ashes were six to eight inches deep in places, with random footprints testifying to the presence of looters after the fire. Arrik adjusted his eye-structure to the inky shadows and searched for some indication that Vango had survived.

He found part of Vango's head.

It was long past midnight when the stolen skimmer

finally came to rest on a nearby hilltop. Radiating annoyance, Fortune strode across the intervening space. The boarding ramp seemed to take forever to swing out and lock into position. At its top sat the Torg, his shape again approximately that of a small dog.

"I'm glad you finally got here," Fortune snapped. "I thought for a while I was going to be stranded in this blasted cemetery."

"Vango is dead," the symbiote said quietly.

"I figured you'd run into some sort of trouble. It's not like you to leave me hanging like that."

"I am not Webley."

"Whatever you say, but let's get out of here."

"No. Stop. Listen to me. The Residency is destroyed. All of our tapes and equipment, everything. Vango is dead. I am as much to blame as if I'd killed him. Don't tell me nonsense; it's true. Malik thought you were dead. Malik thought Vango stole the skimmer. I don't need proof, I can feel it's true. I left him alone and unprotected. If I'd stayed where I belonged this wouldn't have happened. So I killed him. Don't interrupt; I killed him because I wasn't there to warn him. I thought working with you would be more exciting, but I am not Webley. I can't take it any more. Malik thought Vango stole the skimmer and for revenge he smashed the Residency. That has to be the way it happened. Vango was a gentle person, he never hurt anyone. I'm just as guilty as Malik is. Don't think at me; I'm not listening. I am just telling you how it is, and why I can't do it any more. Not with you. Not with anyone. I'm sorry, but there's no way to change my mind. I brought you your skimmer. I hope you succeed in what you have to do. No, you don't need me, Hannibal Fortune. Vango needed me, and I let him down. Working with you has been—instructive—but my place is with Vango. I stop now."

The small, dog-like figure seemed to crumple, losing the sharpness of its outline, and sagged against the top of the ramp, then began to slide slowly downward, leaving a glistening trail, a lump of grayish protoplasm with pieces dropping off, fifteen pounds of still-warm raw material that had already forgotten the dog and everything else.

Hannibal Fortune clenched his fists and stared at the ramp, helpless to do anything about it.

"You," he whispered harshly, "you had no right to do that."

Then, stepping around the streak of slime, he walked up the ramp and into the skimmer.

He could not recall ever having felt quite so alone.

It isn't fair.

It isn't fair at all. And it's so confusing, what with everyone pretending to be somebody else, games within games, just when you've memorized all the pieces the queens and bishops and knights and rooks turn out to be pawns in a bigger game, and the players themselves are puppets controlled by hidden rods and wires in the hands of—of what? It was all right when you were manipulating Scipio and Masinissa and Syphax, themselves controlling the lives of thousands of disgustingly ordinary, unimportant clods whose only purpose was to die for the cause, you were a step removed from all that, most of the time, because the real battle isn't between Rome and Carthage at all, but between Empire and T.E.R.R.A., and all the rest is merely make-believe. But then, just when you've got it all straightened out once again, somebody jiggles the kaleidoscope and the game changes. Adapt. It's your specialty, remember? That's how you got your License to Tamper. That's what you're good at. That's why you're one of the best secret agents in the entire history of secret agenting. Who says it has to make sense, too?

Webley—dead. Heroically, as if that makes any difference.

Luise—there's no point in thinking about Luise. Some other time, maybe.

Vango—he would have been no help anyway.

Arrik—every bit as dead as Webley, but pointlessly, senselessly; instead of wishing himself a new shape he'd wished himself dead. He had no right to kill himself, not when you still might have a use for him.

Malik—even now, the spider is probably spinning a new web, and you don't even know where he is.

All you've got is a piece of machinery which will probably function the way it was designed, but then again it might not. It certainly won't do anything above and beyond what it was designed for. You can't use it to call for help, because the only signals it can generate are the slow, cumbersome speed-of-light variety which would take twenty-seven thousand years to reach anyone who could do you any good, and be lost in the interstellar noise before they'd gone half that far.

Your head keeps doing the thing it's good at, sifting data, making posits, testing them, running reality through the maze marked *What Would Happen If?* and forecasting, to six decimal places, every variable in sight. Your head has worked this way since you were a schoolboy. You couldn't stop it if you wanted to. You can't explain it to anyone else, or teach it, you just do it. With sufficient data you get right answers ninety-eight percent of the time.

But without adequate input you're groping in the dark. One set of eyes vanished into *Doubletime* so you could live; your next set committed suicide. And lacking proper equipment you're about as ferocious as a newly hatched fruitfly. An IntraSystem luxury skimmer is not a T.E.R.R.A. time-ship. So your head still does flashy tricks. How nice. Your clever head informs you that an armless, legless, blind and deaf computer freak has little chance of carrying it off.

You're beginning to see Arrik's point.

You examine the skimmer again, hoping you'd missed something earlier that might give you an edge. A weapon, a code book, a remote doorknob for the mother ship which might or might not still be orbiting Earth. Nothing. You doubt that the Empire force that destroyed the Residency headquarters did so on foot or even horseback. There has to be another skimmer somewhere, outfitted with grenade launchers, heavy-duty sonic beam cannon and assorted other goodies from Empire's arsenal. The Torg swiped the wrong skimmer. Not his fault. It was the only one available at the time. So your opponent has the battle cruiser and you're stuck with a troop carrier. Admittedly, it's a sophisticated piece of equipment which might come in handy for sightseeing, but as a weapon it's useless except maybe in a ramming operation. Of course, there's always the remainder of Vango's Residency kit: a handful of smoke bombs, the ultrasonic scrambler and three short-range stundarts; the rescue beacon is in Sophonisba's fancy limestone coffin, keyed to start squealing some time next week.

When you put it there you still believed someone from your side might come around to take custody of her. That was before you knew the Residency had been demolished, along with the control unit for the buried cross-temporal transmitter, which might still be operable except that you have no idea where it is.

You recompute the odds. With luck, you might stay alive three days, unless you take the skimmer to a far country and sink it in somebody's lagoon. If Malik or any of his henchmen should still be in this time segment —and you must act as if he is—your first decisive move with the skimmer will draw the same kind of firepower they used on Vango.

Perhaps Malik still thinks you're dead. You can't count on it.

Perhaps, as Arrik believed, the spider thinks Vango took the skimmer and hid it somewhere, in which case he's probably still looking for it.

If only the Torg were still alive to scout Malik's seaside cavern. It might be empty, but without weapons you can't risk finding out.

An agent is resourceful—that's what they used to teach you.

But an agent by definition, is also backed up by the entire organization. In over six decades of service you've seldom realized how much you rely on the organization. There are two sides to that coin. Although T.E.R.R.A. Control depends on you for its continued existence, you see now that it's been T.E.R.R.A. Control from which you've drawn your reason for being.

What man wants to continue without a reason for being?

It all tastes flat. A galactic chess player one day, demoted to mere human being the next.

Just making it from one day to another is no longer important.

Webley, Vango, Arrik—these are the lucky ones.

To know you've lost everything and still to be alive—that's the crowning indignity.

Men engaged in battle, you suppose, might fight to the death in hopes that their culture, their friends, their loved ones can survive to eventually win the war itself. But when you're cursed with the sure knowledge that the cause is hopeless, and when you're deprived even of the chance to die fighting . . .

Winning or losing makes no difference now; continuing to play the game is pointless. It's lost already. For a while you wonder how long it will take for the temporal deviation to become critical, to reach the point where the new time-line will be beyond repair, how long before the new version of Earth history acquires the inertial thrust which will erase vast portions of your own base-time reality—and you along with it. Although it's not particularly difficult to imagine a universe in which you no longer exist, you find it a mind-bending impossibility to envision a universe in which you have *never* existed—but that, you know, is what it will be. *At what point along your own time-line, you ask yourself, will you cease to exist? Will it happen all at once, in mid-thought perhaps, or will you gradually fade away and be conscious of your own demise?*

It's a question you've never taken seriously before, perhaps because you've never really believed you could lose. But now you not only believe losing is a possibility, you know you've lost already. The Galactic Federation (at least as you know it) is doomed, billions of people will wink out (or fade gradually?) along with Hannibal Fortune. T.E.R.R.A. Control will never be, the bitter-sweet interlude with Luise will never take place, the camaraderie with Webley will never come about—it'll all be less than a dream because there'll be no one left to do the dreaming. Even Gregor Malik and Empire—they, too, might perish when the cancer of Earth history reaches across space.

Oddly enough, now that you know you'll vanish in a flicker of might-have-been, the certainty of it holds no terror. You're a bit surprised to feel nothing but a vague regret. You find yourself hoping (but not desperately) that it will happen when you are awake, simply to satisfy your curiosity, but that doesn't really matter either. If it's instantaneous, you'll never know about it anyway.

Once you reach the conclusion that whatever happens is of no importance at all, you experience a strange feeling of relief, as if a weight has been removed from your shoulders. It takes you a while to identify the missing pressure as *hopelessness* and to reach a degree of insight you've never attained before: the simple truth that hope and despair are equally meaningless shadows of each other.

Drajne Wokajeni laughs. You might no longer have a purpose, but the world is suddenly a much more interesting place. Anyone looking at you could spot the twinkle in your eye, and probably shake his head in bewilderment, wondering what in the world a big-time loser could find to be so happy about.

Suppressing a grin, you look more closely at your predicament. After a moment you frown, as it dawns on you that your predicament doesn't exist. Aloud, you exclaim:

"And neither does anyone else's!"

Wheee.

And then, in a whisper: "I wonder if Pohl Tausig knows about this?"

SEVENTEEN: "NOW, SEBASTIAN, TELL
ME WHAT WE CAN DO ABOUT ELEPHANTS."

FOUR HUNDRED YEARS of computer technology coupled with the advent of near-total-conversion energy sources had put spaceships into the pleasure craft category. The average GF citizen needed no more than an hour's instruction to be able to "pilot" a private skimmer almost anywhere. It was primarily a matter of learning how to ask it to take you where you wanted to go—and then trusting the ship to work out the details. IntraSystem, Fortune recalled, boasted about the tourist-proof design of its Navigator. Although its powerplant lacked some of the qualities that were most admired at sportscraft rallies, he had to admit that for its class it was a sweet machine. Every skimmer in Empire's fleet had been acquired without the formalities of Registration, nor had prior owners been compensated. The thieves had chosen well. Despite its limitations, a million miles of powered flight was well within this model's weekend capability; vastly different from pioneer times when Earthmen took six to eight days just to get to their own moon and back, roughly half that far.

Less than twenty minutes after he left the catacombs of Carthage, Hannibal Fortune was closing for rendezvous with Empire's orbiting time-craft.

There were two immediately obvious differences between T.E.R.R.A.'s temporal transporter and Empire's version of the same machine. First was the matter of size. Although presumably variously improved since Lipnig and Rudnl's first ungainly creation, Empire transporters were still roughly ten times as big as the T.E.R.R.A. ships. Part of this size differential could be traced to T.E.R.R.A.'s passion for component miniaturization and versatility, while Empire's policy had always been to handle a bulkier assortment of personnel and equipment.

In the second place, since it wasn't intended to maneuver in atmosphere, there was no reason to streamline an Empire time-ship; if anything, the craft which orbited ahead of him was more ungainly than the original.

Hannibal Fortune studied the huge ship as he approached. It was even bigger than the one Malik had used at Mohenjo-daro; clearly, this was the pride of Empire's fleet. Like a shark investigating a whale, Fortune crept closer, matching orbits to within a few feet per second. A voice, raspingly familiar, came from somewhere on the console. "Excellency?" The language was Borian, Gregor Malik's own native tongue.

Fortune smiled tightly and found the talk-back switch. He made his voice dry and silky. "Open the air lock," he hissed. Whoever was on duty inside the transporter had assumed it was Malik himself in the skimmer; Fortune intended to keep that assumption operational.

"Excellency," the voice responded, "I must ask you to clear your viewports before the ship can let you in."

Fortune could see out but the other could not see in. Not wanting to end the masquerade so soon, he swore colorfully in Borian, then added: "The control is jammed. Open the hatch."

"But, sir—"

"But sir nothing, you idiot! Open up!"

While this dialogue was in progress, the IntraSystem Navigator had been efficiently exchanging data with its counterpart in the mother ship; a blinking light on the control panel showed that the two computers had agreed on a docking program and were standing by to initiate the maneuver. Fortune chuckled, remembering that it had been Gregor Malik who had once pointed out that machines don't care which side they work for.

There was a considerable silence on the voice circuit. At last the transporter's cargo hatch yawned open. Fortune grinned and let the Navigator ease the skimmer inside. Ponderously, the cargo doors swung shut again. The inner doors of the air lock gleamed frostily in the skimmer's headlight beam while air pressure mounted in the chamber, then they, too, levered open, revealing a large bay on the other side with mooring spaces for half a dozen skimmers. Two of the berths were occupied.

Warily, Fortune let the stolen craft drift deeper into the mother ship.

Bahrs Tolunem was puzzled but hopeful. His hope was that the Tyrant was at last satisfied with the progress of events on Earth so they could go home. Even the luxury of zero gravity couldn't make him forget all the comforts of his native planet. On the contrary, lack of gravity activated a tiny gland hidden at the base of his muscular, snail-like foot, and the resulting secretions triggered a violent desire to drelb, a yearning so intense that he had difficulty concentrating on anything else. His last drelb had been so long ago he could hardly remember what it felt like. If it had been left up to him, they'd have gone home long ago, but Malik hadn't been satisfied just to destroy his arch-enemy, Hannibal Fortune; the Tyrant had insisted on staying until the entire T.E.R.R.A. operation could be wiped out. Personally,

Tolunem thought Malik was carrying his hatred a bit far, but he was in no position to voice an opinion. The pay was good—and besides, he'd seen what happened to dissenters. Still, his body craved drelbing with an ache he could almost taste. If he'd known he'd have to abstain for so long at a time, Bahrs Tolunem might never have embarked on a life of interstellar crime. Obviously, one couldn't drelb alone in a spaceship. Especially in free fall. He'd tried once to imagine how to do it; if the concept hadn't been so ludicrous it would have been obscene. The prospect of returning home so he could drelb wasn't the only reason he was hopeful, but it might well have been.

His puzzlement was a bit more concrete. It was not like Gregor Malik to travel alone as long as there was anybody else around to chauffeur him—but if he was not alone his pilot would have answered Tolunem's approach challenge. Not only was the Tyrant alone, but apparently the viewports of his skimmer were malfunctioning. Familiarity with the Tyrant's intolerance of anything not in proper working order functioned to increase his caution, which had been seriously impaired by all those thoughts about drelbing.

Ever since you realized that losing yours doesn't matter, you've felt intoxicated with life itself. It's a warm sensation of aliveness, a tingling awareness that you occupy—no, you *are*—a bubble of being, an intense focus of consciousness unexpectedly in love with everything. You even appreciate the dignity/beauty/inevitability of Arrik's suicide, and you marvel momentarily at your acceptance of it. You're glad no one asks you to explain—or even describe—your new awareness, because words could only sketch a tarnished likeness.

You are invading an Empire time-craft, which strikes you as a magnificently inconsequential thing to be doing.

You have no plan for this moment. Your mind is uncluttered by thoughts, removing the usual lag between stimulus and response, which now have become simultaneous.

Now is not quite big enough to contain a heartbeat; it totally involves you. Perception and awareness are one, arising alongside action, so that the instant you see what to do you've done it.

The only other occupant of the giant time-craft apparently had not been paying full attention. You dispose of the orange-fringed corpse and take control of the ship.

It should be recorded here that in his youth, even before his tertiary vascules were fully developed, Bahrs Tolunem had been warned that although drelbing was a perfectly natural, healthy activity, too much thinking about it could be harmful.

Not only was he released from straight-line temporal continuity, but capturing the orbiting transporter had placed three skimmers instead of one at Hannibal Fortune's disposal. Two of them, he discovered, were fitted with heavy sonics. Not bad at all, he reflected, for an impromptu one-man invasion. He doubted that he could have done much better had he planned it.

His next task would be to find Scipio and check on the progress of his war, but first he turned his attention

218

to consolidating his gains. Unlike those of his own transporter, the controls on the Empire monster were plainly marked; the flight computer was a standard commercial job. An orbiting time-ship is not like a hill, which you can occupy as long as you defend it, but more like a submarine, which doesn't have to be defended as long as you can keep it hidden.

Step one, then, was to move it to a different parking place, which called for a new orbit.

Following standard Empire procedures, Malik had parked it in the plane of Earth's equator in a circular twenty-four-hour orbit, which kept it constantly 22,280 miles above a point some 36° south of Carthage. Fortune chose a much faster, closer, elliptical orbit with a perigee so low it punched corridors of silence through the tenuous upper atmosphere. By giving the ship a slight lateral burst of power at the far end of each swing, he caused the perigee to precess neatly around the track, in step with the planet's rotation, giving him sixteen low passes over North Africa per day, each one lasting almost two and a half minutes.

That took care of *where*.

Taking care of *when* turned out to be more complicated, since he wanted to occupy the new orbit for only a few minutes a day, so that even if Gregor Malik and Remnant should stumble upon the proper *where* the odds would be overwhelmingly against his being there at any given *when*.

Achieving such a peek-a-boo effect required only that the time-craft's computer be programmed to give intermittent realtime occupancy of discrete portions of three randomly selected circuits daily from the sixteen which were available, bypassing the rest of the orbit by means of sychronized time-leaps. To an observer limited to Earth's time-line, there'd be so little orbital data revealed by these appearances that making operational predictions about either the orbit or the transporter's realtime schedule would be virtually impossible. Peek-a-boo orbiting was an enormously slowed-down, macrocosmic analogue of subatomic quantum behavior, and had been suggested by one of Linz Lipnig's more devious junior assistants. Scornfully, Lipnig had pointed out that it wasn't needed, since T.E.R.R.A.'s time-ships had the much more efficient Observation Module capacity for optical and electronic invisibility, and told his assistant to apply himself to more pressing problems. Fortune, however, loved the improbable, the impractical and the unnecessary; he'd become intrigued and had promptly memorized the useless technique.

He'd remembered it perfectly, too. Of course, once he got it working he found he agreed with Lipnig: T.E.R.R.A.'s solution was by far the simplest, best and most flexible. This new way, although beautiful in concept, was decidedly clumsy in operation. Take the matter of landmarks, for instance.

When you're sixty miles up and doing three hundred miles a minute you have little time to look for landmarks, but an immediate need for them for your optical scanners to use as sweep triggers. Leaping through time by orbital increments gave Fortune the subjective impression of an uninterrupted panorama that kept repeating itself every two and a half minutes. In the main, the only things that changed from one sweep to the next were cloud formations and the lengths of some mountain shadows. The military situation was somewhat more difficult to assess from sixty miles up.

Castra Cornelia seemed deserted. It took twenty passes to find the Roman army, plus another four before the scanners locked on. Even at maximum resolution the only way he could identify it as Roman was from the stark linearity of the portable encampment.

At such altitudes there remained too many unanswered questions to make speculation fruitful, so he concentrated on data-gathering. By the time he'd prepared a working map of the area, six months had elapsed below.

Fortune mapped the movements of the Roman force. Curiously, Scipio was marching steadily away from Carthage, following the Bagradas toward its headwaters to the southwest.

At last, some sixty miles south of Carthage, Fortune spotted a second army, this one also moving west, apparently in pursuit of Scipio. The orbiting agent turned up his scope magnification to maximum and grinned as he verified the presence of dozens of elephants. That meant the commander was probably Hannibal One-Eye himself. The big one was coming up.

Even further west than Scipio, Fortune found the apparent reason for Scipio's steady march into the interior—a large force of horsemen headed east. Masinissa? Again, it was hard to tell.

Two days later—to Fortune, less than an hour had elapsed—the desert horsemen had halved the remaining distance between themselves and Scipio. Clearly, it was time for him to go down and make his own entrance. Accordingly, he moved the Empire transporter into a somewhat higher orbit, loaded the skimmer with provisions and plummeted swiftly into atmosphere, coming down as he'd done the year before far out over the

Mediterranean in order to approach his eventual target with the least chance of being observed by any residual Empire force that might be accompanying Hannibal. This was one of the times that he really missed the invisibility aspects of his own time-craft.

Parking the skimmer a short distance from the Roman-Numidian camp, Fortune approached on foot, in the guise of Scipio's spy, Sebastian Necropoulis. Several of the Roman officers recognized him; two escorted him to the command tent.

"I thought you dead," Scipio said, smiling as he clasped the Greek's forearm in the traditional Roman grip of friendship. "Where have you been?"

"Would you believe me if I said I'd been flying high overhead, above the sky?"

"Knowing you," the Roman said with a grin, "I wouldn't say you lie until I could prove it. No matter, you are with us now. What can you tell me that I don't already know about Hannibal?"

"Merely that you need me to help dispose of his war elephants."

Scipio nodded. "Sit, Necropoulis. Gaius Claudius, pour my excellent friend some wine, for he has come far and he thirsts, and then send for Laelius. Now, Sebastian, tell me what we can do about elephants?"

EIGHTEEN: "WHATEVER HE'S DOING
HE'S DOING IT ON PURPOSE."

THE WHITE-BEARDED Punic War enthusiast who had furnished the micro-recorder Fortune welded into Scipio's tunic, has one of the best descriptions of the ensuing Battle of Zama ever offered. Although the material is highly opinionated, it is difficult not to agree with Dr. d'Kaamp's conclusions. Originally presented *ad libitum* during a seminar in the spring of GF 89 at the T.E.R.R.A. Control Institute (T.E.R.R.A.C.I.), it is not as formally structured as one might expect a discourse entitled *Strategic and Tactical Deployment of Tandem Special Teams, with Particular Attention to Techniques of Historical Obfuscation,* by A. E. d'Kaamp, F.G.F.A.S., to be. Pohl Tausig contends d'Kaamp was indulging in whimsy when he titled it; according to high G.F. sources, Tausig was secretly pleased when the Archivist dubbed it Training Abstract 44-38/AW, Special Subsection 17. Dr. d'Kaamp was said to swagger when he overheard a graduate assistant subdub it, *What Really Happened at Zama.* By permission of Dr. d'Kaamp and T.E.R.R.A.C.I., exerpts from the audio tracks are included here.

Readers unfamiliar with d'Kaamp might estimate the angle of his bias by considering the following passage from his earlier dissertation, *Some Consequences of Faulty Assumptions Regarding Military Mystique,* privately published by and for the Anomaly Club:

"When I began serious study of the Military History of Earth, which subsequently became my specialty, I was appalled at some of the things Earth-men could find to fight about, and outraged at the bloodthirsty gods they invented, and I felt compassion for them and thought what they were doing to each other was criminal. Now that I've got to know them well enough to become an Authority, I am no longer surprised by their heroic stupidity. I think they richly deserve the worst of their gods and I am forced to view many of their virtues with disgust. Whatever evil they do to themselves is less than they've really got coming. Aside from its militarism, Earthmankind's greatest opportunities to express loutish stupidity are found in its religions. I doubt, on GF-38 at least, that either of the two could long exist without the other to support it, the religious establishment and the military, the political war parties."

Polybius had expressed much the same view some twenty-seven centuries earlier when he said of Roman superstition that it "maintains the cohesion of the Roman state." He echoed Scipio's sentiments, surely, in his assessment of practical Roman politics: "As every multitude is fickle, full of lawless desires, unreasoned passion, and violent anger, it must be held in by invisible terrors and religious pageantry."

Against that background, d'Kaamp boldly outlines events leading up to the crucial confrontation, often with sarcasm, always with vigor:

From the audio tracks:

In an attempt to lure the Carthaginian into the plain, rather than risking an engagement in hilly country,

Scipio had been ravaging the area west of Carthage, pillaging, looting, roping the terrified inhabitants into slave trains, slaughtering livestock, burning crops and the like in accepted GF-38 military manner, and had been sending couriers daily for the last several weeks to find Masinissa and urge him to join the Roman force quickly with the previously promised ten thousand Numidian horsemen. Masinissa, though, had become engrossed in the novelty of being king and was wasting time with orgies, circuses and whatever else those early Earthmen could turn to self-indulgent purposes.

Hannibal, having quit Italy and brought his own army of twenty-four thousand troops to Africa to meet the threat of Scipio, had managed to double his forces, half with Ligurians and Gauls from his late brother Mago's army, plus another twelve thousand raw recruits from Carthage, which gave him a total of forty-eight thousand foot soldiers and, of course, his eighty war elephants. These last were a complete surprise to Scipio, and might have been his undoing were it not for the somewhat unconventional intervention of Special Agent Hannibal Fortune, who'd stolen a transporter from Empire and was watching it all from a spy orbit overhead.

Unknown to Fortune, another team of T.E.R.R.A. agents was on the scene, along with his own symbiotic partner Webley, whom Fortune thought to be dead. Since early the previous winter these three—Agent Luise Little and Torgs Webley and Ronel—had been searching in and around the Carthaginian peninsula and among each of the armies involved, naturally to no avail, for Fortune had hidden himself in orbit and was flickering in and out of realtime just long enough to pass overhead three times a day. They'd found Gregor Malik and some underlings in a fortified cave, but no trace of Hannibal Fortune.

The original Hannibal, whose name the agent a-dopted at the outset of his career, had in addition to his forty-eight thousand infantry some six thousand cav-alry, with more presumably on the way, fanatical fighters calling themselves the Sons of Syphax. On the one side, then, we see Hannibal's fifty-four thousand troops, a mixed bag of talents, temperaments and languages, while pitted against them are barely twenty-six thousand Romans. I caution you, never underestimate the Roman legions—think of them as a precision drill team with but one purpose, to decimate the enemy. Typically Earthian, they were a highly superstitious lot, and their leaders were quick to take advantage of the rabble's willingness to believe. There was a wide enough selec-tion of deities in those days so that for any extreme of be-havior some god or other insisted upon it. At one time Earthmen had a matchless reputation for inventing religious excuses to butcher each other. I mention their compulsive indulgence in religion so you may better understand what happened at Zama, since one might say Fortune's entire strategy hinged upon their astonish-ing gullibility.

One of the characteristics of mass combat in those days was its hypnotic, unreal, quasi-hallucinogenic as-pect which the Romans enhanced by voicing *a capella* the most unnerving minor chords they could construct, as precisely worked out as their footwork or shot sword techniques; Carthaginians chose to augment it with ex-otic herbs and crude medicinals. The evangelical fury of an occasional berserker baptizing with the sword was easy to mistake for a god in human form leading his troops to glory. It was easy for any soldier, even a Roman, to see miracles, and equally easy to discount another's holy vision. If you're involved in an epic and don't want your name mentioned, try to arrange things so your more memorable exploits are seen only by those who consistently strive to prove that all miracles take place in other people's minds, or who have sundry other good reasons to deny it.

This was more than just a conflict between armies. It was a struggle for dominance between two thriving civilizations. Neither could coexist with the other on a friendly, cooperative basis. To be truly viable, nations need fierce pride, like that of a petulant child, easily offended, frequently outraged, always eager to settle some score or other.

Both Rome and Carthage qualified.

Every culture that develops a concept of nationalism does so in the same manner, with individuals banding together into groups in order to coerce other individuals or smaller, weaker groups into acknowledging their supremacy. In such cultures, hostility and fear are virtual prerequisites for cooperation. "If you can't beat 'em, join 'em," is quite practical advice for surviving on a planet full of predators: if you encounter an aggressor you think you can't defeat, maybe the two of you together can frighten someone else into paying tribute.

Rome and Carthage were denied that option, though, because at that time there weren't any other super-nations they could jointly attack. Egypt, Babylon, Crete—already ancient history—while the Greeks had demonstrated that grown men who'd rather play with geometrical theorems than conquer the world could never amount to much.

227

To men of limited intellect, war is surely the most exciting, stimulating and emotionally involving activity ever devised. Nothing else can give so many people so many excuses for such a spectrum of activities. It's the ideal all-purpose purpose.

And of all the wars fought on GF-38, this war between Rome and Carthage, this war known to the local enthusiasts as the Second Punic War, aroused more scholarly controversy than almost any other event in Earth history, mainly because Hannibal Fortune threw away the rules and openly participated in a crucial battle between indigenous cultures.

And got away with it.

Some critics contend that if he'd covered his tracks as agents ought to, the Greek historian Polybius would not have commented about the "times when Fortune counteracts the plans of valiant men," nor would Hannibal of Carthage have said he'd "learned from experience how fickle Fortune is." T.E.R.R.A. Control contends the usage was pure coincidence; *Fortuna* was the Roman goddess of chance. Scipio's statement to his troops that "Fortune offers us the most glorious of prizes" is in the same category, as Scipio knew the agent only as Sebastian Necropoulis.

Bear in mind what I said about religion in that area at that time. Some of you may recall a noted holy man named Jesus who was active in one of the nearby Roman provinces about two hundred years later. The plenitude of superstitious cults which characterized that later time was just beginning to gather momentum when the Battle of Zama took place. The battle was named after a small wilderness settlement near the plain where it was fought. Earth's military historians are unsure even now of the exact location of the battlefield—one of the many mysteries which T.E.R.R.A. feels should be allowed to remain unsolved.

For that matter, we aren't advertising the fact that it was this same T.E.R.R.A. agent who served as Scipio's interpreter when the Roman met with Hannibal on the eve of battle to discuss the necessary limitations and terms of a possible truce. By the time that conference was over, both generals were furious, each determined to destroy the other come morning.

Fortune's participation in the affair actually began several days before the battle itself. Masinissa had not yet returned from the west with his ten thousand horsemen when Fortune convinced Scipio that this encounter called for a more daring approach than Rome had ever attempted against the Carthaginian. He pointed out that starving a nation into submission, as his depradations against the farmlands thus far threatened to accomplish, was not something the Roman Senate would likely throw a triumph for. Still, all of the conventional tactics had either failed or at best had produced limited results: Utica still had not fallen, a direct assault upon the city of Carthage would be suicidal while Hannibal had an army in the field, the Punic navy still ruled the coastline—they'd recently captured sixty of Scipio's supply ships loaded with provisions—and now he was vastly outnumbered by the one-eyed warrior's seemingly slipshod conglomerate of diverse ethnic types.

If ever Necessity moaned in labor to announce the emergence of tender Invention, it was now.

Of all the Roman generals, Scipio was probably the one most willing to ignore traditional tactics—he'd already tried some new ideas in his earlier campaigns, small ones—so he greeted Fortune's suggestions with enthusiasm. The two men agreed that as far as posterity was concerned, the tactical innovations would be credited to Scipio alone.

The most serious challenge, the Roman contended, would be the elephants. Although fantastically disciplined, Roman troops were nonetheless afraid of the great beasts, and thus far no one had been able to devise an adequate defense against elephants.* Imagine yourself standing in the front line of a battle formation armed only with a short sword and spear, while eighty war elephants thunder toward you—and you've no place to run!

Fortune suggested frightening the elephants first, and even offered the means of doing it: a simple bullhorn effect with feedback, using sound equipment already in the skimmer. A scared or nervous elephant is not necessarily less dangerous on account of his fright, but where before he was a tool he has now become a phenomenon, and thus he might be diverted. It took the two of them less than an hour to work out a novel way for the infantry to give the panicky beasts a fast exit from the field.

Scipio sent for his centurions and outlined the procedure in considerable detail; with perfect military spirit they suppressed their individual opinions and assured their commander that the men would have the maneuver mastered in a matter of minutes. Or perhaps hours.

*See GF-chart 004424-1.6 or corresponding cerebrotape for a comparison of human and elephant weight, mass, strength, speed and gestation period.

In its own time, on any of forty-seven GF planets, a Galactapowr skimmer was a very common sight, certainly nothing to excite the viewer even if he came upon it suddenly. The handful of Romans clustered on a minor hilltop below, however, were visibly awed. Ronel could see that much even from her nearly mile-high altitude. With Webley and Luise, she'd been searching daily for traces of Fortune—an Empire skimmer wasn't quite what she was looking for, but it couldn't be ignored.

She watched for a while, then flew swiftly back the way she'd come, and rejoined her two companions. "I found him," she told them. "He's alone and he's flying a Galactapowr sports model."

Absorbing the pertinent data in a matter of seconds, Webley was on his way moments later to see for himself. For the next few hours he observed the situation, probing his former partner from a distance, but giving no hint of his own presence there. When he got back to the Carthaginian army, where Luise was traveling as an ornithomancer who could divine the future by watching the flight of her two "birds," he suggested they leave Fortune entirely alone. "Some of his circuits may be as scrambled as PsychSec says they are," Webley admitted, "but in something like this I'd trust the rest of his head to come up with an approach that works. I don't think he's forgotten that what he's doing is against the rules—whatever he's doing he's doing it on purpose."

Ronel and Luise agreed to let Fortune continue. Since his plan was already in motion, the three resolved to keep themselves available to help out as he needed them, but not to let him know they were there unless a changing situation demanded it, in which event they'd do as little as possible to alarm or annoy him.

From the audio tracks:

Through my own modest involvement in the Zama incident I have come into possession of a voice recording of a meeting between Scipio, Masinissa, Laelius and our own Hannibal Fortune, who was playing the role of a Greek spy named Necropoulis. He'd shown them his skimmer, which bristled with Class Four hunting gear, heavy-duty stuff you'd take on safari to the monster preserves, and they'd agreed for various reasons to keep quiet about his helping them afterward. As few of you speak Latin, I submit the following translation in Unispeak:

MASINISSA: But what if the Carthaginians tell about these wonders?

NECROPOULIS: Does the mighty Masinissa expect survivors?

LAELIUS: There are always survivors.

SCIPIO: My people know Carthaginians as gullible, superstitious foreigners. Rest easily; we Romans are too sophisticated to believe the Punic version of anything.

NECROPOULIS: Remember that, Scipio, the next time you officiate at a celebration of the Megalesia.

SCIPIO: Necropoulis, I wish you'd return with me to Rome when this is over. There's a poet I'd like you to meet.

NECROPOULIS: Quintus Ennius?

SCIPIO: Yes. You know him?

NECROPOULIS: By reputation only. It was he who wrote, "I grant you there are gods but they don't care what men do; else it would go well with the good and ill with the bad—which rarely happens."

MASINISSA: We'll make a liar out of him pretty soon, won't we?

NECROPOULIS: One day, Masinissa, when you are an old man like Syphax, the armies of Rome will again march against Carthage. A new Scipio will be at their head, while your Numidians form the cavalry. You must promise me that when Carthage falls, when not one stone is left upon another, you will seek out every book in that accursed land and scatter them to the winds.

MASINISSA: Why would I do that?

NECROPOULIS: At least one of them will contain the truth about your first night with Sophonisba.

As one might suppose from that exchange only, Fortune was playing a subtly different game with each of these men. Scipio was ambitious for glory and personal power, and anxious for the approval of his equals, of whom he could rightly say there were few. Just because the glory would be Scipio's did not make it any less important to Laelius, who planned to live well in its reflection. As for Masinissa, the official version of his brief marriage starred the swarthy prince as a legendary lover and more of a romantic figure than he'd been before; to have it known that the sultry Sophonisba was referring to someone else—and a filthy Greek at that—in her suicide note would not help his image with the tribesmen. Even if Necropoulis turned out to be a god, as two of the three suspected, publicly acknowledging his help would be risky business because neither one could be sure *which* god he was; Scipio's atheism, then quite fashionable in Rome's better families, made it imperative that Necropoulis *not* be a god, but there is always social merit in knowing and being able to display a cultured Greek.

As for the legionaries themselves, the *hastati, principes, triarii* and various other specialists, many of whom would see the miraculous skimmer in action, Fortune knew he could rely on the reputation combat veterans have in all ages as tellers of tall tales, the height of their lies in exact proportion to how much they've had to drink. The three at the top could think of him in any terms they wished; he was sure of their motives for silence.

The ten thousand horsemen under Masinissa had arrived almost simultaneously with a handful of spies from Hannibal's advancing army. Scipio's forces captured three of the spies; on Fortune's advice, instead of executing them and sending their heads back home Scipio gave them a grand tour of his encampment, instructing his officers to show them anything they wanted to see and to answer all questions honestly, then to provide for them an honor guard back to Hannibal. The Carthaginian, properly offended by the Roman's gratuitous gesture but weary of the war he'd been waging during the sixteen years since he invaded Italy by crossing the Alps, called for a conference.

Thus it was that the two rival generals, each with an interpreter (one of whom, as noted, was Hannibal Fortune), met on the open plain. Hannibal walked into the conference prepared to surrender—all he needed was a graceful way to do it. Such a move fit neither Scipio's ambitions nor Fortune's program for strengthening the time-line. Both were disappointed. With the calculated insult of treating his spies like visiting royalty, they'd done everything they could to guarantee that Hannibal One-Eye would be in a mood to fight. By all rights, the Carthaginian should also have been emboldened by comparing their relative troop strength. But he wanted to quit instead, perhaps because he'd had a premonition that this was the only way he could hope to retire undefeated. To keep him from this ignoble, shameful and cowardly deed, Fortune deliberately garbled Hannibal's offer of peace, twisting it into a springboard for scathing Scipionic rhetoric. History called for a total victory, which in terms of Earthmen's sacred dualism meant total vanquishment for Carthage, a state of affairs that cannot be negotiated but must be earned in honest battle with the spilling of honest blood. The world's most altruistic statesman balks at negotiating his own total defeat. Hannibal offered terms for peace; Scipio found the terms unacceptable. Both retired to their respective camps, honor bound to do battle at dawn the next day.

Before sunup, each army began moving into position. Scipio's thirty-six thousand troops were deployed in a subtly yet significantly different combat formation, as devised by Hannibal Fortune. Across the plain, the military might of Carthage was arranged into what appeared by pre-dawn light to be two distinct armies, one behind the other, with a wall of elephants unexpectedly in front, in what looked like a psychologically valid move to strike terror in the hearts of Scipio's slowly advancing legionaries.

High overhead, the T.E.R.R.A. agent hovered silently in his stolen skimmer, watching for the fracas to begin in earnest.

Cautiously at first, and then with impatient, almost eager steps, the two armies moved to close the intervening gap. Now the elephants began their charge, breaking slowly away from their own front lines, thundering toward the Romans. Answering the cue for his first miracle, Fortune nudged the skimmer into a steep dive, stopping abruptly less than twenty feet from the ground. From the ship came a sound like the coordinated blast of a thousand trumpets. (Indeed, that's what Polybius claimed it was, ignoring the fact that the Roman army didn't *own* a thousand trumpets.) As planned, it completely unnerved the elephants and their *mahouts*.

Scipio's forces, however, knew what to expect—this was their signal to change formation, opening up neatly spaced corridors between the manipules. Most of the terrified elephants, sensibly seeking the avenues of least resistance, lumbered straight through the holes and caused very little damage. Once they were outside the immediate battle area, Fortune tickled them with fine-focused sonics to encourage their further dispersal, burning only those that refused to scatter. The rest of the huge beasts, seeking safety at the sides and the rear, trampled Hannibal's spearmen and completely disrupted his flanking cavalry.

Closing ranks, the Romans moved in for the conventional hack-slash-skewer of man against man Punic warfare, at which they were exceedingly good. Methodically, they chopped Hannibal's front line (Livy describes it as cowardly Gauls and Ligurians) to pieces, until it broke up and scattered. At the same time, Scipio's cavalry (commanded on the left by Laelius, on the right by Masinissa) chased their Carthaginian counterparts off the battlefield and out of sight.

Hannibal's second army, fresh and with unblunted swords, moved into action. It was mid-morning now and although his foot soldiers didn't know it, Scipio could see that Hannibal had still a third army standing in reserve some two hundred yards to the rear of the action.

The legionaries continued hacking at their fresher opponents, with about equal losses on both sides. Scipio's cavalry by now was completely out of sight, presumably still chasing the Carthaginian horsemen. The battlefield was slippery with blood and littered with the dead and the dying before Hannibal's second army finally turned tail.

Now the Roman troops caught sight of Hannibal's third army: his elite corps, twenty-four thousand veterans of the Italian campaign—more than a match for the surviving exhausted Romans. Scipio, watching from his hilltop, still could see no sign of his cavalry; apparently Masinissa and Laelius, intoxicated with victory, had carried the pursuit too far. Hannibal One-Eye, atop the opposite hill, noted that the field was clear for him to close in for the kill—but he could see something else that puzzled him greatly. Rising from behind the Roman lines was a fantastic silvery machine that soared skyward until it was a tiny dot and then swooped suddenly down again.

It was at this point that the two symbiotes, Webley

and Ronel, took action that significantly affected the outcome of the Battle of Zama. They were understandably curious about Fortune's strange maneuver with the skimmer, and probed his mind to find out why, thus learning that he'd merely been looking for the missing cavalry, had spotted them, and that although Laelius and Masinissa were headed back it would be another ten to fifteen minutes before they arrived. Scipio would have to stall for time. As Fortune glided toward the Roman command site to pass along this intelligence, the two Torgs flew to Hannibal One-Eye and landed on his shoulders. Before he could do more than gasp his surprise, they'd invaded his mind with a combined power probe and proceeded to hold the Carthaginian general immobile until Scipio had time to clear his Roman casualties off the field. Later historians would offer vastly different theories to explain this fatal delay on the part of Hannibal. Some postulated an epileptic seizure, others credited it to typical Punic stupidity, a few said cowardice, some blamed it on the gods and at least one flatly denied that it happened that way at all. Hannibal himself was unaware that the delay was lengthy, thinking he'd paused just long enough to wonder what had become of the Sons of Syphax who were reportedly on their way to augment his cavalry.

The officers and men who were with him on the hill-top gaped, almost literally spellbound, their superstitious awe striking them mute, as they witnessed a marvel: the ornithomancer's two birds perched on the one-eyed general's shoulders. Later, when he said he could remember no such episode, they loyally and prudently forgot it.

Having had a few minutes of much needed rest and

a brief pep-talk by their commander, the legionaries regrouped into another unconventional formation. They were still outnumbered. Their remaining enemy, unscathed, had already begun marching toward the final confrontation. Just as the two armies met and began to have at it again, Scipio's cavalry swooped in from two directions.

Too late, Hannibal One-Eye screamed orders to try to meet this new threat, but with no surviving horsemen of his own it was plain that the tide of battle had turned against him. Even Hannibal Fortune could see that.

From everywhere on the battlefield, Fortune and the skimmer were effectively invisible. Staying that way simply meant correcting for the sun, to keep it throwing his shadow on the arena from high enough so the base of the glare cone encompassed both command sites. The net effect would have been a lot easier to get with a T.E.R.R.A. transporter.

He'd been lucky so far: there'd been no trace of Empire, despite his openly brandishing the skimmer the last few days. He'd been uneasy since dawn, holding part of his awareness in fretful anticipation simply because he had insufficient data for any bets on Empire's showing up at all. He knew he'd be busy enough concentrating on one war at a time, although he felt vaguely neglected, too.

He disliked being ignored when he was doing fantastically—

Something dark flowed across his viewports.

Something almost liquid, almost opaque, almost in the shape of a T.E.R.R.A. recog sign, until it sagged and became a peculiar four-spoked wheel.

Webley?

The name burst from his mind like a salmon determined to commit its noble duty. Instantly, he tried to call back the thought, cover it up, scatter sand on it, look innocent and claim someone else did it, nonchalantly lose it in a clutter of mental odds and ends he could pretend to be chucking out—

The stuff outside his viewports quivered in Torgish amusement. Hurriedly, Fortune popped the control room exit hatch.

Before even a pound of him had flowed into the cabin the symbiote had vocal apparatus in operation and was saying, "Long time. Been on the shelf, orders. Sure hate to sit something as big as this one out."

"Web? I didn't dream all that, did I? You *did* take *Doubletime* instead of me—or was Arrik lying to me?"

"No lie. Lipnig says I'm immune, all Torgs are, nobody knew it until now. We're like air or any of the liquids. Far as the continuum is concerned, protoplasm acts like free molecules, only slower. Never had a meal or a drink of water refuse to come along when you jumped, did you?"

"That's fantastic. It opens up all sorts of possibilities. Just to—"

"—mention a few, hold it. Down, Worldsaver, easy there. It happened *once*. Nobody knows the limits, in terms of jump-span, mass, particle size, or just how vigorously to stir before trying it again. Need volunteers to find limits—big shortage of volunteers this week."

"You sound a lot more patronizing than you used to, Web."

"Should hear rest of crew. Was Sons of Syphax in your briefing when all this started?"

Fortune quieted an imaginary pool in his head and waited a moment for something to float to the surface. Nothing did. "Guess not. What are they?"

"Numidian riding club, patriots, loyal to Carthage and sworn to avenge Syphax. Three thousand members. Hannibal has been looking for them to stage a last-minute rescue since yesterday, so they're probably not too far away."

Fortune studied the battlefield for a moment. "Three thousand horsemen," he said, slowly shaking his head. "The Skip doesn't deserve that at all today. What direction?"

"Up around Cirta. I'd go with you but I'm needed here."

Fortune arched an eyebrow. "Oh?"

Webley fluffed his fur importantly. "Tausig gave me a couple of helpers. We're getting in Hannibal's way, messing up his communications, things like that."

The agent nodded. "Just be sure you let him get away. It's important that he gets back to Carthage in one piece."

"Of course," agreed the Torg, already halfway out of the hatch. "We *will* get together after the war, won't we?"

By mid-afternoon the war was over. Twenty thousand Carthaginian corpses littered the field, another twenty thousand were captured while almost fifteen thousand of Hannibal One-Eye's troops fled in dishonor. Hannibal himself managed to escape with a small group of men, no doubt still wondering what delayed the three thousand Sons of Syphax.

Nobody seems to have noticed the departure of the

strange saucer-shaped craft that streaked off to the northwest, or the sleek T.E.R.R.A. time-ship that pursued it. Nobody thought it important to report the improbable brush fire that engulfed a five-mile area of undergrowth just as the Sons of Syphax were approaching and caused them to make a time-consuming detour.

And nobody saw the second Galactapowr skimmer descending from the sky, its thin shaft of bright orange light splashing on the control surfaces of the first, causing them to glow bright red and emit sparks as the stolen skimmer crashed into a hillside.

STUNNED BY THE impact, Fortune lay sprawled across the tourist-proof Astrogator for almost a minute before realizing that his survival probably depended on his quitting the skimmer immediately. Through shattered viewplates he could see his opponent settling down on a ridge commanding the area. Opposite him across the control room, the emergency exit hatch cover interrupted a wide rip in the side of the ship. There was no way to tell the true extent of the damage. It was an academic question anyway, he realized, as he had no way to make repairs and it obviously couldn't fly without them.

Although its rangers had snapped off, the ultrasonic rifle seemed otherwise intact, so he grabbed it up on his way to the ruptured exit hatch. Flames lapped at the base of the Astrogator as Fortune squeezed through the jagged rent, slid dizzily along the glazed, friction-free curve of the impeller housing and dropped to the ground below. Running, sliding, rolling, he gained the shelter of a nearby cluster of rocks. A powerful explosion *whumped* loudly inside the skimmer—the cabin he'd just vacated began to glow dull red.

There was a slim chance his attackers hadn't seen him dashing to safety, but it was too slim to count on. For that matter, all the odds were distasteful, but even as he computed them he realized his job was finished. From here on there was very little Empire could do to save Carthage; the Roman juggernaut had too much momentum, now that Zama was Scipio's victory, for Carthage ever to make a comeback. The time-line had been repaired, the Mediterranean was becoming a Roman lake, Earth-history once again supported his own base-time reality. And even though it didn't matter whether Hannibal Fortune lived or died, at least he wanted the pleasure of taking one or more of his opponents along with him.

Accordingly, he leaned around the edge of the rock, took aim, fired. The grass under the remaining skimmer puffed into flame. He ducked back into shadow just as ultrasonic energy crackled the air and ignited the ground on either side of the rock.

Their cannon made his rifle seem a slingshot. Recollections of David and Goliath were no comfort at all.

The crackling stopped and he could hear the stator-field's rising whine as the skimmer lifted from the smoldering ridge. He was getting set for another dash elsewhere when he heard the familiar *pop* of a materializing transporter and saw it about thirty feet away. Its hatch was already starting to cycle open.

A T.E.R.R.A. handgun protruded part way from the hatch. Now a thin violet beam of coherent light lanced toward the skimmer, still hidden from Fortune's view by the huge rock.

The whine of the skimmer's stator-field collapsed and the craft fell noisily to the ground. He could see the figure in the T.E.R.R.A. ship's hatchway now as the girl took aim once more.

He chanced a quick look over the top of the rock. The enemy craft had landed on its leading edge; its cannon, still on, was pointed into the sand, industriously making glass. The laser beam playing back and forth across the ship's power section caused a series of small explosions as it groped for the main energy cells. As if to prove the craft still alive—if more proof was needed than the impromptu glass-forge—the skimmer's entry ramp began sliding out at an awkward angle.

"Drajne, hurry!" the girl called.

There was movement in the shadows of the ramp's aperture. Carefully, he filled the hole with sonic death.

Luise kept the laser steady, slicing methodically at the power section, her target three human-head-size metal spheres mounted on a torbar. Square pieces of hull fell into the crippled skimmer as the beam doubled back on itself. A moment later the ramp stopped moving. Molten glass hiccuped slowly in its crucible of sand while the cannon continued to burn.

The control room exit hatch eased open just enough to accommodate the lethal end of a sonic rifle, probably a twin to the one in his hands, which he'd found racked to a bulkhead in the other skimmer. He lifted his, forced by the broken rangers to guess at focus, and pressed the firing stud. He was not far off target, and doubted if faster focus was possible. The pinpoint of ultrasonic heat showed on the skimmer's hull as a spot of smoldering frictionless glaze. He moved it up to the hatch cover and the rifle-tip and changed his stud pressure to full on, welding the exit hatch shut and at the same time fusing the target rifle to the skimmer's hull and probably scorching the Empire who'd been about to use it. It all happened one-two-three, as effortlessly as sneezing, although once in progress the sequence of discrete events seemed interminable.

The cannon flickered twice and went out just as a metallic crash came from the mutilated power section. Fortune felt relieved that she'd found the ship's energy cells before the handgun's charge was exhausted; he hoped there were enough effective milliseconds left in it to take care of the crew, for lasers could punch through places where sonics merely warmed the surface.

Luise set the gun on twenty-five b.p.s. repeat, and began stitching a line of holes through the passenger section, systematically starting another grid. Mentally, Fortune forgave her for kicking him out of her last Residency; any time she got the urge to drop in on an assignment of *his* she'd be most welcome, even if she *stayed* Chinese.

Another flash at the ramp opening; Fortune shifted his welding ray to cover it and grinned when a beam gun bounced on the ramp and skittered over the edge. It would be a while—maybe even fifteen or twenty seconds—before anyone tried anything from there again.

All he needed was five or six.

He launched himself from behind the rock and dashed for the rescue ship while Luise provided covering laser fire. The eight or ten steps involved seemed like a hundred, all uphill with weighted boots, then suddenly he was pulling himself into the transporter, squeezing in past Luise and slapping the hatch mechanism on his way to the pilot's chair.

"I'm delighted you could come," he said, checking his coordinates and reaching for the control that would warp them safely into the Secondary Module, clockwise ninety degrees from *now*. The hatch sighed shut, Fortune moved his hand and the time-craft did its trick. "I know the invitation said refreshments will be served, but you . . ."

Turning from the controls, he found himself staring at the charred, pulpy lump that a moment ago had

been the head and shoulders of Luise Little. The laser
handgun clattered on the deck as she slid wetly down
the bulkhead.

From the audio tracks:

The history books merely note that the Sons of Syphax arrived about six hours too late to do Hannibal
One-Eye any good, and that they were cut to pieces by
the remnant of Scipio's army. Carthage, as a world power, was no more. The occupants of the fortified city followed Hannibal's advice and surrendered to Rome.

You sit for a long time just staring at the thing while
the breath drains silently out of you.

Ordinary people have a supply of pre-programmed
"appropriate" responses to violent situations, responses
which generally have little to do with the events that
trigger them. You have some too. Those owned by ordinary people are probably the more comforting.

You use the weapon Luise should have used at the
outset, the high energy laser cannon built into the top of
the transporter. You have to aim the whole ship to line
up the cylindrical lens with the disabled skimmer, but
this you can do safely out of sight in the Secondary Module. You return to the objective *now* just long enough
to push the red button and watch the flash as the skimmer disintegrates. Your pleasure is intensely sharp and
disappointingly brief. You take aim again, this time at
the remains of your own crippled skimmer, and blast
it, too, out of the reality world, along with half a ton of
North African desert. Already the ritual annihilation be-
gins to pall; destroying the first one was twice as much
fun.

So much for the "appropriate response."

You find it helps to look at her. The face and hair, of course, are gone completely, so it could have been anybody, except that you know it was Luise. Had been Luise. Luise doesn't live here any more. The right side of the body is charred, all of it that the heat ray had touched directly. The rest is relatively normal. Doesn't matter. Isn't Luise any more. Even those parts that still look like Luise aren't Luise.

You have already begun to forget what she looked like.

Maybe you never really knew. (It matters?)

But you loved her.

At any rate, the thing in front of you once functioned as part of an entity you knew as Luise Little and it is not functioning that way any more. You recall being angry with someone for making her look Chinese. You were angry with her, too, over something more important than that, and at Pohl Tausig for either the same thing or something else. No matter; you'd loved her. That's what was important. You loved her and she loved you.

You had it sorted out a while ago, a few days, a week, a month—it all runs together now. Whenever it was, you'd discovered that none of it really makes any difference, that both Predicament and Peril are nonthings that don't exist until you say they do. It was so beautifully simple, and you felt good afterward exploring the implications in it for the rest of your values.

But now you see that that was only the beginning.

The concept needs expanding. You suspect you'll be expanding it for the rest of your life.

Odd you never discovered this way of thinking/perceiving before. (You are a viewpoint with recurrent delusions of being a conscious entity!) Whoosh. Who'd ever guess so much of your head could be awake at the same time?

How many others are aware? Luise?

You look again at the corpse, but *it* doesn't know, because it's no longer participating in a functional Luise. Had she lived, maybe you could have explained it to her. Maybe not. You suspect seeing it is something each individual must stumble across himself. You can't imagine how to teach it. Not your problem. But the corpse is.

Considering all that's happened, it might be fitting to give the remains a proper GF-38 funeral. Some respectful noises, maybe a little poetry, some sort of marker. An Earth-style funeral would be most appropriate, seeing that if you hadn't fallen in love, Earth-style, there'd be no corpse to bury. You can see why some people, especially in Earth-style cultures, would find funerals something to wallow in.

Since it is fittingly Earthian, you wallow briefly in this one.

You realize now what happened. You'd gifted Luise with virtues that existed only in your imagination, and then been angry when she couldn't live up to your fantasy image of her. You were desperately, classically, insanely in love with a concept of Luise that bore little resemblance to the real Luise. When she'd expressed honest concern that you were endangering both of your missions it only made you feel tremendously rejected—you'd returned to your assignment completely miserable, because *your* Luise would never have treated you so unlovingly!

The massive irony of it strikes you now—your love psychosis caused you to screw things up masterfully—somehow this made it necessary for Luise to come to your rescue and be killed herself. You're guessing, but that's good enough for a funeral.

You don't bury her, though, despite how fitting it would be. And you don't take her home with you—there's nothing left worth salvaging.

So you lay her out on a hilltop, return to the transporter and take careful aim with the big laser. You pause for a moment, recalling the words, then very quietly you say them. "Remember, and in remembering leave no regrets, that what has passed, though gone, was good."

Then you push the red button.

Hannibal Fortune watched the multicolored streaks of light that had long ago replaced the stars. Almost an hour and a half had elapsed since he'd collected Webley and Ronel from the battlefield. At first he'd feared that Ronel, learning about Luise, would opt for the same sort of symbiotic suttee Arrik had committed, but evidently Webley refused to allow it. For the last twenty minutes the two had been silent, presumably communicating on another level. Web would have his pseudopods full for some time. The symbiotic weld, Fortune knew, was an even more intense blending of individuals than he and Luise once had achieved. He wished he knew more about the emotional structure of Torgs.

He checked the coordinates, read the twin clocks and punched an address into the computer. Almost instantly it displayed the looked-for answer. He set the controls for entry into the Secondary Module and thumbed the button.

The threadlike streaks of light collapsed into bright pinpoints and the surface of Sfarua loomed dead ahead, its omnipresent ocean sparkling with reflections of the four nearest stars. Efficiently, he moved the time-craft toward the crescent-shaped cluster of islands to hover over the area where he'd drilled Luise in temporal navigation.

Recalling the exact sequence of events on that long-ago day was difficult—so very much had happened since—but he forced his head to sort it out. Hovering closer, he moved the trolling lever forward a notch. The landscape below took on a reddish tinge and seemed more animated. Ahead was the gleaming time-craft.

Fortune eased nearer, scanning the grounds, one hand nudging the trolling lever, until he spotted the two figures scurrying toward the waiting transporter. He pulled the control back slowly, restoring the scene outside to a near-normal entropy rate. The pair talked for several minutes, then the man removed a remote control unit from his belt, touched the activating stem and the time-craft's hatch swung open. Luise waved to him as he climbed through.

"This isn't T.E.R.R.A. Control," Webley said suddenly, sharding the silence.

"No," Fortune agreed, stripping off his battle-smudged and bloodied clothing. "And I wasn't wearing a Greek tunic when I got aboard just then, either."

"Are you all right?" the symbiote persisted. "Do you know what you're doing?"

"Perfectly." Fortune opened his mind to the expected confirming probe and added in loudthink: *See?*

"All right. But wipe the hatch before you open it."

Outside, the other time-craft abruptly vanished. For-

tune eased this one into the space the other had va
cated, phased the transporter into the objective *now*
and then rose and spent an agonizing few seconds scrub
bing stains from the entryway. Throwing the blood·
rag to one side, he opened the hatch and looked out

The girl facing him seemed almost a complete stranger
Fortune stared at her for a moment, reading the as
tonishment in her eyes.

"Drajne!" she exclaimed.

Belatedly, he willed a smile to his lips, then swung
down to the ground.

"Where've you been?" Her banal question carried
overtones of concern.

"Classified," he told her, grinning broadly now. Yes
he realized, this was the girl he'd shared an improb
able adventure with in Mohenjo-daro several lifetime
ago, the girl with whom—by now, here—he'd spent al
most half of their year's sabbatical afterward. Yet she
was different; even her face didn't match exactly the
mental picture he'd carried with him to Carthage. "I
meant to bring you a present," he said, forcing a banter·
ing tone into his voice, "but the natives weren't as
friendly as I thought they'd be." He could tell as he spoke
that she didn't believe him, but he couldn't let her guess
the truth. Coming back, he realized, had been a very
foolish indulgence, climaxing a great many foolish in
dulgences; now he had to make the incident as harmless
as possible. *Lightly,* he cautioned himself, *but with just
enough conviction so she'll take me seriously.* He tried
to make it sound like an afterthought:

"Incidentally, darling, this visit is highly irregular. It
might be dangerous for me to know about it later."

"All right," she replied, almost matching his apparent casualness. "I'll try not to mention it to you."

But her eyes gave lie to her vocal nonchalance. He wondered if he was only imagining that her eyes were saying *Hold me, convince me you're real*. Trying to ignore the tightness in his throat, he reached for her.

As she thrust herself into his arms he could sense the futility loitering like fussy stacks of emptiness around them. "I love you," he said, and the words triggered other words which tumbled after them. "I loved you as much right now as I did tomorrow. Time is arbitrary. You realize, we really can't afford each other. We—" He bit back the rest of it while she waited for him to finish the sentence.

"We what, darling?" she said at last, her unaltered lips pursing quickly with the question.

He pulled her closer, whispering, "I love you no matter what you look like." Then his mouth was on hers and her supple body burrowed fiercely into him. She tried to begin another question but he shook his head warningly. "Don't ask me. We only have a few minutes."

She hid her face against his neck and murmured agreement. *Time!* he thought bitterly. *It keeps running out, even with a technology like ours. . . .* He was content just to hold her for a moment, savoring milliseconds. "You have to pretend," he told her, "that these last few minutes didn't exist." Even as he said it he was conscious of an eerily familiar feel to the situation.

"I promise," she replied, and then smiled as if she'd just realized a true thing. He knew what it was an instant before she said it: "There's only now, isn't there? For as long as we live, all we've really got is now. That ought to be enough for anybody."

Not trusting himself with words, he drew her to him once again, trying to trap for all time the feel of her lips on his, the softness/firmness of her body, the aliveness of her hands pressing on his shoulder blades. Reluctantly they parted. Neither spoke, although Fortune felt that Luise knew, by some intuitive sense, what it was all about.

Abruptly, blindly, he climbed back into the open time-craft, slapping the hatch control on his way. The hatch sidled shut. Fortune stumbled to the control seat, set the dial, then activated the countdown. The twin clocks showed them still within the safety margin.

The bell chimed softly.

The bubble clouded and cleared.

"What was that all about?" Webley inquired testily.

Fortune watched the star-streaks outside, then re-checked the controls. Only after he'd satisfied himself that they'd achieved normal cross-temporal, sub-spatial operation did he turn in his seat and look at the two symbiotes huddled together against the bulkhead. "Sometimes," he said, "it's impossible to say goodbye."

Her voice echoed softly in a warm, remote corridor of his mind: "For as long as we live, all we've really got is now. That ought to be enough for anybody."

Not hearing it ever again, he realized, would be a desperate thing.

Perhaps.

AUTHOR'S NOTE:

The preceding is a true account of the curious manner in which Publius Cornelius Scipio managed to defeat Hannibal of Carthage in the Battle of Zama. All of the facts have been carefully checked against the archives at T.E.R.R.A. Control and accurately reflect the events chronicled. For any reader curious to see how generations of poets, militarists and other pedantic fictionalizers have garbled the facts, the author recommends the following books:

A Greater Than Napoleon—Scipio Africanus, Captain B. H. Liddell Hart, Wm. Blackwood & Sons, Edinburgh & London, 1926.

Hannibal, Enemy of Rome, Leonard Cottrell, Holt, Rinehart & Winston, New York, 1960.

Hannibal: One Man Against Rome, Harold Lamb, Doubleday, New York, 1958.

The History of Rome, Titus Livius (Livy), translated by Spillan and Edmunds, G. Bell & Sons, Ltd., London, 1919.

The Histories of Polybius, translated by W. R. Paton, William Heinemann, London, 1922.

The serious scholar is cautioned, when reading any of the above, to bear in mind Mark Twain's observation on the Punic Wars: "The researches of many antiquarians have already thrown much darkness on the subject, and it is probable, if they continue, that we shall soon know nothing at all." In this fashion are the sinister forces of Empire confounded.

—*Larry Maddock*